'Patrick McGrath's new novel immediately grabs the reader's
attention with his frightening story of familial
murder and abuse ... The writing is spare, direct and understated –
an approach that actually serves to heighten
the narrative's grisly effects. *Spider* is a small classic of horror –
a model of authorial craft and control' –
The New York Times

'This thriller's grasp for the peculiar chill of mental
anguish interspersed with everyday detail is undeniable ...
a black hole of a book' –
Financial Times

'Disturbing, wholly absorbing ... a combination murder mystery/
dark-night-of-the-soul ... touchingly, menacingly brilliant' –
Chicago Tribune

'The narrative voice is, as ever in McGrath, tricksy
and suspect. His London is a vague, smoky, downtrodden
place, redolent of the rich, seamy smells of the pre-plastic age:
liver and onions, flannel, sawdust and beer' –
New Statesman & Society

'The sensuous world that Mr McGrath creates is intense
in its beauty ... mesmerizing' –
The New York Times Book Review

ABOUT THE AUTHOR

Patrick McGrath was born in London and, after several years in British Columbia, moved to New York in 1981. He is the author of the critically acclaimed collection *Blood and Water and Other Tales*, which was published in the Penguin Originals series in 1989, and the novel *The Grotesque* (Penguin 1990).

PATRICK McGRATH

SPIDER

PENGUIN BOOKS

PENGUIN BOOKS

Published by the Penguin Group
Penguin Books Ltd, 27 Wrights Lane, London W8 5TZ, England
Penguin Books USA Inc., 375 Hudson Street, New York, New York 10014, USA
Penguin Books Australia Ltd, Ringwood, Victoria, Australia
Penguin Books Canada Ltd, 10 Alcorn Avenue, Toronto, Ontario, Canada M4V 3B2
Penguin Books (NZ) Ltd, 182–190 Wairau Road, Auckland 10, New Zealand

Penguin Books Ltd, Registered Offices: Harmondsworth, Middlesex, England

First published in the USA by Poseidon Press, a division of Simon and Schuster, Inc. 1990
First published in Great Britain by Viking 1991
Published in Penguin Books 1992
1 3 5 7 9 10 8 6 4 2

Printed in England by Clays Ltd, St Ives plc

For my parents, Helen and Pat

My name is Ozymandias, king of kings:
Look on my works, ye Mighty, and despair!

SHELLEY

I've always found it odd that I can recall incidents from my boyhood with clarity and precision, and yet events that happened yesterday are blurred, and I have no confidence in my ability to remember them accurately at all. Is there some process of fixing, I wonder, whereby time, rather than causing memories to decay (as you would expect) instead does the opposite—it sets them hard, like concrete, the very reverse of the sort of fluid mush I seem to get when I try to talk about yesterday? All I can tell you for certain—about yesterday, that is—is that there were people in the attic again, Mrs. Wilkinson's people—and here is a curious thing, something that escaped me until this moment: the woman who runs the boarding house I'm living in (just temporarily) has the same last name as the woman responsible for the tragedy that befell my family twenty years ago. Beyond the name there is no resemblance. My Mrs. Wilkinson is an altogether different creature from Hilda Wilkinson, she's a sour, vindictive woman, big, it's true, as Hilda was big, but with none of Hilda's sauce and vitality, far more interested in questions of control—which brings me back to the people in the attic last night; but of them, on reflection, I think I will speak at another time.

It takes me about ten minutes to walk from the canal back to Mrs. Wilkinson's. I am not a fast walker; I shuffle, rather than walk, and often I am forced to stop dead in the middle of the pavement. I forget how to do it, you see, for nothing is automatic with me anymore, not since I came back from Canada. The simplest actions—eating, dressing, going to the lavatory—can sometimes pose near-insurmountable problems, not because I am physically handicapped in any way, but rather because I lose the easy, fluid sense of being-in-the-body that I once had; the linkage of brain and limb is a delicate mechanism, and often, now, for me, it becomes uncoupled. To the annoyance of those around me I must then stop and make decisions about what it is that I am attempting to do, and slowly the basic rhythms are reestablished. The more involved I am in memories of my father the more frequently it seems to happen, so I suppose I must look forward to a difficult few weeks. Mrs. Wilkinson gets impatient with me at such times, and this is one of the reasons why I intend to leave her house, probably at the beginning of next week.

There are five others living here, but I pay no attention to them. They never go out, they are passive, apathetic creatures, dead souls such as I encountered frequently overseas. No, I prefer the streets, for I grew up in this part of London, in the East End, and while in one sense the changes are total, and I am a stranger, in another sense nothing has changed: there are ghosts, and there are memories, and they rise in clusters as I catch a glimpse of the underside of a familiar railway bridge, a familiar view of the river at dusk, the gasworks—they haven't changed at all—and my memories have a way of crowding in upon the scene and collapsing the block of time that separates then from now, producing a sort of identity, a sort of running together of past and present such that I am confused, and I forget, so rich and immediate are the memories, that I am what I am, a shuffling, spidery figure in a worn-out suit, and not a dreamy boy of twelve or so. It is for this reason that I have decided to keep a journal.

This is actually a most peculiar house. My room is at the very top, immediately beneath the attic. The trunks and suitcases of Mrs. Wilkinson's tenants are all stored up there, so quite how they manage to make as much noise as they do I

cannot imagine, unless they are very small. Before I leave I
intend to go up and have it out with them, for I have not
had a good night's sleep since I got here—though of course
there's no point in telling Mrs. Wilkinson this, she doesn't
care, why else would she have put me up here? There's a
small, rather wobbly table under the window, which is where
I sit when I write. I am sitting there now, in fact; in front of
me lies my exercise book, all its pages neatly lined, and in
my long slender fingers I hold a blunt pencil. I'm wondering
where I should hide the book when I'm not using it, and I
think for the time being I will simply slide it under the sheet
of newspaper lining the bottom drawer of my chest of drawers; later I can find a more secure place.

Not that there are so many possibilities! I have a narrow
bed with a cast-iron frame and a thin, tired mattress that lies
as uncomfortably upon its few functional springs as I do upon
it; this bed is too short for me by about six inches, so my
feet stick out the end. There is a small threadbare rug on the
cracked green linoleum, and a hook on the back of the door
from which a pair of wire hangers dangle, jangling tinnily
when I open the door. The window is dirty, and though I
have a view of the small park across the road I can never be
sure that I see what I think I see down there, so poor is the
visibility. The wallpaper is a dingy yellowy-green color with
a very faint floral pattern, worn away in places to reveal the
older paper and plaster beneath, and from the ceiling hangs
a bulb in a hat-shaped shade of some parchmentlike material,
the switch being by the door so that I must cross the room
in darkness after turning off the light, a thing I hate. And
this, for now, is where I live.

But at least I'm not far from the canal. I've found a bench
by the water, in a secluded spot that I can call my own, and
there I like to while away an afternoon with no one disturbing
me. From this bench I have a clear view of the gasworks,
and the sight always reminds me of my father, I don't know
why, perhaps because he was a plumber, and a familiar figure

in this neighborhood as he pedaled along on his bicycle with his canvas toolbag slung over his shoulder like a quiver of arrows. The streets were narrow in those days, dark poky little slum houses all crammed together with narrow yards behind—there was outside plumbing, and washing lines stretched from wall to wall, and the yards backed onto narrow alleys where thin stray cats scavenged among the dustbins. London seems so wide and empty now, and this is another thing I find odd: I would have expected it to work the other way round, for the scenes of one's childhood tend to loom huge and vast in the memory, as they were experienced at the time. But for me it's all backwards, I remember everything narrow: rooms, houses, yards, alleys, streets—narrow and dark and constricted, and all pushed together beneath an oppressive sky in which the smoke from the chimneypots trailed off in vague, stringy wisps and strands, a sky filled with rainclouds—it always seemed to be raining, and if it wasn't raining it was always about to rain. There was blackened brickwork, and grimy walls, and against them gray figures in raincoats scurried home like phantoms through late winter afternoons before the lamps were lit.

This is how it works, you see. I sit on my bench with my back to the wall. The sky is gray and overcast; there is perhaps a spot or two of rain. An air of desolation pervades the scene; no one is about. Directly in front of me, a scrubby strip of weeds and grass. Then the canal, narrow and murky, green slime creeping up the stones. On the far side, another patch of weeds, another brick wall, beyond the wall the blotchy brickwork of an abandoned factory with shattered windows, and beyond that the great rust-red domes of the gasworks hulking against the gloomy sky, three of the things, each one a dozen towering uprights arranged in a circle and girdled at the top with a hoop of steel. Within those slender, circling masts of steel sit the wide-domed cylinders of gas, paintwork flaking off them, wheel attachments on their rims to run in the rails of the uprights and permit them to rise and fall with fluctuations in volume and demand. But I try not to look at them, for reasons I will explain later; I gaze south instead, toward a humpbacked bridge a hundred yards away crested with an iron railing and framed on this bank by a dead tree, and beyond it a perspective of gray slate roofs, with ranks of spindly red chimneys drifting smoke. I roll my cigarettes, and somehow time slips by me.

Yes, I roll my endless cigarettes, and as I do I watch my fingers, these long, spidery fingers that seem often not to belong to me at all; they are stained a dark yellow round the tips, and the nails are hard and yellowy and hornlike, and come curving over the ends like hooks, hooks that Mrs. Wilkinson seems now determined to snip off with her kitchen scissors. They are always slightly trembling, these days, these long, yellowing, hooknailed fingers of mine, I really don't know why. But it was a dingy place, the London of my boyhood, a clotted web of dark compartments and narrow passageways, and sometimes when I recognize one of its features I return in my mind to those days without even realizing what I'm doing. This is why I intend to keep a journal, so as to create some order in the jumble of memories that the city constantly arouses in me. Today's date: October 17th, 1957.

ANOTHER gray and cheerless morning. I was up early to write my journal (I'm not very easy in my mind about hiding it in the chest of drawers; later maybe I will try and get it under the linoleum) and whenever I glanced up at the grimy little window over the table I saw merely a thick blanket of grayness that grew slightly paler as somewhere behind it, somewhere out beyond the North Sea, the sun rose into a bleak wintry sky. This house often feels to me like a ship, did I mention this already? It points east, you see, toward the open sea, and here I am up at the top of the east end of it, like a sailor in the crow's nest, as we slip downstream with our cargo of dead souls!

We take our meals in the kitchen here. Mrs. Wilkinson has a small bell; she stands at the foot of the stairs and shakes it, and slowly the dead souls emerge from their rooms and come drifting down with blank faces and rigid limbs, and when I appear—I'm always the last, living as I do on the top floor—they will all be seated around the table in the kitchen, silently eating porridge. The cook is a squat little foreign woman with a wispy black mustache; she stands at the stove with her back to the room, peering into her steaming pots of giblets and offal, smoking cigarettes and wiping her nose with the back of the same hand that stirs the stew.

I take my place at the end of the table. There is a stiff plastic cover spread over the table (like a tarpaulin), already spotted with gobs of porridge and smears of milk—we don't get real milk here, the woman mixes up a powder, so it's a watery sort of a fluid with lumps floating in it. Cups and plates are of thick off-white porcelain, and we're permitted to use real knives and folks. Mrs. Wilkinson is never present unless she has something to say, she is in her office off the hallway by the front door. I attempt a spoonful of porridge; it is poisonously bad. The dead souls pay me no attention. In stupefied, wordless abstraction they hungrily devour the porridge and slurp their tea, various small body sounds escaping from them as they do so, little farts and burps and so on. One by one they finish and drift off to the dayroom. The foreign woman gathers the plates and scrapes off the porridge into a dustbin by the stove. Already her pots of weeds and innards are bubbling energetically; without removing the cigarette from her mouth she leans over, sniffing, to give them a stir; ash falls into the stew.

After breakfast I try to get out as fast as I can. This is not easy, for Mrs. Wilkinson sits in her office by the front door like the three-headed dog of hell. "*Mis*ter Cleg!" she barks, looking up from her paperwork. I freeze; the woman terrifies me. I stand there shuffling guiltily as she gets to her feet and takes off her spectacles and eases her great frame sideways round the desk. "*Mis*ter Cleg!" she cries. She is such a loud woman! I cannot look her in the eye. She leans against the frame of the office door. Seconds tick by with excruciating slowness. She holds a pencil in her plump, strong fingers; she toys with it, and I imagine she will snap it in two—as a warning! "We won't be late for lunch again, will we, Mr. Cleg?"

I mumble something, my eyes on the floor, on the wall— anywhere but her stern face! At last she releases me. "Enjoy your walk, Mr. Cleg," she says, and off I scuttle. It's not surprising, is it, then, that I spill my tobacco on the ground when I've reached the haven of my bench once more, my hands are trembling so? It's not surprising that I should relish my solitude here, my solitude and my memories—she is a tartar, that woman, a harpy, and thank God I shall soon be seeing the last of her.

When I was growing up we lived on Kitchener Street, which is on the other side of the canal, east of here. Our house was number twenty-seven, and like the rest of the houses on the street it had two rooms upstairs, two rooms downstairs, and a walled-in back yard with a door into the alley and an out-house containing a toilet. The front door had a grimy fanlight over it in the form of a setting sun and there was also a coal cellar that you reached through a door that gave off the down-stairs passage and down a steep flight of stairs. All the rooms in the house were small and cramped, with low ceilings; the bedrooms had been wallpapered so many years before that the paper was moist and peeling, and badly discolored in patches; the large spreading stains, with their smell of mil-dewed plaster (I can smell it now!) formed weird figures on the fading floral pattern and stimulated in my childish imag-ination many fantastic terrors. The downstairs passage ran past the front parlor (which was rarely used), past the cellar door, and into the kitchen, where above the sink and beside the back door there was a window that looked out onto the yard. My bedroom was directly above the kitchen, so my window had a view of the yard, and also of the alley beyond and the backs of the houses on the next street over. Perhaps the only way in which our house differed from the other houses on Kitchener Street was that we owned it: my mother's people were in trade, and they'd bought the house for my parents when they were married. I remember hearing this brought up when my mother and father argued in the kitchen at night, for my father believed that my mother's family looked down on him, and I think they did. Nonetheless it was a rare family that owned its house in those days, and it must have been a source of envy for the neighbors; perhaps this helps account for my parents' curious isolation within those teeming streets and alleyways.

On Sunday mornings I often watched my father leaving for the allotments, where he had his vegetable garden. I'd see him outside the back door, in the cool, misty air of the early morning, his breath turning to smoke as he pulled on his cap and wrapped a scarf tightly about his throat, then went down on one knee to knot a piece of string round each of his ankles so his trousers wouldn't be caught in the bicycle chain. The bicycle was leaning against the outhouse wall; he'd wheel it down the yard and through the gate into the alley, and shortly afterwards I'd see him cycling away.

He rode a bicycle in a rigid, upright manner, my father, and I can picture him now, on autumn mornings, in the old threadbare jacket he used for gardening, his cap pulled low, gliding through the deserted streets and taking a sort of grim pleasure in the fresh, smoky silence and in his own solitude within it. He passed the milkman, whose horse snorted and pawed the ground before unloading a steaming heap of ginger-colored bricks of dung upon the cobblestones, and as it snorted great clouds of smoke issued from its blackened and distended nostrils. Sometimes my father would get off his bicycle and trowel the fresh dung into a paper bag, later to add it to his compost heap. Then on through the quiet narrow streets in a southwesterly direction toward the gasworks which, lightly cloaked in the early morning mist, achieved a sort of grandeur, and mystery, despite the smell. Across the canal, then up a long rise and down Omdurman Close to the railway embankment. Halfway across the railway bridge, when he was within sight of the allotments, he dismounted and took a moment or two to roll himself a cigarette. By means of this small ceremony he was able to savor for a few sweet seconds more the prospect of the day that lay before him.

I haven't yet been back to Kitchener Street; I feel apprehensive about crossing the canal and seeing again those blackened bricks, imbued as they are in my memory with the sounds and smells of the tragedy that occurred there. One day I must do it, I know, but not yet, not yet. I did, however, climb the hill to Omdurman Close last week, and even stepped out onto the bridge over the railway lines, clutching tight to the railing. From a point exactly halfway across the bridge—I dared not look down at the meshwork of tracklines far below—I saw that the allotments were still there, beyond the embankment on the far side, and still apparently in use, for the smoke of a gardener's bonfire was sweeping into the turbulent air of that windy October afternoon. But barely had I decided to go further, and see what had become of my father's garden, and of the shed he'd built at the bottom of it, than a goods train went wildly shrieking beneath me, and in a sort of shambling panic I scampered back the way I'd come and was a few moments later clinging limply to a lamp-post with my heart leaping and racing in my chest and my ears ringing with the sound of the train, a terrible sound that for a few seconds turned into a howl of mockery from some tribe of invisible imps, so it seemed! How easily I am thrown into turmoil, these days.

I'm something of a gardener myself, you see. In fact gardening is probably the only good thing that came of the years I spent abroad, learning how to grow vegetables, though I never took to it with the same passion as my father. For him that narrow strip of soil was not merely a source of fresh vegetables, it was, I believe, a sort of sanctuary, a sort of spiritual haven. Having crossed the bridge he would wobble down the narrow path beside the embankment, past the allotments of his fellow gardeners, working men like himself who would already be hoeing, perhaps, or digging, or perhaps simply pacing up and down between the rows with their hands clasped behind their backs and their brows knit as they contemplated their potatoes or their runner beans or their carrots or cabbages or peas. "Morning Horace," they would murmur, as my father slowly steered his bicycle along the path. Silent and abstracted these men may have been, manifestly anxious about slow growth, or blight, or wilt, or a damp summer and marauding crows, but these men were at peace, as I have been at peace in a garden, they were happy.

The first hour of the Sunday morning was when my father reflected on the state of things in the garden, and it was an hour from which he derived a measure of quiet joy incomprehensible to any but a fellow gardener. That hour, in the crisp, early air, with the dew still wet on the cabbage leaves, was in a way what he worked for, for he experienced then a sense of fulfilment that I don't believe he found anywhere else in his narrow, constricted existence. He inspected, he pondered, he poked at the soil with the toe of a boot, he squatted on his hams to examine this plant or that, laid a veined and tender vegetable leaf upon the calloused skin of his palm, and peered at it through his spectacles. Then after a while he would go to his shed, a trim, square structure knocked together from waste lumber and tar paper, and there, in the cobwebby gloom, he would hang up his jacket and fetch out what tools he needed, and the day's work began. This is the barest sketch of my father's allotment (I shall show you more of it in due course), but it was by means of this thin strip of soil and its shed that he was able to carve out within the larger frame of his life a compartment in which to enjoy autonomy and fellowship; and it was this that made existence tolerable for him, and for others like him. In a very real sense the allotment was the spiritual core and flavor of a life that was otherwise loveless, monotonous, and gray.

I HAVEN'T even told you my name yet! It's Dennis, but my mother always called me Spider. I am a baggy, threadbare sort of a customer, really—my clothes have always seemed to flap about me like sailcloth, like sheets and shrouds—I catch a glimpse of them sometimes as I hobble through these empty streets, and they always look vacant, untenanted, the way the flannel flaps and hollows about me, as though I were nothing and the clothes were clinging merely to an idea of a man, the man himself being elsewhere, naked. These feelings disappear when I reach my bench, for there I am anchored, I have a wall behind me and water in front of me, and as long as I don't look at the gasworks all is well. But I had a bit of a shock yesterday, for I discovered that nothing fit me anymore. I noticed it first when I got up from the bench: my trousers barely reached the tops of my ankles, and from the ends of my sleeves my wrists were poking out to an absurd length, like sticks, before flowering suddenly into these long floppy hands of mine. When I arrived back at the house everything seemed to have returned to normal, and it occurred to me that the problem might be with my body rather than my clothes? Of course I wouldn't think of speaking to Mrs. Wilkinson about any of this, she has already made her views clear on the subject: she has forbidden me to wear more than one of any article of clothing at any one time, no more than one pair of trousers, one shirt, one jersey, and so on, though naturally I defy her on this as I like to wear as

many of my clothes as I can, I find it reassuring, and since
returning from Canada reassurance is something I am simply
not getting enough of. Probably the whole thing was just
some sort of perceptual error, I have occasionally been troubled this way in the past.

I am a much taller man than my father was, but in other
respects I resemble him. He was wiry and shortsighted; he
wore round, horn-rimmed spectacles that made him appear
owlish. His eyes had a deceptively mild, watery sort of look
to them, and when he took his spectacles off you realized
what a startlingly pale-blue color they were. But I've seen
those eyes of his fire up with anger, and when that happened
there was nothing mild and watery about him at all, and as
often as not I'd be taken down the coal cellar and feel the
back of his belt. Not that he'd let anyone else ever see his
anger, he was much too careful for that—but my mother and
myself, we saw it, he had no other outlet for it, we were the
only people in the world weaker than he was. I remember
my mother used to say, "Run down the Dog, Spider, and
tell your father his supper's on the table," and that's when I
knew I'd see that furious pale light come up. The Dog was
the pub on the corner of Kitchener Street, the Dog and Beggar. It was not a big pub; there were four rooms, the public
bar, the saloon bar, and two small snugs where private conversation could be had, each room separated from the others
by a wooden screen inset with panels of frosted glass. My
father drank in the public bar, and I can still recall pushing
open the door and being immediately assailed by a welter of
sounds and smells, men's talk, their barks of laughter, thick
smoke, beer, sawdust on the bare boards, and in the winter
a small coal fire burning in the grate. Above the mantelpiece,
I remember, was a mirror with a black toucan on it and the
words GUINNESS IS GOOD FOR YOU. I couldn't read the first
word, I only knew that something was good for you. There
wasn't anything good for me in the public bar of the Dog
and Beggar: I'd see him at the bar, his back bent, leaning

with his elbows on the counter and one boot up on the brass rail that ran the length of it at ankle height; someone would say, "Here's Horace's boy," or, "Here's your boy, Horace," and I'd see him turn toward me, a cigarette hanging from his lips, and in his eyes there'd be only that cold loathing that came of being reminded, again, of the fact of his family and the house to which he must return from the careless sanctuary of the public bar. I'd blurt out my message, my little voice piping like a tin whistle among those shuffling, grunting men, those cattle at their beer, and he would tell me to go on back to the house, he'd be along shortly. No one would know, only I, only I, how intense, how venomous, was the hatred he felt toward me at that moment, and I'd hurry away as quick as I could. I was never able to tell my mother how much I disliked going into the Dog and delivering her message, for my father disguised his feelings so effectively she would have laughed to hear me explain what was really going on.

When he was in this frame of mind—and drinking only made things worse, drinking broke down his reserve—mealtimes were hell. I would sit at the kitchen table gazing at the ceiling, where an unshaded bulb dangled on the end of a braided brown cord. I tended always to slip into reverie in that poky little kitchen, with its clanging pots and dripping tap and ever-present smell of boiling cabbage, it made those ghastly meals tolerable. Outside the twilight darkened into night, and from over by the railway embankment came the scream of a whistle as some suburban train went steaming by. My mother put in front of me a plate of boiled potatoes, boiled cabbage, and stewed neck of mutton, the meat coming away from the bone in stringy grayish patches. There was a terrible tension in the room as I picked up my knife and fork. I knew my father was watching me, and this made things worse, for I was a clumsy boy at the best of times, only poorly in control of those long, gangling limbs of mine. I stuffed a large lump of potato in my mouth, but it was too

hot so I had to cough it back onto my plate. "For Christ's
sake—!" he hissed between clenched teeth. My mother
glanced at him, her own fork poised over a potato that sat
like a plug in a greasy puddle of thin gravy. "Don't lose your
temper," she murmured, "it's not the boy's fault."

The meal progressed in painful silence. There were no further train noises from over by the railway embankment, nor
was there anything moving on Kitchener Street. Cutlery clattered on cheap china as we ate our neck of mutton and the
tap dripped into the sink with a steady plop plop plop. The
bulb overhead continued to spread a sickly yellow light over
the room, and having devoured my food I sat once more
gazing at the ceiling with my lips faintly moving, pausing
only to pick at a shred of mutton caught between my teeth.
"Put the kettle on then, Spider," said my mother, and I rose
to my feet. As I did so I banged one of my kneecaps against
the side of the table, jarring it violently such that my father's
plate moved several inches to the left. I felt him stiffen then,
I felt his grip tighten on his fork, onto the end of which he
had just scraped a soggy pile of pale limp cabbage; but mercifully he said nothing. I lit the gas. At last he finished eating,
laid his knife and fork across the middle of his plate, placed
his hands on the edge of the table, elbows arched outward at
a sharp angle, and prepared to get up from the table. "Off
down the pub, I suppose," said my mother, still at work on
her last potato, which she had cut into a number of very small
pieces, and without lifting her eyes to my father's face.

I cast a quick fearful glance at him; and in the way his jaw
worked I knew what he thought of the pair of us, his gangling,
useless son and his mutely reproachful wife, who sat there
making little pokes and stabs at her potato and refusing to
meet his eye. He took his cap and jacket from the hook on
the back of the door and went out without a word. The kettle
came to the boil. "Make us a nice cup of tea then, Spider,"
said my mother, rising from her chair and brushing at her
cheek as she began to gather the dirty plates.

*   *   *

Later I would go up to my bedroom, and I think I should tell you about that room, for so much of all this is based on what I saw and heard, and even *smelled*, from up there. I was at the back of the house, at the top of the stairs, and I had a view of the yard and the alley beyond. It was a small room, and probably the dampest in the house: there was a large patch on the wall opposite my bed where the paper had come away and the plaster beneath had started literally to erupt— there were crumbly, greenish lumps of moist plaster swelling from the wall, like buboes or cankers, that turned to powder if you touched them. My mother was constantly at my father to do something about it, and though he'd replastered the wall once, within a month they were back, the problem being leaky drainpipes and decaying mortar in the brickwork, all of which my mother thought he should be able to fix but which he never had. I would lie awake at night and by whatever moonlight penetrated the room I would gaze at these shadowy lumps and nodules, and in my boyish imagination they became the wens and warts of some awful humpbacked night-hag with an appalling skin disease, a spirit damned for her sins against men to be trapped, tormented, in the bad plaster of an old wall in a slum. At times she left the wall and entered my nightmares (I was plagued by nightmares, as a boy), and then when I woke in the night in terror I would see her sneering in the corner of the room, turned away from me, her head cloaked in shadow and her eyes glittering from that horrible knobbly skin, the smell of her breath befouling the air; then I would sit up in bed, screaming at her, and it was only when my mother came in and turned the light on that she returned to her plaster, and I would then have to have the light on for the rest of the night.

As for school, I was never happy there, and I tried to avoid the place as much as I could. I had no friends, I didn't want any friends, I didn't like any of them, and over the years they'd learned to leave me alone. I shudder to think of those days, even now: there were long rows of desks in a vast, high-ceilinged barn of a classroom with wooden floorboards, and sitting at each desk a bored child with a pencil and an exercise book. I was at the back of the row closest to the windows, which were set high in the wall so I could not gaze off into space and escape the tedium, and through those windows streamed the light of the day, and in it there was a constant thick drift and swirl of dust. The effect of dust dancing in sunlight has always for me been soporific, doubly so when there came from the front of the room the dull flat weary tones of some disaffected teacher in a shabby suit and heavy leather shoes who paced back and forth in front of the blackboard—a distant world, dusty eons from my own— interrupting himself to chalk up a word, or some numbers, the chalk scraping on the board with a hideous screech that had the pupils squirming, and the dust swirled as they shuffled on the floorboards with their shoes, and your Spider drifted further and further away, further into the back parts of his mind where no one could follow. Rarely was I called upon in class to answer a question; other boys and girls were better at that than I was, confident clever children who could rise smartly to their feet and tell the teacher what he wanted to hear. These children sat at the front of the classroom, closest to the blackboard; back here in the netherlands was where the "slower" children sat, a fat boy called Ivor Jones who was less popular even than me and was made to cry in the playground every day as a matter of routine, and a very messy girl named Wendy Wodehouse whose nose was always running with snot, and whose dress was always filthy, and who smelled, and who craved affection so avidly that she'd pull her knickers down behind the toilets if you asked her, and there were rumors she did other things as well. These were my closest neighbors at the back of the class, Ivor Jones and Wendy Wodehouse, but there was no sort of alliance possible between us, in fact we hated each other more bitterly than the other children hated us, because to each other we presented an image of our own pathetic isolation. I doubt I was missed when I stopped going to school; there would have been a neat line of *absents* in the register, and one less set of homework to mark. Nobody cared.

On Saturday nights my mother and father always went to the pub together. From my bedroom window, where I sat with my elbows on the sill and my chin in my hands, I'd see them leave through the back door and go down the yard, then through the gate and into the alley. They always sat at the same small round table in the public bar, close to the fireplace. They didn't have a great deal to say to one another; from time to time my father went up to the bar, and the landlord, a man called Ratcliff, served him. "Same again, is it, Horace?" he'd say, and my father would nod, his cigarette between his lips as he fumbled for change in his trousers.

I've mentioned that I lived in Canada for the last twenty years. About those years I intend to say nothing at all, apart from this: I spent much time, in Canada, thinking about the events I am here describing, and I arrived at certain conclusions that would never, for obvious reasons, have occurred to me at the time; these I shall disclose as we go forward. As regards my father's first glimpse of Hilda Wilkinson, my guess is that he heard her before he saw her—she was a loud woman (especially when she had a drink in her hand), and there was a slightly hoarse edge to her voice, a sort of huskiness, that some men seem to find attractive. I see my father sitting stiffly in the Dog in his hard-backed chair by the fire, while on the far side of the room Hilda stands at the center of a lively group of drinkers. Up comes that laugh of hers, and for the first time he becomes aware of it. I see him startled, I see him turning, I see him frowning as he seeks the source of the noise—but he cannot locate it, for the Dog is crowded and he is not wearing his spectacles. He is far too guarded a man to allow my mother or anybody else to know what's going on, so the image he constructs of Hilda that night is assembled from the gleanings of a series of furtive, short-sighted glances, taken when he goes to the bar, or out to the Gents—he catches a glimpse, perhaps, between a group of men, of her neck (flushed pink with warmth and alcohol) and the back of her head, the blonde hair piled and pinned atop it in an untidy heap; or, a little later, he sees her hand for a moment, with its pale plump fingers grasping a glass of sweet port and a cigarette; or staring, apparently absently, at the floor, he discovers a white ankle and a foot in a scuffed black high-heeled shoe—and all the while he hears that hoarse-tinged voice erupting in husky laughter.

As he walked my mother home, his hobnail boots ringing on the stones of the alley, my father still held in his mind's eye these scraps and fragments of the laughing woman in the public bar. My parents had sexual intercourse that night, as they did every Saturday night, but I don't think that either of them was really in the here-and-now. My mother was distracted by a headful of her own concerns, and my father was still thinking about his blonde; and in his imagination, I would guess, it was with her that he copulated, not my mother.

He was back in the Dog the next night, and Ratcliff had leisure to rest a forearm on the bar and drink a small whisky with him and pass a few remarks about Saturday's football. It was in the course of this exchange that my father fleetingly glimpsed, behind the other's head, in the snug opposite, a large, flushed face beneath an untidy pile of blonde hair; and a moment later he caught the tones of that boisterous voice again. A rapid flare of heat inside him, and he lost all interest in the landlord's talk. "Customer, Ernie," he murmured, indicating the snug, and Ratcliff glanced over his shoulder. In a low voice he said: "It's that fat tart Hilda Wilkinson"—then made his way in a leisurely manner down the bar to serve the woman.

Little enough occurred that night in terms of an actual encounter. My father stayed in the public bar, straining to see and hear what went on in the snug, while at the same time attempting to learn what he could from Ernie Ratcliff, though the landlord proved disappointing, for this night he wished only to talk about football. At one point my father noticed another woman come up to the bar, one of the group that had surrounded Hilda the night before, a small woman in a hat who pushed empty glasses across the counter and asked in quiet, mannish tones for a bottle of stout and a sweet port.

He did not leave until closing time. The night was cool, and a slight rain had begun to fall. He stood on the pavement with his cap pulled low and spent some moments rolling a cigarette. A sudden splash of yellow light some yards away, at the corner, told him that the door of the snug had opened, and glancing up he saw that Hilda Wilkinson and her friend had emerged. For a moment she gazed straight at him, and he met her gaze from the corners of his eyes, his tongue on the edge of his cigarette paper. For the first time he saw her clearly—and what a glorious woman she was, a spirited woman, bosomy and fair-skinned, a *yacht* of a woman! With her ratty fur coat flapping about her, and the rain drizzling down on her bare head, and lit still by the glow from the pub, she gazed squarely at my father, her big chin uplifted, and suddenly dear God how he wanted her, this he knew with more certainty than he'd ever known anything in his life before! Then the door swung closed, the glow disappeared, and the two women hurried off together into the rain and the night.

I CLOSED the book and, leaning over in my chair, pushed it under the linoleum where it peels away from the floor by the skirting board. I felt drained by my effort of memory and conjecture. It was late, the house was silent and in darkness, even the attic above me was still. I lay down on the bed, on top of the thin blankets, without getting undressed. I smoked, staring at the light as it swung almost imperceptibly on its cord. The silence seemed to grow thick all about me. I continued staring at the ceiling, and slowly became preoccupied with the light bulb, a glowing filament inside a fragile shell of thin gray brittle glass. For some minutes I continued staring, my exhausted brain empty of all images but the bulb, which had begun to crackle at me; and then I became aware of the smell of *gas*. It was very faint, so faint that for a few moments I thought I must have imagined it. But then I smelled it again. I lifted my head from the pillow and looked about me. There is one outlet in the wall where there used to be a gas lamp, and there is an upright gas fire installed in the fireplace like a screen, but it too has been shut off for years. I got off the bed and, pulling the chair across the floor, clambered onto it to sniff the dead pipe in the wall. Nothing. I went down on my hands and knees and put my nose to the gas fire. It was hard to tell what was there, it was so indefinite, at one moment leading me to think it was here inside the room, the next convincing me that it was only the memory of a smell, a memory that some obscure chain of associations had set off as a result of my writing.

There was a third possibility, though it took several minutes for it to dawn on me: that the smell was coming from *me,* from my own body.

This was a shock. I straightened up and tried to smell myself. Nothing. I staggered upright, clutching the end of the bed, and opened my shirt and trousers, fumbling clumsily at the buttons in my haste. Was it there? Again that awful uncertainty—I would seem to have it, then it was gone. I sat hunched on the bed, cluching myself round the shins, my forehead on my knees. Did I have it? Was there gas? Was it seeping from my *groin?* I lifted my head and turned it helplessly from side to side. Gas from my *groin?* It was at that moment that I became aware of a noise in the attic overhead, quiet laughter followed by a sort of bump—then there was silence again.

I had little sleep the rest of that night, and the light stayed on. I tried to put the whole thing out of my mind, but it wouldn't go away, a terrible nagging uncertainty persisted. I was particularly uneasy at breakfast, for I had the feeling that they could destroy me, any of them, with just a glance; I felt like a light bulb. It wasn't until I reached the canal that some semblance of normality returned, and as with trembling fingers I rolled a cigarette, and the minutes slipped by me in that lonely place, so did the events of the night come to seem like a waking nightmare of some kind; after a while I was able to shrug it off.

But gas—why gas? I was at a loss to know what to make of it. Was it connected to the gasworks on the far side of the canal? They don't have gasworks in Canada, so when I'd looked at the three great domes behind the factory it was the first sight I'd had of such things in two decades, though it's the structural character that disturbs me, nothing more, the uprights comprise thousands of steel modules, and each of the four faces of each module is a frame with diagonal crossstruts; and stacked as they are to a great height, they repeat this crisscross pattern almost to infinity, and if I look at them too long I become absorbed in the pattern and the effect is horribly vertiginous—this is foolish, I know, but the sensation is real nonetheless. Is this why I suffered those bizarre sensations last night? I failed to find a connection.

I walked home slowly through the wet empty streets. It had begun to rain earlier in the afternoon (I had not gone back to the house for lunch), and the drizzle had persisted for several hours now. I was soaked through, but I didn't care, it felt cleansing, and after the peculiarly unwholesome events of the night I welcomed this. On I went as the damp day thickened to dusk, past a long series of grimy brick arches, a smoke-blackened viaduct supporting the railway lines that slice across the East End streets, many of the arches bricked up now, or sealed off with sheets of corrugated tin behind which scrap-yards and garages did their furtive business. From one of them a humped man in a shabby wheelchair suddenly emerged then went lurching round the corner, and I followed him under the arch, and coming out on the other side I saw, again, to the east, the gasworks, the rusty bulk of its trio of domes stained and streaked a dark reddish-brown in the drizzle.

I crept back into the house and went straight up to my room, where I intended to smoke, for I had smoked very little all day. I stood by my table as I groped for tobacco and papers, and gazed out of the window at the shabby square below, in the center of which stands a little park with spiked iron railings, a few bushes, a tree or two, a small pond, and some grass where the children play. It was almost dark. At the gate of the park, padlocked since 5:30 P.M., stood a single lamppost, a black iron stem rising from a fluted base, a short knobbed crosspiece near the top, and a glass box that housed an orb of light that spread a hazy, yellowy-gold glow through which the drizzle came drifting like flecks, like hints, or suggestions. My clever fingers plucked and spread tobacco in my paper, then I rolled the thing and licked the edge. I have a squat tin lighter with a hinged cap; with this I lit the cigarette, and then I smoked. Night fell, and the yellowy haze of the streetlamp strengthened and brightened in the blackening air, and still the rain came misting down through its corona on the slant, like so many memories drifting across some lost and benighted mind. I seated myself at the table and reached down for my book.

The following Sunday had dawned bright and clear, and before eight I heard my father in the kitchen downstairs, filling the kettle and turning on the gas. I heard the clatter of the big black skillet as he set it on the stove, I heard the bread tin being opened for the heel and crust of yesterday's loaf. Then silence—the smell of bacon fat drifting up the stairs— he is sitting at the table drinking his tea from a chipped white enamel mug and dipping the bread into the hot fat. The scrape of chair legs—he is lacing up his boots—then out the back door, and from my bedroom window I watched him go down the yard to his bicycle.

It must have been some time that afternoon that Hilda Wilkinson crossed the railway lines by the bridge off Omdurman Close and made her way along the path to the allotments. My father was in his shed sorting through a basket of potatoes he had dug that morning. That shed—what a shudder it still arouses in me, the very thought of the place! It was very dark inside, and it smelled strongly of earth. There were always piles of boxes and sacks and baskets in there, tools of course, spades and rakes and hoes and so on, seed packets in bundles tied with string on the shelves, and up in the shadows, draped between the rafters, the cobwebs. Sometimes I would close the door behind me and watch them for hours, and in the shed's deep gloom—it had no window, and what light there was slipped in through chinks and cracks— I would at last see a great web tremble as its maker scuttled rapidly along a fine gossamer trapline for its meal. At other times I would fling open the door and let daylight for a moment flood the shed, and then the webs would shimmer in the sunshine as I gazed entranced at the filmy delicacy and perfection of their construction. But I never had enough time, somehow, to examine them properly in the light. There was also a battered, leaking, horsehair armchair in there, and beside it a wooden box on which a candle was stuck in a puddle of old wax; and lastly—and where this came from I've not the faintest idea—on a shelf on the back wall there was a stuffed ferret in a dusty glass case. It was snarling, exposing its little white pointed teeth, one paw raised, its sleek lithe body frozen in a posture of sudden alarm, and though one of its glass eyeballs was missing, and stuffing oozed out of the socket, the other glittered sharply in the shed's gloom and always upset me if I looked at it too long, malignant creature it was.

My father, as I say, was selecting potatoes to bring back to Kitchener Street, and he didn't hear Hilda come up the path. It was a bright day, that Sunday, but cold. Then he looked up sharply and saw her framed in the doorway with the light streaming in all around her, hair disheveled, breast heaving from the exertion. He stood there, bent over his basket in the gloom as he turned guiltily toward this woman with whom, by this time, he had more than once imagined copulating. In a leisurely manner she surveyed the inside of the shed. Slowly my father straightened up, unconscious that he had a potato in each hand though clutching them so tightly that his knuckles turned white. Hilda's hands were deep in the pockets of her big fur. "Mister Cleg?" she said hoarsely, lifting her chin and her eyebrows in a sort of interrogatory gesture.

"Yes," said my father, at last finding his voice.

"Horace Cleg?" she said. "The plumber?"

"That's right," said my father, dropping his potatoes into the basket. He was recovering his poise now.

"I'm having a spot of trouble with my pipes," said Hilda. "I was told you could help me."

M y father's relationship with Hilda Wilkinson properly began when he went to work on her pipes. She had not lingered long on his allotment; an appointment had been made, the pair of them behaving in an adult, businesslike manner throughout, and then, without a single bubble of hoarse laughter, with no saucy lift of that big pink chin, off she'd gone, swaying and yawing to right and left as she picked her way carefully down the garden path. My father had watched her from the door of the shed, then gone back inside and lowered himself into the armchair. Picking a potato from the basket beside him, he turned it slowly in his fingers, reflecting on what had just occurred.

Hilda lived over a tobacconist's shop on Spleen Street, which runs under the gasworks on the side farthest from the canal; she shared a flat with a woman called Nora Temple, the woman in the hat my father had noticed with her in the Dog and Beggar. A few days later then we find him leaning his bicycle against the lamppost outside the tobacconist's. Glancing up at the looming domes that cast a small sea of shadow on the shops and houses of Spleen Street, he entered the tobacconist's and went through the back and up a dark flight of steep narrow stairs. It was when he was halfway up those stairs that a peculiar thing happened. From above, the sudden sound of heavy footsteps descending; then a fat man in a thick black overcoat with the collar turned up came clattering down and without a word pushed by my father, forcing him against the banister and almost knocking him back down the stairs. A moment later he could be heard stamping out through the shop and into the street, the little bell on the tobacconist's door tinkling feebly in his wake. My father was astonished and annoyed; frowning, he resumed the climb. At the sound of his knock the door of the flat was opened a crack, and through the crack peered Nora, who was hostile and suspicious until he said he was the plumber. There would then have been some difficulty about getting the door open, as Nora wouldn't want the cats to get out, for they had dozens of the creatures, mangy things always yowling and shedding hairs. So my father edged in sideways through the crack and followed Nora as she clumped off on heavy shoes down a short dark passage far more constricted than it need have been on account of the bulky coats hanging from hooks and pegs along the walls, his progress further hampered by the cats swarming about his ankles. At the end of the passage Nora threw open the door of the lavatory. "In here," she said. But before my father could go in, a familiar voice spoke: "That the plumber?"

He turned. She was standing in the doorway of her bedroom. She was wearing a dressing gown of some silky material, low-cut at the breast and tightly belted. Her hair was freshly brushed, and she was smoking a cigarette. Without her high heels she was an inch or two shorter than my father, and this fact alone provoked in him a vivid flare of the familiar heat. "Afternoon," he said, standing stiffly in front of her with his toolbag in one hand and his cap in the other. She was leaning against the doorframe; her room, my father saw, was crowded with furniture. The bed, unmade, was huge, the headboard a dark plate of lacquered wood wedged between two stout posts with knobs at the top. At the foot of the bed stood a dressing table, a mere splinter of space separating it from the bed, its big mirror and two flanking wings almost obliterating the window, which was curtained with a piece of dingy lace, and through which he glimpsed the vast looming bulk of the gasworks; and upon the dressing table a chaotic litter of cosmetics and hairbrushes and pins and grips and bits of colored elastic. Between bed and wall on one side was a small table, also littered with female stuff, and from the depths of that litter rose a half-empty bottle of port and a pair of unwashed glasses. On the other side of the bed was a chair, so heavily draped with skirts and blouses and stockings and underwear that it was more a hump of fabrics, a hillock of silk and cotton, than anything else. Then the banging started: suddenly, a series of harsh metallic clangs in the pipes. "Hear that?" said Hilda. "We get that three times an hour."

"Water-hammer," said my father in his short gruff way.

Hilda shifted slightly on her doorframe and blew smoke at the ceiling. "That what you call it?" she said.

My father nodded. "Blockage in the vent stack, I shouldn't wonder."

She gazed at him frankly. "It's driving me mad," she said. "Can you fix it, plumber?"

My father sniffed, adopted his cagey artisan manner, as if to suggest that this was a matter of delicacy and tact. "I'll have to test the system," he said.

"Live round here, do you?" said Hilda.

"Kitchener Street."

"I thought so." She was examining her fingernails. "I thought I seen you down the Dog." Suddenly she yawned, stretched her arms above her head and then, with a lazy smile, folded them back across her chest. "You going to stand there all day, then?" she said. "I thought you was here to do my pipes."

Her skin, my father noticed, was a much paler pink than he'd first thought, white, almost, and her dressing gown left exposed all the top part of her bosom. He also realized for the first time that her chin was really quite abnormally prominent, but her skin was so clear, and her hair so gloriously wheaty (though black at the roots), that after a moment or two you simply didn't notice the square, puggy jut of the thing, and the bad bite of her ill-occluding lower teeth. "Some sort of clogging," said my father, still standing in the doorway, still with his cap in one hand and his toolbag in the other. Then, as Hilda bent down to scoop up the cat purring at her ankles, he saw them: a glimpse, a clear view, for just an instant, as the dressing gown fell forward, of her breasts: perfectly framed within the silky material, a pair of white, bell-shaped breasts with little rose-colored nipples. He tore his eyes away. "Air in the pipes," he said—and at that moment, as suddenly as it had begun, the banging stopped.

"Bad air," said Hilda, absently stroking the cat. "Can't you smell it?"

"It's coming from your lavatory," said my father.

Hilda smiled. Because of her jaw it was a queer little smile, more of a short slit with slight openings at either end, and my father was oddly touched. "I sincerely hope so," she said. "Shocking, the state of the plumbing in this place." Still smiling, she permitted her eyes to drift languidly up and down the dour man rigid in her bedroom doorway. "Well, you going to stand there all day?" she repeated. "You going to do my pipes or what?"

My father found, as he'd thought he would, that there was no water in the toilet bowl and hence no seal, or trap, to impede the passage of sewer gases. Back-siphonage had occurred as a result of a pressure differential caused, like the water-hammer, by blockage or clogging in one of the vent stacks. It was his task to locate the blockage and eliminate it, and his first thought was of nesting mice: they often got into the plumbing of these old buildings. He would test the system by closing all the pipes then turning on the water; an inspection of the various valves and faucets should then lead him to the source of the dysfunction.

I put down my pencil. I was deep in unknown territory. I only knew Hilda Wilkinson later, and by that time her relationship with my father had progressed far beyond these early, formal contacts. So I am moving forward in the darkness, with little to guide me but my intuition.

I presume my father fixed Hilda's back-siphonage and water-hammer problems; these are straightforward tasks for a competent plumber, though whether it was nesting mice I can't say. When I was a small boy my father used to talk to me about his work, he'd show me his tools, explain what they were for, and if he had a job to do about the house I'd be his apprentice, it'd be up to me to hand him his blowtorch or his number-eight spanner, or whatever. Oddly enough there always seemed to be something wrong with our lavatory too, in the outhouse in the yard; when you flushed it the water came right to the top of the bowl, and sometimes slopped over onto the floor. But it was like the plaster in my bedroom, for when he fixed it it would only work for a month or two and then the problem started again. I don't think my mother is to be blamed for nagging him about it, he was, after all, a plumber, and when the thing overflowed it was her who'd have to mop up the mess. How she worked, my mother! I can remember coming home from school and finding her on her knees scrubbing the kitchen floor, a bucket of dirty water beside her as she pushed about a big, stiff-bristled brush with both hands. I knew what happened to the hands of women on Kitchener Street: they'd murmur to one another over the back wall about working their fingers to the bone, but the very reverse was true; years of hot water and coarse soap piled heaps of sodden nerveless flesh on those bones, they were red, raw, flabby things, and had my mother lived I imagine the same would have been true of hers. But she was young, still, when all this happened, she had not yet lost the bloom of her young womanhood.

When did it all start to go sour? When did it start to die? There was a time when we were happy; I suppose the decay was gradual, a function of poverty and monotony and the sheer grim dinginess of those narrow streets and alleys. Drink, too, played its part, and so too did my father's character, his innately squalid nature, the deadness that was inside him and that came in time to infect my mother and me like some sort of contagious disease.

Two or three evenings later he was in the public bar of the Dog and Beggar when he heard Hilda's gusty tones issuing from the snug. He drained his pint of mild and made his way out onto the street and along to the door of the snug. He pushed it open; Hilda was seated at the table with three of her friends. They turned toward him. Hilda's face was flushed, and at the very moment my father appeared in the doorway a glass of port was halfway to her lips. There it stayed as she lifted her eyebrows and smiled that puggy smile of hers. Nora sat on one side of her; on the other, a dark, tarty-looking woman and a thin young man with long hair. It was a dry, cold, moonless night in late November, and in the sudden silence that descended on the room only the distant murmur of traffic was audible from three streets away, and the muted hum of conversation in the Dog's other bars. Hilda's eyes shifted from my father to the three others seated at the table. Then she set down her glass—my father still stood in the doorway—rose to her feet, and swept across the snug and past him into the street. As he let the door swing closed behind him a ripple of quiet laughter erupted at the table.

Using the alleyways that ran between the backs of the houses they made their way down toward the canal. Hilda was in good spirits. She'd forgotten his first name though. "Horace!" she exclaimed. "Always been one of my favorites. I'd a cat called Horace once." She talked about the weather. "Nippy, eh?" she said. "I'm glad I've got me fur." What was going through my father's head? What did he think was going to happen? He glanced at her from the corner of his eye. She was marching along with her shoulders hunched and her hands deep in her pockets. "Lovely job you did on them pipes," she said. "Barely a squeak out of them now. Smell didn't go away though." They talked about plumbing for some minutes. Hilda knew very little about it, and appeared impressed by my father's obvious mastery of the trade. She was a jovial woman, and soon had him silently chuckling. Most people, he remarked, were bored stiff by plumbing. "I don't believe it!" she cried. "Well, not me, Horace. I love plumbing."

They had reached the bridge over the gasworks canal. She led him to a set of slimy stone steps that gave onto a narrow quay just above water level. "Come on, then, Horace," she murmured, gingerly descending, "down we go." They were now effectively hidden from the view of any passerby. Hilda opened her coat, unbuttoned her cardigan and showed him her breasts. Then she slid an arm round his waist and with her other hand rubbed his trousered groin, grinning at him as she did so. "How do you like that, Horace?" she whispered. She was exactly the same height as him in her heels, but probably a little heavier, and to feel the big swelling weight of her pressed against him almost overwhelmed the man. He slipped his hands inside the fur coat and hesitantly touched her breasts, then tried to kiss her on the mouth, but she turned her face aside. His penis was stiff in his trousers; Hilda continued whispering to him as she rubbed it with the inside of her palm, then deftly undid the lower buttons of his fly and pulled it out. "What's this then?" she murmured. It was an unusually thin penis, my father's, but stiff as a pencil, and twitching. Hilda spat on her hands. "Ooh, Horace," she whispered. She brought him to climax in half a dozen quick strokes, then shifted aside as he spurted into the canal. She stepped away from him then, tucked her breasts back into her cardigan, and closed her coat with a shiver. My father was standing at the edge of the quay with his back to her, urinating into the canal. He could see his sperm drifting away through the black water, filmy strings of the stuff, grayish and translucent. "Hurry up then, Horace," said Hilda, her teeth chattering, "I'm bloody freezing." But my father wanted to be alone; he told her he was going to stay out and have a smoke. "Suit yourself," she said cheerfully, "I'm off back up the Dog."

When my father reached the top of the steps a few moments later Hilda was marching up the street. Frowning, he leaned against the railing and groped for his tobacco. He watched the fur-coated figure pass under one streetlamp after another, trailing clouds of smoky breath behind her as the tap tap tapping of her heels on the pavement grew fainter and fainter, and when it had vanished altogether he was still standing on the bridge in the cold night air.

THERE was a time when we were happy. My mother was so quiet, so patient; even when my father began spending all his spare time on his allotment or in the Dog she never became shrill or bitter, she never turned into a *shrew*, as most of the women on Kitchener Street did; her sweetness of temper persisted against all odds. Sometimes we would sit together in the kitchen, she and I, in the evening, and we'd play games of the imagination. There was a large stain on the kitchen ceiling, and the game was to make up a story about it. Mine were always horrible—I'd see a twisted dwarf up there, and describe to my mother in lurid detail the evil done by this creature at dead of night when good people were asleep. My mother, her knitting in her lap and her needles peacefully clacking, would shiver at the things I said. "Spider, what an idea!" she would murmur. "However did you think of such a thing!" When it was her turn she would set down her needles and tell me that the stain on the ceiling was a haystack, or a cottage, or a loaded wagon—she'd grown up in Essex, and had never lost her feeling for the countryside. And as she talked, and the tapping of her needles resumed, a restful, rather dreamy expression softened her features, and the dark terrors of my own tale would be dispelled, replaced by a mood of lyric tenderness, by pictures of fields and farms, birdsong in summertime, fresh cobwebs glistening in the elms at sunrise. She used to tell me about the spiders, about how they did their weaving in the quiet of the night, and how, early in the morning, she'd cross the field and see the webs they'd woven draped in the branches like clouds of fine muslin, though as she got closer they'd turn into shining wheels, each with a spider motionless at the center. But it wasn't the webs she'd come to see, she said, for hidden in the lower boughs, if you knew where to look, you'd find a little silk bag the size of a pigeon's egg hanging from a twig by a thread. Inside the bag, she'd say, was a tiny ball of orange beads all glued together and no bigger than a pea—and those were the spider's eggs. She'd been busy all night, spinning from her own insides the silk she'd need to weave the egg-bag and the coats it wore to keep it warm and dry. And look, Spider, see how perfect her work is! Not a thread out of place! Then in my mind's eye I'd see the little egg-bag dangling on its thread, and yes, it was a perfect thing, a tiny bulb of compact white satin with black silk and brown laid across it in broad ribbons, in spindle-shaped patterns, in elaborate wavy lines. I imagined cutting it open and finding inside a thick quilt of wadding, and under that the fine silk pocket in which lay the tiny eggs themselves. But it was the ending of the story that I loved best: What happened to the spider, I'd say. My mother would sigh. When she's finished (she said) she just crawls off to her hole without a backward glance. For her work is done, she has no silk left, she's all dried up and empty. She just crawls away and dies. The knitting resumed. "Put the kettle on, Spider," she'd say, "and we'll have a nice cup of tea."

I'd be in bed by the time my father came home. Sometimes I heard nothing; I knew then he was sullen and silent, unresponsive to her talk and her concern. Soon I'd hear him come heavily up the stairs, leaving her to see to the lights and the doors. At other times he came home angry, and then I'd hear his voice raised, the sharp bite of his sarcasm, the quiet tones of my mother as she tried to soften his temper and blunt the spike of his drink-quickened grievance against the world and her. Often he reduced her to tears, he abused her with such fierce spite, and once, I remember, she came hurrying out of the kitchen, along the passage and up the stairs into my room, where she sank onto the edge of my bed, clutched my hand and sobbed into a handkerchief for several moments before bringing herself under control. "I'm sorry, Spider," she whispered. "Sometimes your father upsets me so. It's my fault—you go to sleep, it's all right, I'm fine now." And she leaned over to kiss me on the forehead, and I felt the dampness of the tears on her face. Oh, I hated him then! Then I would have killed him, were it in my power— he had a squalid nature, that man, he was dead inside, stinking and rotten and dead.

I W A S feeling better, much better, by the time I closed the book and pushed it back under the linoleum. I think it comes of talking about my mother, or at least talking about the hours I spent with her alone. It was different when my father was present; then there was tension, and ugly silences, and neither of us could properly be ourselves. I pushed back my chair and rose to my feet and stretched. I really did feel remarkably well. I leaned on my hands on the table and gazed out of the window. The rain had stopped, though droplets still clung to the bare branches of the trees in the park, glinting in the light of the streetlamp then dripping onto the dead leaves below. A figure with an umbrella went hurrying along the pavement, and somewhere a dog began to bark. The moon was a slender crescent of yellow light, and I imagined that light rippling on the dark swells of the river a mile or so to the south. I knew I would sleep well tonight, and there would be no more of this business about gas. I think it's the house that's to blame—I am a sensitive individual, highly strung, and Mrs. Wilkinson's establishment is not suitable for such as I. Tomorrow or the next day I would hand in my notice and find more sympathetic accommodations. I might even move away from the East End altogether—the memories it arouses are so relentless, somehow, and so grim, for the most part, perhaps if I was away from here I could think about the past with more detachment?

I was up early the next morning, and still in excellent spirits.

The day was gloomy and damp, and this I welcomed, for I have always enjoyed rain and mist and darkness. I sat at my table until I heard the bell for breakfast, smoking, gazing at the blanket of cloud, and working out what I would say to Mrs. Wilkinson. I was one of the first in the kitchen that morning; I sat at the table, drumming my fingers, and as the dead souls appeared one by one I greeted them loudly. Little response, of course; in they came, shuffling and grunting, settling down to their porridge with lowered eyes. I couldn't eat; I drank tea instead, cup after cup, with plenty of sugar and no milk. My fingers were drumming, my feet were tapping, I was smiling at the world. I announced to the dead souls that I would shortly be leaving them. Little response to this either, though a few fishlike eyes did flicker up from porridge bowls and cast glances my way. Yes, I told them, soon they wouldn't be seeing Mr. Cleg anymore, I was taking lodgings elsewhere in town (I remained vague about precisely where). Yes, I said, I should be taking a suite of rooms, my residence in the garret—I pointed at the ceiling—was purely temporary, a stopgap measure while I found my feet. In Canada, I told them, I had been accustomed to certain amenities, a billiard table, a library—how could a person live in a house that lacked a library? I drank more tea; I expanded upon my theme. But barely was I launched than I saw them turning toward the door. Mrs. Wilkinson was standing there with her arms folded across her chest. I fell silent. "Go on, Mr. Cleg," she said. "This is most informative."

Her sarcasm was like acid. "Mr. Cleg," she said, advancing into the room. I turned sideways in my chair, averted my face to the wall and crossed my legs. I began to fumble with my tobacco. "Mr. Cleg," she said, "I do sincerely wish I could provide you with a billiard table and a library, but this is not a rich house, and so we must shift for ourselves—as you do, Mr. Cleg, I wish more of the residents would get out for a stroll."

Still sideways in my chair, my face still averted, I grew

rigid. I burned with humiliation. From my trembling fingers shreds of tobacco spilled onto my trousers. Several moments passed. A weary sigh, then, from my tormentor. "Mr. Cleg, how many shirts are you wearing? What about our agreement?" Agreement! I was frozen stiff by this point. I abandoned the effort to roll a cigarette. My fingers hung poised and immobile, a paper between two fingers of the left hand, a pinch of tobacco in the right. Silence. What was she doing? Then, from one of the dead souls: "She's gone, Mr. Cleg," and I slowly relaxed, though my fingers kept twitching for at least another quarter of an hour.

Not until I was safely out of the front door did my spirits begin to rally. The woman is a monster! But I put her out of my mind, I was in much too good a humor to let her spoil it, and soon I was bubbling with exuberance once more. For some reason I felt reluctant to sit by the canal, and I wondered, as I do every morning, whether today I would cross the bridge and revisit Kitchener Street. But I didn't revisit Kitchener Street, not that day, nor did I go to the canal, I went to the river instead, for I knew that I should only become morbid if I watched the rain spotting the black surface of the canal, for the rain carries ideas, this I learned in Canada, where it rains almost all the time. Along the towpath I went then climbed up to the main road—how fast everything seemed to be moving in the rain!—crossed over, then threaded my way through narrow streets to an alley between the warehouses, then to a set of worn stone steps descending to the river itself. Oh, the river! Great broad swirling stream, old Father Thames in the raw gray day! On the far side, the cranes of Rotherhithe poking at me through the mist like fingers, or insects. On the lower steps, as I gingerly descended, a creeping green slime, and one of the steps was eaten away and the rest were crumbling and pocked. At the foot of the steps the water churned and eddied, gray-green like the sky, the thick, lowering blanket of sky, spitting rain, soaking me through, my cap a soggy, useless thing by this point so I tossed it into the river and watched it float away. I love the wetness of a day like this, I love wetness and darkness and skies like thick gray blankets, for it is only at such times that I feel at home in the world.

I made my way in a state of some exhilaration back across the main road (there was some honking and emotion in the traffic, for I had one of my forgetful moments, I became uncoupled), then back along the towpath. Close to my bench I left the canal and quite on impulse moved up the hill to Omdurman Close, until I stood on the bridge across the railway lines. Far below me the rails glistened, bedewed iron cobwebs, but no imps could terrorize me in weather like this, this was my day! Over the bridge then, a damp ecstatic squelch it was, for the rain was really very heavy now—and at the other end I stood and gazed upon the allotments spread beneath me, strip by strip, in a sort of haze, each one fenced off, tenanted by its shed. Nothing, nothing had changed here! Down the path I shuffled, muddy, puddled path though it was, careless of its mud and its puddles, until I stood again at the gate to my father's allotment.

Nothing had changed. I opened the gate and advanced down the path, the potato plants to either side of me bedraggled and flattened like prostrate courtiers, as the rain splattered onto the soil and formed pools in the troughs between the rows. Set back from the shed, off to the right of it, the compost heap, a soggy thing this day, its eggshells and peelings congealing in a slick moist fecund mash, and there before me the shed itself, cleansed by the rain, I felt no black horror from it, none of the sheer giddy waves of horror that my father provoked from the place and which came in time to haunt him to the very threshold of his sanity—none of that, nor, as I turned toward the soil again, did I feel the horror there either, there was peace in the soil, for the rain brings peace to the living and the dead, to all things under the ground and under the water, they all rest in the rain. I knelt down in the potato patch and laid my head on the soil;

and then a voice said: "Here! What do you think you're doing?"

Here! Here! Here here here here here! It echoed as I turned, stumbling, toward the source, a bearded figure in a cap and raincoat on the other side of the fence. Here! Here! Here here here here here! The imps took up the cry, damn them, damn their filthy souls to hell! Oh, I fled, I went squelching and weeping back up the path and over the bridge with the sounds of their filthy voices ringing in my ears until I was back on the bench, a damp and heaving wreck, I should have known, I told myself, I should have known, they never rest, I must be cunning, I must be like the fox.

Mrs. Wilkinson saw me coming in, soggy bit of flotsam that I was, and she wasn't at all happy that I was so wet. But I ignored her as I shuffled upstairs, heedless also of the dead souls who emerged from the dayroom to peer at my dripping and beleaguered shell. I sat on the side of my bed with my elbows on my knees, a sad and sorry water-spider indeed— and then she came barging in, without knocking, all brisk matronly zeal. "Out of those wet things, Mr. Cleg," she said, "we don't want you catching your death of cold."

I was totally debilitated by this point, my exuberance, my energy, all evaporated, vanished like the mist. I rose rather wearily to my feet and permitted her to make a start on my buttons. After a moment I felt more engaged, I brushed her fingers from me and continued with the buttons myself. She swept out. "A hot bath for you, Mr. Cleg," she cried, "I'd no idea you'd get yourself soaked to the skin." I could hear her in the bathroom down the passage, humming to herself as hot water came coughing and gushing from the old brass taps. When I was ready I wrapped myself, shivering, in the faded old dressing gown I'd had since the colonies, and padded down the passage.

It is an old house, Mrs. Wilkinson's, with an old bathroom;

the tub itself is a vast, claw-footed, cast-iron affair that stands beneath a sloping skylight on a floor of black and white lozenge-shaped tiles. When the pipes are coughing forth their scalding torrents the room quickly fills with steam, and this is how it was when I appeared in the doorway. Mrs. Wilkinson was bending over the tub, one hand on the rim and the other testing the water. Turning her head toward the door she stared at me for a moment or two then straightened up. "Come along, Mr. Cleg," she said, "let's warm up those chilly bones of yours."

I hung my towel on the hook on the back of the door and cautiously approached. The water in this house always has a faintly reddish-brown tinge to it, copper oxide in the pipes, I imagine. Mrs. Wilkinson stood by her bath of steaming brown water with hands outstretched to take from me my dressing gown. Naturally I drew back. "Don't be bashful, Mr. Cleg," she wheedled, "I've seen plenty of men in this bath."

I bet you have, I thought, as I retreated toward the door. "Mr. Cleg," she said, "don't be silly." Still moving backwards I groped behind me for the door handle. She was a big woman, but I felt I could handle myself if I had to; fortunately it did not come to that. "Then I leave you to your own devices, Mr. Cleg," she said, and went out, shaking her head. There is no lock on the bathroom door (there are no locks anywhere in this house except, significantly, on the door to the attic stairs, and of course the dispensary) but through careful arrangement of my towel I managed to cover the keyhole; and then at last I clambered into the bathtub and stretched my lanky limbs: there was no smell at all.

I FIND myself for some reason thinking about the coal cellar in Kitchener Street. My mother once trod on a rat down there, so she'd always have me go down for her. After a while I began going down for no reason at all, I simply grew to like it there in the darkness with the smell of coal dust in my nostrils, and I can never smell coal these days without remembering the cellar, and perhaps this is why I'm thinking of it now. My sense of smell has always been acute, and it occurs to me that this whole thing about gas might have something to do with it—I am oversensitive, in an olfactory way, and this could cause me to detect nuances of odor that are perhaps imperceptible to a normal nose, or that perhaps don't even exist at all? But I shan't dwell on it any further; the smell has disappeared, it was probably a mistake, and I was a fool to make such a fuss about it. Oddly enough I remember now how the streets used to smell when I was a boy: of beer. There was a brewery not far from the canal, and most days the air would be filled with that distinctive brewery smell—malty, yeasty, whatever it is. My mother hated it, but then she hardly ever drank—a glass or two of mild on a Saturday night—because for her drink was associated with my father's moods. She once told me when we were sitting by ourselves in the kitchen that she thought ours would have been a happy house if my father didn't drink. I don't believe this; I believe that my father's cruelty to my mother would have occurred even if he'd never touched a drop, though perhaps in a different form. This is because it had to do with his nature, with what was—or rather, was *not*—inside him.

But it's strange that I should have liked the cellar, because that's where he belted me. I remember once (I'm not sure if this was before or after my mother's death) he told me to stop scraping the tines of my fork across my plate, he said it irritated him. Well I did it again, and he went off the deep end. The cellar's natural gloom was always thick with coal dust, which drifted in the air like tiny points of blackness, the devil's germs, I used to think, and they invaded your eyes and mouth and nostrils, even the very pores of your skin, and I always came up feeling blackened by the place, and this, too, was a sensation I enjoyed, for I liked to imagine myself a coal-black boy who could move through darkness without being seen. I also remember the sounds: how the stairs creaked when I went down, and how they creaked differently when my father was coming down behind me. Then, as well as the creaking, there would be the unbuckling of his belt—the clank of prong and buckle, and the slither of leather pulled through trouser loops—and I can never hear those sounds now without thinking of pain, though the pain of the belting was never as bad as the minutes that preceded it: my father's rage, the way he ground his teeth together and pulled his lips apart and hissed at me to get down the cellar—the *anticipation,* I mean, was worse than the event itself.

The cellar was lit, like the kitchen, by a single bulb on the end of a braided brown cord, and cramped and low-ceilinged as it was down there this bulb did little more than emphasize the depth of the shadows that colonized great blocks of space around the walls. I used to have fantasies down there involving ghosts and chains and torture—how gleefully I tortured my father! I took a sharp knife to those little webs of skin between his fingers, and sliced them open! In the middle of the floor stood a beam, a blackened, worm-holed, hoary beam that supported the floor above; beside it dangled the light bulb, shedding a circle of dim, yellowy light on the floor. Into this circle I stepped and began to unbutton the thick gray wool trousers that came down to my kneecaps and were held up by a pair of striped braces, which all boys wore in those days. The trousers would fall in an untidy heap about my boots, followed by my thick winter underpants, and then without a word I'd cross my arms on the beam and lean my head on them, and bend over at the waist. I'd pretend then that there was a different Spider leaning against the beam, or even tied to the beam, or even *nailed* to the beam—with me taking the belt to *him!* Often I'd imagine my father nailed to the beam.

He would take up a position behind me, stamp his boots once or twice, the belt now folded back upon itself and gripped just below the buckle. There was an old nail half-driven into the beam, just above where I laid my arms, and I'd curl my little finger round it and think of something else. Often I thought about the rats that lived in the cellar and were regularly caught in the traps my father set out and baited with poisoned cheese. I used to check these traps at least once a day, and if there was a rat I'd put it in my pocket and later, when I went fishing in the canal, I'd use it for bait by hammering a nail through its ear then bending the nail and tying it to a piece of string. I don't know what I expected to catch in the gasworks canal, there was nothing down there but old boots and a few mud-colored carp, perhaps a rusty bicycle— what a fool I was, in my thick gray trousers, squatting on the edge (not far, I realize, from where my bench is today, though on the other side) with my socks bunched about my boots and my big kneecaps jutting out to either side as I dangled the string in the water and watched it seamlessly fuse with its own reflection and then sprout, on the black surface of the canal, an image of my own hunched form that a moment later, with the breeze, would shimmer into a thousand shardlike fragments! I was, I suppose, in my imagination, a black boy, deep in some jungle, hunkered on a log in loincloth and facepaint. . . . Then my father's hatred came slicing through, and all I knew was pain.

He was doing his drinking at the Earl of Rochester by this stage. This was a much larger pub than the Dog and Beggar; it was where Hilda and her friends generally spent their evenings, being close to Spleen Street, and this was fortunate, for in his dealings with Hilda the further he was from Kitchener Street the better. Often I followed him when he left the house after supper, I'd slip down the alley behind him, flitting from doorway to dustbin, holding to the shadows, and he never suspected a thing. I'd watch him through the window of the Rochester, I'd see him sitting there with Hilda and Nora and the others, and often he seemed isolated, excluded—he did not belong to their world, I realized later, the world of tarts and bookies and crooks, his world was the lonely, circumscribed world of the jobbing plumber, and he was not an innately sociable man. Sometimes, peering in at him from the pavement, I thought of how I sat at the back of the classroom each day without ever really being present: this was how my father sat in the pub with Hilda and the rest, gazing into the crowd with an absent expression on his face, just letting the hubbub swirl about him—until, that is, she laid a palm on his thigh, and this brought him back to life. Oh, Hilda was at her "best" in a pub, she loved to laugh and be saucy, she loved to banter with the men, and weep with the women, and she loved her port, how that woman did love her sweet port! So she'd bring him back to life and he'd take a drink of his mild, produce a twitch or two of that furtive grin of his, bask a moment in the glow of Hilda's warm boozy light; then her attention would be drawn elsewhere, and off he'd drift again. Back and forth went the banter, others joined them, rounds of drinks came and went (somehow there was always money for another round, though often it was my father who paid for the last of the evening), and then, finally, after sitting quietly in his chair all night, like a good child he was rewarded: for when time was called he got to walk Hilda back to Spleen Street. I'd follow them at a distance as they veered off into the back streets and alleyways, and in one of those alleyways, deep in the shadows, they would spend some minutes in each other's arms. Then Hilda would undo his fly buttons, ease out his thin, stiffened cock, and bring him to climax in a few deft strokes. She would slip away from him soon after, and he would walk home. I wasn't always present for the last part of their evening, for I had to be back before he got in; but I can imagine it all too well.

It's not hard, then, for me to see my father stamping off down the alley of an evening, after yet another unhappy meal in his own kitchen, and imagine what he was thinking. I wonder if he ever contemplated the idea of simply going down the Dog as he used to, avoiding the Earl of Rochester altogether, avoiding Hilda Wilkinson altogether, quietly subsiding into his old life which, narrow and constricted though it was, promised at least the mild benefits of predictability, and a sort of harmony? He did not, of course; only a wistful nostalgia could resurrect his old life, his life before Hilda; he had felt too often her breasts beneath his hands, the softness of her belly pressed against his own, best of all the sheer giddy euphoria of her fingers fumbling at his fly buttons—and as the memory of these sensations flooded him he stiffened, even as he strode forward, in his trousers, and all doubt, all wavering, vanished. The thing was beyond his control.

There was one night in the Rochester that I remember very well. It was a bloody awful night, made more bloody than it need have been because my father was still stewing in the bad feeling he'd carried away from Kitchener Street with him. He seemed more ill at ease than usual as he sat there among Hilda's people, amid the gilt and mirrors of the big busy pub, and I wonder if he didn't see one of the regulars from the Dog come in—this would have caused him anxiety, I know, the thought that Ernie Ratcliff would hear about this, Ratcliff a man who loved gossip and slander above all else. So there he sat, for more than an hour, frowning and morose, and not even Hilda could warm him up. When they left the pub she was cool and haughty, she wouldn't let him take her arm as they walked off together into the night. Going down an alley near Spleen Street (I was close behind them at this point, creeping silently through the darkness and black as a shadow) my father tried to push her up against the wall. She was having none of it! Oh, she turned on him then, and he shrank back from her—what a spitfire she was when her dander was up! Her eyes blazed. "Don't put yourself out, do you, plumber?" she cried. "You don't make much of a bloody effort, eh? I don't know why I bother with you, sitting there all night like an undertaker—what *is* your problem then? Eh?" She was warming to it now, the chin was out, the coat was pushed back, hands on the hips of a straining skirt. My father had turned away and was facing up the alley, toward where I was crouched behind a dustbin. "Give it a rest, Hilda," he said wearily, pulling out his tobacco.

"Give it a rest? That's a laugh, coming from you. Give *me* a rest, plumber. Sit there all night like a bloody corpse and then want to feel me up down an alley. What's your problem? Ain't you been paid for the pipes yet?"

I saw him stiffen then, for this one cut him to the quick. At the other end of the alley the streetlamp cast splinters of light into the cracks between the cobblestones and along the edges of the bricks. Paid for the pipes? Paid for the pipes? Was that what it was all about? He'd had no cash from her for his work, he knew he'd never be paid—is that how she saw it, though, payment for services rendered? All color drained from him, he slipped his tobacco pouch back in his pocket. Hilda glanced at him, assumed an airy nonchalance, tossed her big chin. "That it, plumber? That the truth of it?"

He stood there, white with rage, still with his back to her, and struggled to bring himself under control. He wanted nothing so much as to hit her very hard, this I could see, I knew that look—he wanted to hurt her really badly, hurt her as she'd just hurt him. "Come'ere, plumber," he heard her say.

He didn't move.

"Come on, plumber." A silky tone now. Sweet Hilda now. He turned. Coat still pushed back, hands still on her hips, she was leaning against the wall with one knee crooked so her skirt rode up, and she was grinning at him. "Come'ere," she murmured. Over he went, meek dog he was. One hand still on her hip, with the other she clasped the back of his skull, drew him to her, kissed him softly on the mouth. His hands were on her thighs, working the skirt up; suddenly he was inflamed, overwhelmed with desire for the woman, he wanted to have her *now,* this moment, up against this wall, he was stiff in his trousers and already fumbling with the buttons, he was blind and panting with passion—but Hilda, still kissing him, reached down, took hold of his wrists, pushed his hands off her, broke away from him. She laughed once, quite hoarsely, and with a shiver closed her coat. "No more, plumber," she said, catching his wrists as he came crowding in on her again, "I'm off home." My father began whispering furiously, again reached for her, was again pushed away. Then I saw her put her hand on his cheek. "I'm off home," she said again, "it's cold out here. Goodnight, plumber"—and shaking her head as he tried for the last time to hold her, she slipped away, went swaying down the alley toward the light, leaving my father in a heated confusion of anger and desire, a very flux of contradictory emotion.

H I L D A was a prostitute, you see. She was a tart, and she paid my father with the services of a tart, though he didn't realize it until that night in the alley. When he got home half an hour later—he had smoked a cigarette by the canal, despite the cold of the night—he found to his annoyance that my mother was waiting up for him. I heard his boots in the yard, and then I heard him come in through the back door. My mother was sitting at the kitchen table in the dark, with a cup of tea, and he did not see her until he switched the light on. Her face, as she turned toward him, was puffy around the eyes, the way it got when she had been crying. "Still up?" he muttered as he sat down heavily at the other end of the table and bent to unlace his boots. He could not look at her.

"Where have you been, Horace?" she said quietly. There was a trace of accusation in her voice, accusation tempered with misery. The door from the kitchen into the passage was open, so I crept out of bed (I'd only been home a short while myself) and sat at the top of the stairs, in my pajamas, to listen. Did my father, even at this stage, have any decency at all left in him? Did her unhappiness catch at his heart and tear him, tear him between an involuntary spurt of compassion for my mother, for whose pain he alone was responsible— and his intense irritation with her, not only because she was a hindrance to him in his tawdry affair with Hilda Wilkinson but also because she complicated the clean hard thrust of his desire? His heart was not yet completely turned to stone, I believe; she aroused in him still, I think, traces of the responsibility he'd once felt for her, but the guilt triggered by these feelings he was forced violently to suppress, and for one simple reason: he could maintain his lust for Hilda only if he simultaneously hardened himself against my mother—if, in other words, he made a sort of unnatural compartmentalization of his emotions: the only alternative was to flounder about in muddle and indecision, a flaccid, unmanly condition he was anxious to avoid. So while one tiny voice cried out to him to comfort my mother, to wipe away the tears from those bleary eyes, take her in his arms and make everything all right again—an opposite and equal impulse told him to *make* her suffer, intensify the crisis, provoke the breakdown and dissolution of whatever frayed bonds still held them together. So he did not comfort her, he set his jaw in a thin, hard line, pulled off his boots, one by one, and rubbed his feet. "Down the pub," he said.

"Down the Dog?"

"Yes."

"Liar! You're a liar, Horace!" she cried. Oh, it was hard for me to hear her voice cracking like that, she such a stranger to anger! "I went down the Dog and you weren't there!" Now she was sitting upright at the end of the table with the tears streaming down and a sort of watery light gleaming in her eyes, fury and misery combined.

"I went somewhere else after a bit," my father said angrily. "What were you down the Dog for? It's not Saturday."

She didn't answer this, just sat there staring at him as the tears came flooding down her cheeks, not even bothering to wipe them away.

My father shrugged, dropping his eyes and rubbing his feet once more. "I went down the Earl of Rochester." I heard him say it, and I thought, why would he tell her that? How could he go down there again, with her likely to come looking for him? "What are you chasing after me for?" he said angrily. "Can't a man have a drink after his work?"

"I won't live like this," said my mother, quiet again after

her outburst, and wiping her face with her apron. "I wasn't meant to live like this."

"That's not my fault," said my father, as a voice in his head said: oh yes it is.

"Yes it is," said my mother, for an uncanny moment becoming the articulation of his conscience.

"It's not!" he shouted—and I could stand no more. Down the stairs I pattered, along the passage, barefoot and feigning sleepiness. My mother turned toward me, and the sight of her tear-streaked face upset me badly. "It's all right, Spider," she murmured, blinking once or twice as she rose wearily from the table and smoothed her apron across her stomach in that way she had. "Your father and me, we're just having a talk."

"You woke me up," I said, or something of the sort, I don't remember exactly.

"It's all right now," she said again, "we're all coming to bed now." She took my hand; I was taller than her, even in my bare feet. "Come on, my big Spider," she said, "back up to bed," and up the stairs we went. My father sat there at the table for another ten minutes or so, then I heard him turn off the light and come upstairs. My mother was awake, lying on her back in that huge bed of theirs and staring at the ceiling; the glow from the streetlamp outside sifted through the curtains and created queer rhomboid grids of light and shadow overhead. My father undressed and climbed in on his side, and the pair of them lay there in the darkness, silent and sleepless, for more than an hour.

When my father rose the next morning, and dressed for work, and went downstairs, he found my mother at the kitchen stove frying bacon. She had laid a clean white cloth on the table and poured his tea. She was all quiet bustling activity; she broke a couple of eggs into the skillet and a moment later set the plate before him: bacon and eggs, fried tomato and fried kidneys. "I popped out and got you something nice for your breakfast," she said. "You need a good breakfast in the morning, you work hard." Then she cut three slices from a fresh loaf and smeared them with dripping for his lunch. My father ate his breakfast; he said nothing, but dead as he was he couldn't have been unaware of the meaning and quality of her gesture. "Drink your tea while it's hot," she murmured as she wrapped his sandwiches in newspaper. He left for work a few minutes later, out through the back door; I watched him from my bedroom window. She was at the sink as he went out, I heard the water running. He paused a moment in the doorway, and looked back at her. She gave him a small smile, without lifting her hands from the washing-up water, and he produced an expression about his mouth, a sort of squeezing together of the lips, that was part resignation, part regret; and then he nodded once or twice. Cycling to work in the sharp fresh early morning air I imagine him feeling oddly at peace; it was the night that brought the passion and the confusion and the pain, in the morning it was different.

Several times over the course of the day he resolved to have done with Hilda Wilkinson altogether. He reminded himself of what she'd said to him the previous night, he remembered how much he disliked the people she drank with, and not least, he thought about the devastation of my mother, should she ever find out what was going on. That truly gave him pause; flaccid and unmanly it may have been, but *that* he was not prepared to face. No, this brief affair with Hilda Wilkinson, this brief encounter—best put it behind him, forget about it, return to the routines of everyday life, those stable routines that he'd known, so it seemed, forever.

My father's resolution remained firm until, I would guess, about the middle of the afternoon. He was overhauling the plumbing of a warehouse in East Ham with his mate Archie Boyle, a cheery fat youth with hair the color of a carrot. I see him on a wooden stepladder, his shins braced against the top step, working with hammer and wrench on a length of old lead piping high in the dust and the gloom. Every clang of his hammer echoes dully through the empty building, and over this reverberating clangor comes the sharp, thin sound, from down the other end, of Archie's whistling; he is at work preparing sections of new pipe for my father to install. In his left hand my father grips the wrench, which is locked upon an antiquated octagonal nut that over the years has fused with its pipes, and with the right he wields the hammer, and with it delivers a series of steady blows to the shank of the wrench, in an effort to loosen the nut. Each hammer blow resounds through the warehouse like the tolling of some awful funereal requiem bell, flakes of rust drift free, and he has to turn his head to keep them from getting in his eyes. Slowly the nut starts to turn. My father's mind, lulled by the steady dirgelike clangor of his hammer blows, superimposed, in that big empty chamber, like some sort of eerie gothic symphony, on the slow tuneless whistling of Archie Boyle, has drifted, again, to the events of last night, to the sight of Hilda with her coat pushed back, her hands on her hips, bare-legged, one knee crooked so her skirt rides up her white thigh, grinning her chinny grin from the shadows—and with that image the idea of having her, there in the alley, that *tart* (how he savors the word!), up against the wall, with her skirt pushed up round her waist—

Suddenly from out of the pipe leaps a great hissing spurt of cold water. It hits him square in the chest and almost knocks him off the ladder. From all around the loosened nut spring jets of hissing water—the pipes have not been shut off at the mains. Archie comes trotting down the warehouse as my father descends the ladder, dripping wet and cursing, while the water sprays the ceiling and the top of the wall, then runs down to form a spreading puddle on the concrete floor. "Bloody hell!" shouts my father as he strides away to shut off the water. He does not need to be told that this is his fault.

When he returns, Archie, still whistling, is hard at work with bucket and mop. No great problem, after all; but as my father angrily resumes work on the eight-sided nut he knows that if it hadn't been for Hilda this wouldn't have happened. The pair resume their tasks; but all the while, outside the dusty warehouse windows, the light is thickening in the bleak gray November afternoon; and as it thickens my father cannot keep his thoughts from turning, again and again, to Hilda, to his tart, and the longing comes back like a fever, and his resolutions are all forgotten.

Soon afterwards the two plumbers left the empty warehouse. With the descent of darkness a damp, chilly fog had drifted in from the river, and my father pulled his cap low and tied his scarf tightly about his throat. After parting with Archie he mounted his bicycle and pedaled off in the direction of Kitchener Street. The moisture of the fog gathered round his spectacles and made his eyes smart as through obscure, deserted streets he rode, past black walls that glistened slickly where they caught the diffuse glow of the streetlamps, then retreated once more into inky indistinctness. Occasionally a figure hurried by, the footsteps becoming suddenly loud then just as quickly receding into silence. My father's route carried him along streets that tended down toward the docks, and as it did so the fog became denser, the city more deserted, the atmosphere more eerily muffled. Chill and damp though the evening was, with the onset of darkness, and the fading of his morning's resolutions, my father's physical desire had grown stronger, and now he was flushed and distracted with it; he could no more remember his decision to end the affair than he could have risen on his bicycle over the roofs and chimneys of the East End and left the imperatives of the flesh beneath and behind him forever.

On he crawled through the dark drear fog, his body on fire with the longing for Hilda Wilkinson. It smoldered inside him like the molten coke at the heart of a forge, it burned and seethed in the fog so that by the time he wheeled his bicycle into the back yard of number twenty-seven he was a man diseased, a man in fever, no longer responsible for his actions.

He entered the kitchen. I've told you what this room was like, it was a poky, ill-lit room, and one would be hard-pressed to call it cosy. Nevertheless my mother had taken pains to render it warm and homelike. The curtains, as shabby and faded as her apron, were drawn across the grimy window over the sink, and from the stove issued the sizzle and odor of liver frying in onions. She had washed the dishes, swept the floor, and even brought in from the front parlor her only plant, a wilted and failing aspidistra. Wiping her hands on her apron, she gave my father the same small smile he had seen early that morning—an eternity ago, so it seemed!—and reached into the cupboard for a bottle of beer. Me, I was at the table, gazing at the ceiling; I wanted no contact with my father, none at all, not after last night. He stood in the doorway stamping his boots on the doormat as the fog came swirling round him into the room. He did not return my mother's smile, he did not even attempt the equivocal pursing of the lips he'd managed in the morning. My mother was standing at the kitchen table with her back to him, pouring out a glass of beer. "Close the door, Horace," she said, "the fog's coming in. I've fried you a nice bit of liver—" She was cut short by a loud *bang!* as my father slammed the back door. He stamped across the kitchen floor, frowning, sat down heavily at the table (ignoring me as I was ignoring him) and drank the glass of beer. "Don't drink so fast," murmured my mother, busying herself at the stove. In response to this my father refilled the glass, and in the process the thing frothed over onto the tablecloth, a nice piece of embroidered cambric that had been a wedding present from his late mother-in-law. "Oh Horace," cried my mother, "now see what you've done! Be a little more careful, please." But still her tone was mild, she was determined that they wouldn't fight.

My father didn't care. He was a changed man now, hard as granite and cold as ice. A new sort of anger burned in him, and it burned with a cold, hard, gemlike flame: I could see it in his eyes when he took his glasses off, the hard flame burning in those hard pale-blue eyes of his. He had been a surly, humorless husband and father for years, but never before had I seen in him an anger as fierce, as cold, as this. It was as if he'd crossed a line of some sort, lost the ability to feel even a *spark* of human sympathy toward my mother. The tablecloth, the smiles, the sizzling liver—none of it could touch him, he knew only an urge to push her roughly out of his path, and so strong was the feeling he could barely suppress the violence her very presence aroused in him. He sat at the table without taking off his scarf or his jacket or his boots, without looking at me, without rolling a cigarette, he sat there with a face like tortured thunder and threw back glass after glass of beer until the big quart bottle was almost empty. My poor mother, the effort she was making was immense, and in return she was getting nothing but this wordless fury. "What is it, Horace?" she whispered as she put his plate of liver and onions on the table, pushing aside the houseplant as she did so. "What's the matter with you?" She stood there peering at him with her head slightly to one side and a mass of pained, bewildered wrinkles working on her brow. Nervously she kept wiping her hands on her apron although they were quite dry. My father glared at the steaming liver, his fists to either side of the plate clenched so tight that the knuckles were like billiard balls trapped and straining beneath the skin. "Tell me, Horace," came the voice again, and still he glared, fighting down a wave of sheer black rage, grimly clutching for control, grimly holding on. Get away from me! screamed a voice in his head, but my mother, my poor foolish mother, did not get away, instead she drew closer, reached out a hand, made as if to touch him. At last he turned toward her—the kitchen was silent, for the skillet was no longer sizzling, only the drip of the tap—and what a face he showed her! Never will I forget that face, not for as long as I live: brows knit in agony, lips pulled back from his teeth, all his mouth frozen in a terrible rictus that expressed both violence and utter helplessness, tortured helplessness in the face of that violence, and the eyes!—his eyes were burning not with the hard, gemlike flame now but with the same pain that contorted his brow and his lips, his whole sorry physiognomy, it was all there, and my mother read it and was shocked by the suffering that was in him, and she drew closer. "No!" said my father as her fingers fell upon his shoulder, "No!"—and then, with a strangled sound that half choked him in the utterance he rose clumsily to his feet, knocking the chair over backwards with a clatter, and stumbled across the kitchen to the back door, and out into the fog. My mother stood a moment gazing after him with her fingers pressed to her lips. Then she darted after him, down the yard to where the gate at the end stood open, and into the alley beyond. "Horace!" she cried. But night had fallen, the fog was thicker than ever, and she could see nothing, nor did any sound come back to her through the darkness, and after taking a few steps in one direction, and then in the other, she came back into the yard, back into the kitchen, and closed the door behind her. The chill and stink of the fog could be felt within the room's warmth, and she stood for a moment and hugged herself and shivered. "Oh Spider," she whispered; I was still sitting there, stunned by what had happened. She gazed at the plate of cooling liver and the stain of spilt beer on the tablecloth, and then she sank onto a chair and laid her head on her hands and wept.

RAIN again today. I love rain, did I tell you this already? Also I love fog, and have since I was a boy. I used to love going down to the docks in a fog to listen to the foghorns as they hooted and honked at one another, and watch the pallid glow from the lights of vessels slipping downstream with the tide. It was the cloak of spectral unreality I loved, the cloak it spread over the familiar forms of the world. All was strange in a fog, buildings grew vague, human beings groped and became lost, the landmarks, the compass points, by which they navigated melted into nothingness and the world was transfigured into a country of the blind. But if the sighted became blind, then the blind—and for some odd reason I have always regarded myself as one of the blind—the blind became sighted, and I remember feeling at home in a fog, happily at ease in the murk and gloom that so confused my neighbors. I moved quickly and confidently through fog-blanketed streets, unvisited by the terrors that lurked everywhere in the visible material world; I stayed out as late as I could in a fog. Last night, as I sat scribbling in my garret room at Mrs. Wilkinson's, I got up from time to time to stretch my limbs and gaze down at the rain as it came drifting through the halo of the streetlamp opposite; and I realized how little I'd changed, how my emotions in the rain that day (yesterday, I mean) so closely matched the feelings I'd had for fog as a boy. What lies at the root of it all, I wonder, what force is it that once drew a lonely child out into foggy streets and still exerts its attraction in heavy rainfall some twenty years later? What is it about the misting and blurring of the visible world that gave such comfort to the boy I then was, and to the creature I have since become?

Queer thoughts, no? I sighed. I bent down to pull my book out from under the linoleum. Nothing there! I groped. Momentary lurch of horror as I assimilated the possibility of the book's absence. Theft? Of course—by Mrs. bloody Wilkinson, who else! Then there it was, pushed just a bit deeper than I'd expected; no little relief. My father was stumbling blindly through a fog, barely conscious of his whereabouts, the chaos within him further befuddled with the beer he'd just drunk. Great relief, in fact; what on earth would I do if she got her hands on it? Is the best place for it really under the linoleum? Isn't there a *hole* somewhere I can tuck it into? The streetlamps were smears of light in the fog, flecks and splinters of weak fractured yellowy radiance that picked up the glitter of wild light in his eyes, the fleeting blur of whiteness of his nose and brow as he charged by. Somewhere I've seen a hole, I know I have, but where, where? On he blundered until at last he saw a building aglow, and like a moth to the flame he drew near, and found himself outside the Dog and Beggar. In he went, into the dry warmth of the place, and suddenly there was the smell of beer and tobacco in his nostrils and the murmur of talk in his ears. I just can't afford to take the chance.

For a few moments he stood there in the doorway, his chest heaving violently as he brought his breathing under control. His eyes were still wild, his skin damp and sleek with the wet. He glanced about the room, with its scattering of small round tables; there was a thin drift of sawdust on the bare wood floor, and standing at the bar was an old man reading the racing results. Two more old men sat at a table near the fireplace, where a small coal fire was burning, their lips working silently over gray toothless gums. All the talk came from the saloon bar, beyond the glass partition, and from that direction Ernie Ratcliff now appeared. Glancing at my father as he laid a thin hand upon a beerpump, he murmured: "Well come in, Horace, if you're coming." And my father, his passions still roiling in his breast, nodded blankly once or twice and closed the door. Like a man in a dream he approached the bar. Ratcliff noticed nothing amiss—or if he did, it was not his way to mention it. "Nasty out," he remarked, "real pea-souper. Pint of the usual, is it, Horace?" My father nodded, and a few seconds later had carried his pint to a table and sat there gazing at the fire.

Then all at once he seemed to awaken, to recognize his surroundings. He picked up his glass of beer and drained almost the entire pint in one draught. He rose to his feet and made his way back to the bar. "Same again?" said Ratcliff amiably. "Nice drop, this"—and he pulled my father another pint.

An hour later my father was once more out in the fog. He had not grown calm in the meanwhile, very far from it. The manic turmoil had subsided, but from that subsidence had emerged a decision. Decision, I say; it was more of an impulse, even an instinct, than a decision, a sort of simple blind drive toward the satisfaction of a hunger—and I need hardly tell you what that hunger was. Unsteadily he'd emerged from the Dog and Beggar, buttoned his jacket and tied his scarf about his throat. Then he'd set his steps toward the Earl of Rochester, and been quickly swallowed by the fog, which was thicker than ever.

By the time he reached the Earl of Rochester my father appeared to be under control. He did not lurch, he did not slur his speech, but he was in fact drunk, and no less in the grip of instinct than he had been when he left the Dog. The Rochester was full when he arrived; this was a Friday night, and it was already close to nine. He pushed open the door and stepped quickly inside, a wisp or two of the fog clinging to him as he entered. A wave of chatter and laughter, smoke and warmth and light rolled over him. He pushed his way through to the bar and ordered whisky. When he had it he turned, looking for Hilda.

She was at a table in the corner with Nora and the rest. She glanced up, then promptly rose to her feet and made her way through the crush toward him. Odd, this; you would expect her to make him come to her. I think I know what accounted for her behavior in the Rochester that evening, and for much that occurred afterwards, for I believe she'd learned something about my father since the events in the alley the previous night, something specific; when the time comes I shall explain all this in detail. Now, though, she came pushing through the crowd, her face flushed and a glass of port held aloft in one hand like an ensign, and as she came she bantered with the men, who made way for her, laughing, as a brisk sea parts before a vessel under sail. Then she was beside him, and as he had the first taste of the whisky the bite of the spirit added fuel to the desire he'd been feeling since nightfall. With one boot on the brass rail at the bottom of the bar, and his eyes never leaving her face, he pulled out his tobacco. "So, plumber," said Hilda—she too had been drinking, and she recognized the wildness in him—"feeling better tonight, are we?"

My father was rolling a cigarette, his head lowered and his fingers busy with Rizla paper and Old Holborn, but his eyes were still on her. When it was rolled he lit it with a match and said: "Come down the allotments."

Yes, she could feel how wild he was, and it excited her. "Down the allotments?" she said, lifting her eyebrows and resting her tongue on her top lip. He turned toward the bar, nodded, and drank off the whisky. "When?" she said.

For a few moments he was silent, waiting for the barmaid. He bought himself another whisky, a sweet port for her. They stood among the milling drinkers, and it was as though invisible threads bound them together. "I'll go now," he said, "you come down in a bit."

Hilda brought her port to her lips. She allowed a small pause to occur. "All right, plumber," she said, "I don't mind if I do."

I remember where I saw a hole: it's behind the gas fire. It used to be a fireplace. There's an empty grate and a chimney; that'll do me nicely, I'll just slip it in there. But I must stop for a minute, all night I've had the strangest sensation in my intestines, as though they were being twisted like a length of rubber hosing. Something odd is going on down there, though just exactly what I don't know; probably something I ate.

O N I scribbled, on through the hours of darkness, getting down on paper my exact and detailed reconstruction of that terrible night, all I'd thought about during those long, empty years cooped up in Canada. I was in my bedroom when, not long after my father had stormed out, my mother called up the stairs to me. I came out onto the landing and there she was, down by the front door in her coat and headscarf. "I'm going out, Spider," she said, "I shan't be long." She had put some lipstick on her mouth, I noticed, and a spot of rouge on each cheek—this was how she looked when she went out with my father on Saturday nights. It was only Friday, but after what had happened she could clearly sit no longer in the kitchen. "I'm going to meet your father," she said, the last words I ever heard her say in life. I saw her leave the house through the back door, and I watched her as she stood pulling on her gloves in the yard. She'd left the light on in the kitchen and for a moment she was bathed in its glow; this I saw from my bedroom window. Then down the yard she went, a neat little woman off to meet her husband, and soon she was swallowed by the fog and lost to my view. But I was *still with her,* you see, I was still with her as I leaned on my windowsill and clouded the glass with my breath, I was with her as she moved down the alley, clutching her handbag, cautiously advancing by the dim gleam of the lamppost at the end of the alley. She did not know if my father was in the Dog, nor what sort of reception to expect should she come upon him there, but she could no longer sit weeping in the kitchen as he stayed out drinking and seethed with resentments she did not understand but which apparently, and through no fault of her own, were directed at her. She reached the Dog, stepped bravely into the public bar, and walked right up to the counter. "Evening Mrs. Cleg," said Ernie Ratcliff. "Looking for your old man? He was here, but I believe he's gone." He peered about the room with his little weasel eyes. "No," he said, "no sign of him, Mrs. Cleg."

"I see," said my mother. "Thank you, Mr. Ratcliff." She was turning away from the bar when a fresh thought struck her. "Mr. Ratcliff," she said, "can you tell me where the Earl of Rochester is?"

I see my father striding through fogbound streets toward the allotments. Down Spleen Street he strides, the looming gasworks barely visible above him, along Omdurman Close and across the bridge over the railway lines, a small dark figure striding through fog, the ring of his hobnailed boots muffled and dull on the pavement. When he reaches the top of the path he pauses; the fog is less dense up here, up on the high ground, and he can just make out the moon, and off to his left the first of the sheds. He stands there a moment or two, his figure smudged but distinct against the gray-black night with its dim blur of moonlight, with the allotments beneath him and beyond them a maze of streets and alleys falling away over toward the docks, whence through the fog comes the mournful hooting of the ships; and a few moments later he is unlocking the door of his own shed, and then he is in, and fumbling in his pockets for a match. It is cold and damp in the shed, and in the darkness, with its strong smell of earth, it is, he thinks, like being in a coffin. Then the match flares, he lights the candle on the box by the horsehair armchair, and the flame throws a dull unsteady glow upon the place. He opens a bottle of beer and paces the floor, his shadow huge and misshapen in the dim flickering light that the candle flame casts upon the crude plank walls and raftered gables of the roof. From out of the shadows of the back wall the eye of the stuffed ferret suddenly catches the candle flame and casts a sharp glittering sliver of light across the shed. The alcohol in my father's system allows him no pause, no peace, in which he might consider what he is doing; he remains in a sort of fever, still driven by that single fixed instinct.

Finally she comes. My father hears her outside and throws open the door. Cursing and stumbling, she picks her way up the path in her bare feet, clutching her shoes in one hand and a bottle of port in the other. "Shit!" she shouts as she sets a foot down in the potato patch. My father is grinning now, and against the dull light spilling from the open shed Hilda sees his white teeth shining as he comes forward to help her. She steps out of the soil back onto the path and he puts an arm around her shoulders; instantly they are cleaving to one another beneath the smoky moon; instantly the heat that has been simmering in my father since nightfall rekindles to a fury as they rock back and forth, pressed close to one another, there on the path outside the shed. Muffled snorts of laughter from Hilda, her face buried in my father's collar, then slowly they come apart, and move toward the shed, then through the door, the door closes, and silence descends once more upon the allotments.

(Dear God I wish silence would descend on this house! They've started up again, and they seem to be *stamping* up there now, they keep it up for minutes on end and then collapse, helpless, apparently, with laughter. I've been standing on my chair and banging on the ceiling with my shoe, but it does no good at all, in fact it only seems to make things worse. Mrs. Wilkinson has much to answer for, and the disturbance of my sleep by these creatures is not the least of it. And my insides still hurt!)

*   *   *

My mother stood just inside the door of the Earl of Rochester and gazed about her, bewildered. The pub was full, and by this hour a sort of collective madness had infected the patrons so that they talked and laughed and gesticulated like carica tures of men and women, like grotesque puppets, and my mother, meek of heart, and sober, was deeply intimidated. The air was thick with smoke, almost as thick as the fog outside; and in the crush of these people, whose loudness seemed to increase their size while diminishing their human- ity, she could get no sort of an idea whether my father was present or not. Meek and sober though she was, she had determined upon a course of action: gripping her handbag she began to push her way through, with frequent mumbled apologies, glancing all about her as she advanced.

At last she reached the bar. She waited patiently for the attention of a barmaid. Whenever one came near, however, some large, florid man would come crowding in from behind her, reaching over her shoulders with huge red fists clutching beermugs and spirit glasses, and begin to recite a long, com- plicated list of drinks; and the barmaid would be sent scur- rying this way and that. This happened several times, and still my mother stood there at the counter, dwarfed by these giant boozers, until at last she won the undivided attention of a friendly young woman who said: "What can I get you, dear?"

"I'm looking for my husband," said my mother. A snort from the man beside her, and a series of uproarious comments from his companions as he repeated her words.

"Who's your husband, dear?" said the harried barmaid, not without sympathy, raising her voice to be heard over the racket.

"Horace Cleg."

"What's that?" said the barmaid.

"Horace Cleg," said my mother.

"Horace!" shouted the man beside her. "You're wanted!"

"Is he here?" said my mother, turning to the man.

"Not if he's got any sense he's not!" said the man, and they all shouted with laughter.

"Horace Cleg?" said the barmaid. "I don't know him, dear. Regular, is he?"

"No," said my mother. "At least I don't think so."

"Sorry, dear," said the barmaid. "Can I get you something?"

"No thank you," said my mother, and turning away from the bar she pushed back through the crowd to the door, and a moment later found herself out in the fog once more.

She had crossed the bridge over the railway lines and was standing on the path that ran along the allotments; she was staring at my father's shed. The land behind it sloped away steeply, and the gabled roof stood out in sharp definition against the wispy fog and the night sky, in which the moon now seemed more a lump than a globe, like a huge potato. From round the edges of the door seeped a dimly flickering light, so she knew he was in there; what kept her out on the path were the odd muffled noises issuing from the shed; clearly he was not alone.

After several minutes it grew quiet, and my mother, chilled by the night, began to think that she might quite simply walk up the path and knock on the door. But still she didn't move, still she stood there shivering at the gate, staring at the shed and clutching her handbag tight. From the streets beyond the allotments came the desolate barking of a dog, and from the river, the foghorns; then suddenly, behind her, a goods train went steaming by on its way into the city and gave her a start. With no small effort, and no little courage, she opened the gate and walked quickly up the path to the door.

I WAS plagued, as a boy, with nightmares; and that night I dreamed about the gasworks canal. A wild storm raged in my sleeping mind: the water was blacker than ever, violently churning, and darts of lightning sprang crackling, close overhead, between dense, lowering rainclouds, bulbous black things flecked and streaming at the edges with smoke. I was standing close to the edge of the canal as a skeleton surged up from the water, carried on the back of a wave, a skeleton housing some sort of sleek, seal-like creature squeezed tight within its rib cage. The whiskered snout of this awful black lumpy thing was pushed out from between the bones, and it exposed a set of tiny white teeth as it bleated pathetically at me; it was lifted by the canal waters almost to within my reach, then sank again with continued terrible bleatings, and I saw that all around me the canal was throwing up horrible things, a huge gray fish struggling in a sheathlike string bag whose tip was densely woven over its eyes and jaws like the toe of a sock; a boot made of tiny white bones; other whiskery seal-creatures, many of them trapped and struggling within sheets of netting, and several with human faces that bleated as they rose on black waves then sank again. With every cresting wave some new horror was lifted from the depths and exposed to me, and I knew with utter certainty and utter terror that I would be unable to keep my footing on the bank of the canal but would fall in among these bleating horrors. Suddenly then the picture of my father in shirtsleeves and flat cap digging a hole in the middle of his potato patch. It was foggy out there, but not foggy enough to obscure the pitted, knobbly lump of the moon. In the door of the shed I saw Hilda leaning against the woodwork with her ratty fur coat draped about her shoulders, smoking, the candle in the shed throwing a dim glow around her. After some minutes my father fell to his knees and with enormous care lifted from the soil a potato plant, cradling with one hand the leafy shoot, in the other the stemlike rhizome and its trailing, lacey root-lets. He placed it off to one side—how uncanny to observe the tenderness with which he handled the plant! The digging continued, the row of potato plants beside the hole grew longer; Hilda disappeared back into the shed and came out with a bottle of port and a teacup. Foghorns hooted from the river. Then I saw that my father was shoulder-deep in the hole, damp with sweat despite the chill of the fog. He tossed up the spade, then with some difficulty clambered up after it. The earth crumbled beneath his fingers, and several times he slipped back in. Hilda picked her way over from the shed, and still clutching her coat about her shoulders peered in. Worms, faintly visible, gleaming in the moonlight, writhe from the soil in the hole's steep walls. Now my father emerges from the shed, in his arms a bundle partially wrapped in a bloodstained sack. It is a body, the head wrapped in sacking and tied round the neck with string. He lays it down at the edge of the hole, then rises from his knees and glances at Hilda, who is standing there among the uprooted potato plants. She pulls her coat tightly about her shoulders. My father nudges the body with his boot and it tumbles into the grave, coming to rest flat on its back with one arm pinned under it and the other flung untidily across its sack-tied head like a rag doll. Hilda comes to the edge of the hole and kicks in a little loose soil; then she shivers and returns to the shed. My father picks up the spade and begins to fill in the hole; it is with the greatest care that he replaces his potato plants.

*   *   *

I woke screaming and slipped out of bed and darted along the landing to my parents' room, but the bed was empty, so I ran downstairs and along the narrow passage, all in darkness, to the kitchen.

I opened the door. My father was sitting at the table with a woman I had never seen before. "What is it?" he said. "What's the matter with you?" He rose to his feet and led me out of the kitchen into the passage, closing the door behind him. "Back upstairs," he said, guiding me down the passage, "back to bed, Dennis."

"Where's my mum?" I said, trying to resist his forward propulsion.

"Come on, son, back to bed."

"Where's my mum?" I cried. "I don't want to go back to bed, I had a dream!"

"That's enough," he said, pushing me down the passage.

"I want my mum!"

"Don't make me angry, Dennis! Your mum's in the kitchen."

"No she's not!"

"*Upstairs!*" he hissed.

"You're hurting me!" He was gripping my wrists too tightly as he forced me up the stairs, and his lips were pulled back from his teeth. "You're hurting me," I wailed—and he let me go, and leaned against the wall at the bottom of the stairs. "Go and get back into bed," he said quietly, all his anger suddenly dissipated. "You can leave the light on. I'll be up to see you later."

I too grew calm. I began to climb the stairs. Halfway up I stopped and turned. "Who's that lady?" I said.

He glanced up at me and took his glasses and rubbed his eyes with his thumb and forefinger. "What lady?"

"The one in the kitchen."

"Don't make me angry, Dennis. Go on up now." As I climbed the stairs he returned to the kitchen and closed the door behind him.

I T wasn't until close to Christmas that I fully grasped the fact that my mother was dead. Even so, the events of the hours that followed were vivid in my mind, not only those I witnessed with my own eyes, but those that were so painful, later, in Canada, to reconstruct. Horace and Hilda walked home together in silence, and as they made their way through the narrow, empty, foggy streets she leaned on him, and for the first time he was allowed to support her, to put an arm around her shoulders and bear her weight. Having murdered he felt clear and calm, exhilarated even, though these emotions owed their existence more to a numbed state of shock than to any genuine emancipation; my father was a fool to think he would be spared the harrowing of guilt, and indeed this soon followed.

Hilda slept with him in Kitchener Street for what remained of the night. She hung her skirt and blouse in the wardrobe, among my mother's clothes, then flung her underwear over a chair and climbed into bed. My father was eager for intercourse, but she permitted him no contact at all. Early the following morning I crept quietly into the room, and stood beside the bed, gazing at the bulk of her body beneath the blankets where my mother's should have been, and at the pillow where her hair straggled across it in clumps of tangled yellow with black roots. The light that filtered through the curtains was gray and dim, and the room stank of stale alcohol. My father awoke with a start. His first sensation was

of me standing mutely by the bed, the second, the foul taste
of the phlegm in his mouth. Then the night came back, and
he turned and cast a glance at Hilda's body in the bed beside
him. Then he looked at me again, and I saw that he was
suddenly very frightened, and wanted a drink; but there was
never anything in the house (this at my mother's insistence)
apart from an occasional bottle of beer. He felt an impulse to
turn to Hilda for comfort, but she seemed to have become
tainted by association with the events of the night and with
his own guilty terror. At last he remembered a small bottle
of whisky he had bought last Christmas and never drunk. I
was back in my own room when he climbed out of bed,
pulled on his vest and trousers and went down to the outhouse. Back into the kitchen a few minutes later, and into
the parlor, where he found the whisky in the cupboard. There
he sat in the gloom of that weird Saturday morning, not the
least of the weirdness being his use of the parlor; I'd never
known him sit alone in there before. The parlor was for
company, and my parents very rarely had company—they
weren't very sociable people.

An hour later he was a little steadier, and he felt he could go
up and see Hilda. The whisky had blurred the stark outlines
of the night's doings; the terror that had grown for a few
minutes almost intolerable had receded, and been replaced by
a sort of fragile confidence that they were going to get away
with it (he must, I think, have thought from the start in terms
of a "they," in terms of a mutual, shared responsibility).
Slowly, heavily, he climbed the stairs; I was in my own room,
at my window with my chin in my hands. The morning was
well advanced, but the fog still clung to the city and cloaked
it in twilight. While he was downstairs I'd crept along the
landing and had another look at the woman in my mother's
bed. She was still fast asleep and snoring; at one point I heard
her mumble a few words, but they were indistinct. The room

was dark and the awful sweet smell of port was still thick in the air; and there was another smell, I detected it at once, familiar as I was with my mother's fragrance: this too was a woman's smell, but it was Hilda's smell, a warm, fleshy smell colored by strong perfume and the emanations of her fur, which, impregnated with fog, hung from the wardrobe door. There was also the smell of her feet, and the whole effect was of some large female animal, not terribly clean, possibly dangerous. Into the lair, into the *den* of this creature came my father, fortified by whisky; I listened closely from my own room, my door slightly ajar and my ear pressed close to it. I heard him get undressed and then climb into bed.

Her back was toward him, for she lay facing the curtained window and the gasworks beyond. Gingerly my father fitted his body to hers (I could hear the springs creak), his groin and belly forming a snug pocket for her bottom. With an arm laid lightly across her, he pressed his face into her hair (which smelled of cigarette smoke) and tried to fall asleep.

He could not sleep. The terror rose in him again. She stirred, and I heard a heaving in that big bed. Silently I crept out of my room and along the landing until I was outside the door, which was open a crack (it would never close properly, that door). Silently I sank to my knees and edged my head round the side of the door till I could see them. Hilda had turned in the bed, and without awakening she gathered my father into her arms. Again she mumbled indistinctly and the heavy breathing resumed, her bosom rose and fell, and my father, clasped tight, lay peacefully at last, and soon he too was asleep.

For some minutes I watched the sleeping couple, then I crept back to my room and busied myself with my insect collection, listening for when they should awake. I suppose what I wanted was to hear something, something that would help me find out where my mother—my *real* mother—had gone.

*   *   *

My father awoke in the middle of the afternoon. The room was still dark, for the curtains were closed and all that sifted through the cracks was the gray dimness of the persisting fog. Hilda was wakening too, disentangling her limbs from his, and as she did so the big flabby mattress heaved beneath her, the springs and joints of the old bed creaked and screamed, and once more I slipped down the landing to the bedroom door. Hilda stretched her limbs and yawned, and then, turning toward my father, sighed: "Plumber." She gazed at him sleepily. It was hot in the bed, and I imagined my father wanting to wash his face and brush his teeth (I would), but Hilda had gathered him into her arms—and a moment later she came to life. On my knees at the bedroom door I saw movement in the blankets, then suddenly he was on top of her, in the gloom he was making a hump of the pair of them under those hot blankets. A small muddle as she hauled a pillow down under her bottom, then the bedclothes *tented,* they hollowed and bulged, flattened and billowed, the whole shifting shadowy mass groaning as one creature as the creaks and screams of the old night-machine settled into a rhythm that affected the watching young Spider strangely; and then, like a sportive whale, this quaking hill turned itself over (hoarse laughter, stifled grunting during this clumsy maneuver) and her blonde head came up from the hill and turned toward the window with chin lifted and she sank and rose, sank and rose, as if breasting heavy seas, and groaned. The old bed was creaking and grinding beneath her like the spars and booms of a galleon now, her groaning the howl of the wind in its topsail as on she plowed, lifting and plunging, her chin straining to the ceiling then sinking onto her breast, her thick white arms like columns beneath her as the tangled blonde clumps fell forward to conceal her face from the avid eyes of the watching Spider. Then at last she subsided, she expired, with a sustained wail that could have been pleasure and could have been pain, and after that a stillness settled on the room, the only sound an exhausted panting that steadily waned as the moments passed. Silence; then she heaved herself off my father and seated herself on the edge of the mattress, facing the door with her feet on the floor, and yawned.

Still I knelt there by the door, gazing at the woman; I dared not move. From behind her in the bed my father murmured something and I saw her shake her head. Absently she scratched her ear, and this set her breasts wobbling. Her belly swelled like a soft white cushion; I was fascinated with the triangle of soft flesh beneath its crease, and the little tuft of curly black hair between her thick thighs. Again she yawned, and turned toward my father, and I drew back from the door. A moment later I heard her cross the floor to the wardrobe, I heard the hangers jangle as she pawed through my mother's clothes; and on soundless feet I slipped back to my own room.

Later she wanted to look over the house. I watched her pick her way carefully down our narrow stairs, descending in a sort of cautious sideways movement in a tight-belted dark blue dress with small white spots: *my mother's Sunday dress*. I watched her go down, her bottom bulging and a plump hand on the banister, and as I listened to the clack of her heels I couldn't help remembering the soft slushy shuffling sound my mother's slippers made when she moved around the house. She had painted her mouth with my mother's lipstick and fixed her hair with my mother's comb; the scent, how-ever, was all Hilda. Her belly was prominent in the thin material of the spotted blue dress, it was a generous, fleshy belly that sloped away at the flanks to the firm, trunklike roundness of her upper thighs, between which the material clung like a veil or curtain concealing a shadowy concavity. "Two-up two-down, is it?" she said as my father descended the stairs after her (she'd already stuck her nose into my room, but she hadn't seen me, I was under the bed), then, without waiting for his answer: "I like a little house like this, Horace, I've always wanted one of these, Nora can tell you that."

Then—and note how casually she tossed this out—"You own it, eh?"

You own it, eh: this is significant, we shall return to this later. Suffice for now that Hilda Wilkinson, a common prostitute, had spent her whole life drifting from lodging to lodging, often at the dead of night; a man who owned his own home was an attractive proposition—how much more attractive, should that man's wife have disappeared! On she went, her awful boisterous voice ringing through the house, her motives plain as day: "Put your money in real property, that's what I always say. This the parlor, is it, Horace? Now this *is* a nice room, you could entertain your friends in here."

Horace and Hilda spent an hour in the parlor and drank the rest of the whisky. From what I could hear she was comfortable in there, it seemed to appeal to some submerged yearning she had for gentility. She filled it to overflowing with her presence as she admired the modest fireplace with its polished brass scuttle, its poker and irons, and she expressed pleasure as well in the tiled mantelpiece, the oval mirror above it, and the five china geese hanging on a diagonal across the wall. She also liked the pattern of the wallpaper and the chintz cushion covers. The glass-fronted cabinet with its three pieces of Wedgwood: this pleased her too. "I do like a parlor, Horace," she said, more than once, "gives a place respectability." What did my father make of this, staving off, as he was, with whisky, an utter *maelstrom* of guilt when with every passing hour the murder like a virus gnawed deeper into the tissue of his vital organs?

There was bacon in the house, and after finishing the whisky they moved to the kitchen. They ate their breakfast as night fell; I smelled the bacon from upstairs, and it sharpened the edge of my own ravenous hunger, for I had eaten nothing all day; but I would not go down. I sat at the window and gazed at the glow from the kitchen, which barely penetrated the darkness in the yard. I saw Hilda go through the back door to the outhouse, and I was tempted then to go downstairs but the prospect of encountering her when she came back in deterred me. "You should fix that toilet of yours, Horace," she said on her return. "Fine state of affairs when a plumber's own toilet don't work!"

Ten minutes later they left for the Earl of Rochester, and I came downstairs. There was no bacon left, so I had to make do with bread and dripping.

WOULD that awful day never end? I could think no more about it, that long evening I spent alone in the house with the smell of Hilda everywhere in my nostrils. I went out into the fog after my bread and dripping, and made for the canal, where I wandered along in a morose state, at times desperate, at times tearfully furious, kicking stones into the black water and taking what small comfort I could from the foggy darkness of the night. Where was my mother? Where *was* she? I returned to number twenty-seven after nine and came in through the back door; the house was empty. I ate more bread and dripping then went up to my room and got out my insect collection again. I heard my father come in late, alone; he sat up in the kitchen drinking beer until he passed out. I crept down around midnight and saw him slumped in a chair by the stove, still in his cap and scarf, and a cigarette adhering to his lower lip even as he slept.

The next day was Sunday. As was his habit he went to his allotment. The fog had dissipated somewhat, it was a cool, cloudy morning, and it looked as if it might rain later. As he cycled through the empty streets he was still very much a man in crisis: barely thirty hours had elapsed since the murder, and he had not yet adjusted to the new territory he occupied. Murder sets a man apart, moves him into a separate world, narrow and constricted, bound and constrained by guilt, complicity, and the fear of betrayal. None of this he had fully realized, for he was still to some extent in shock; he pedaled his bicycle past curtained windows behind which slept a world from which he was now exiled forever, though this, as I say, was not yet apparent to him.

That soon changed! There has always seemed to me to be a sort of bleak poetic justice in the fact that the allotment, to which my father had so often fled from his domestic life, should now be charged with the horror of my mother's murder. He himself felt this only dimly as he pedaled through the streets that Sunday morning, but the closer he came to the railway bridge the stronger the impulse was to turn around and get as far away from the place as possible. But he did not turn round, for he was also aware of a vague, perverse stirring of excitement at the prospect of seeing again the ground beneath which she lay.

Nothing, however, prepared him for the wave that hit him when he opened the gate and stood at the end of his path. For some moments it swirled about him in a sweeping, spinning movement, as though the allotment had become an active force field in a state of intense disturbance. It warped his perceptions: the shed and the vegetables seemed to *turn black* in front of his eyes, and before he had taken one step down the path he sensed a sort of thrashing and writhing all about him, and then for the few interminable moments it took him to reach the shed the suddenly dark, damp air of the morning swarmed with tiny malignant germs, and to pass through these swarms required no little determination. The effect was weakened somewhat when he gained the interior of the shed and shut the door on the garden's malevolence, but outside it did not abate for a moment, the whole of that Sunday.

(I *know* this feeling, I too have been tormented in this way, I too have felt them clacking and clicking round the back of my head like the teeth of a hound, like a cloud of chattering gnats, in fact the sound is rarely absent, though most of the time it is mercifully subdued, more of a hum than anything else.)

*　　*　　*

While my father was experiencing the first wave of horror that came off the soil of his allotment, I was back in my room at number twenty-seven. I didn't yet know that my mother was dead, only that she wasn't at home, and that a fat woman had been in her place in my parents' bed. I was again busy with my collection, which helped distract me from all the worry and perplexity these changes were producing. As a boy I collected insects, flies mostly, which I pinned in boxes in artistic formations that I called tableaux. Dead leaves of various colors featured heavily in the boxes I'd set up in the autumn, but by this time many of them had become so brittle that they'd broken up into fragments and fallen away from the pins, forming little heaps at the bottom of the boxes. These I cleared out, also the feathers and twigs, and got out the fresh materials I'd been carefully collecting and which I kept in a cardboard box under my bed. All sorts of things were in that box, anything that looked as if it might come in handy, and I made no distinction between natural objects, twigs and feathers and so on, and matchsticks, bottle caps, bits of string, the cardboard and tinfoil of empty cigarette packets. I tried some pieces of eggshell, also a furry ball of blonde hair that I'd pulled off my mother's comb earlier in the afternoon; a few fish bones, a few fins. It made a curious sort of assembly, and I wasn't sure whether I liked it or not. At some point during the afternoon, occupied thus, I heard footsteps outside. Rising from the floor I went to the window and coming down the yard was the woman I'd seen in bed with my father.

I moved away from the window. I decided that I wouldn't let her in, I wouldn't go downstairs, she wouldn't even know that I was in the house. All in vain; she came straight in through the back door without knocking, and I heard in the kitchen the familiar clatter of the kettle at the sink, the dull pop of the gas being lit, and the scrape of chair legs. I sank back onto the floor, careful to make no sound that would alert her to my presence. That too was all in vain; after she'd had her cup of tea she spent a few minutes in the parlor and then came up the stairs. I was at my door when she reached the landing, and I was gripping the knob tightly. She was on the other side, trying to turn it, and she was too strong for me; the knob turned, the door opened, she peered in at me. "Hello Dennis," she said. "What you doing up here?"

I wanted her out of my room! I mumbled something about my insects; in my mind's eye I saw her on top of my father, going up and down and gasping like a fish. Suddenly she shuddered. "Those flies!" she said. "Do we have to have them in your bedroom?"

I was downstairs in the kitchen with her when my father got home from the allotments. The strain of the past two days was quite apparent in his features. He had done no work on his garden; on the one occasion he'd stepped out of the shed and braved the allotment's peculiar atmospheric energies he'd found himself unable to touch the soil. He'd gone back inside, back to the remains of the bottle of port. A cold rain began to fall late in the afternoon, slashing down in sheets and drumming on the roof over his head. It quickly grew dark, and the sense of horror became intense, rising to the pitch it'd been at when he'd first experienced it in the morning. As he left the shed the leaves of his root vegetables turned black once more and flailed about wildly like seaweed in a running tide. With his collar turned up and his cap pulled low he cycled back through the icy rain to Kitchener Street.

It must have been a shock to him to see me sitting at the table with Hilda. "Raining, is it?" she said as my father dumped a string bag filled with potatoes into the sink. "I thought I heard rain. Still, you expect it, this time of the year." My father made no reply to this; after taking off his jacket and cap he began washing the potatoes. I took the opportunity to slip off my chair and leave the kitchen. My father heard me. "Where you going, Dennis?" he said, turning from the sink, a paring knife in one hand and a half-peeled potato in the other. "Up to my room," I said. He frowned like black thunder but said nothing, just turned back to his potatoes. The guilt was his, not mine!

Oh, I throw down my pencil. The psychology of the murderer—how do *I* know anything about this? How do I know anything about *any* of this? All acquired overseas, during the long, uneventful years I spent in Canada. Enough, it is very late, I am tired, there is stamping in the attic but I cannot go on. The pain in my intestines has not gone away, it's spread instead to my kidneys and liver, and I suspect that something very wrong is happening inside me, that it's not the food at all (filthy though it is), but that something far worse is involved. I suspect, in fact, that my internal organs are starting to shrivel up, though I'm not clear why this should be so. How will I be able to function if my organs shrivel up? I am not possessed of great vitality, and can ill afford any shrinking or shriveling internally. Perhaps it's just a transient phenomenon, like the gas smell, which thankfully has not returned.

I'd been writing about the death of my mother. I'd been sitting at my table describing the events of that terrible night and the day that followed, and in the process the memories had somehow become more vivid than the immediate situation— that familiar *running together* of past and present had occurred, and I must have gone into some sort of a trance. For when I came to I found myself in Mrs. Wilkinson's bedroom.

I don't know how it happened. It was very late, the house was dark and silent, and she was fast asleep. She was wearing some kind of headscarf tied beneath her chin and her hair was in rollers. There was white cream on her forehead and cheeks, and in the glow from the bulb in the corridor it shone with a ghostly pallor. I don't know how long I stood there, nor what I was thinking of; I only came to when she awoke with a shudder and started up, one hand groping for the lamp on the bedside table. "Mr. Cleg!" she cried. "For heaven's sake, what on *earth* do you think you're doing? Get back to your own room!" She began clambering out of the bed. When I reached the door I turned back, intending somehow to explain that which was then, and remains now, inexplicable. She was sitting on the side of the bed, a curious figure in her night-gown, curlers, and facepaint, gaping at me, and in some odd way vulnerable as she'd never been before; an emotion stirred within me, something strong, though how precisely to define it is beyond me. I paused in the doorway. She flapped a hand at me as with the other she covered a yawn. "Out! Out!" she cried. "We'll discuss this in the morning!"

When I got back to my room I found the journal where I'd left it, open on the table with the pencil down its spine. I immediately replaced it in its hole, the grate behind the disused gas fire; and it was ironic, I thought, down on my hands and knees at the fireplace, keeping a journal was sup-posed to help me sort out the muddle I made between mem-ory and sensation, and here it was simply increasing the confusion. I slept badly; my insides were still hurting, and there was much activity in the attic; later they began hauling trunks about. This was followed by a period of silence, and then I heard them outside my door. I must have tiptoed across the room half a dozen times and flung it open, but the wretched creatures, imps or whatever they are, were always too quick for me.

The next day it rained, and I thought seriously about going back to Kitchener Street. I don't know what it was that pre-vented me—hardly the need to preserve in my memory some sort of aura about the place, some glow of innocence; Kitch-ener Street was blackly contaminated long before any of these events occurred, every brick of the place oozed time and evil, and not only Kitchener Street, the whole festering warren was bad, bad from the day it was built. So no, it wasn't that, perhaps it was the very *reverse* of that, the prospect of seeing (as only I, only I, could see) how much darker the brickwork

was, how much more it oozed, how much more it had absorbed of the moral squalor such an architecture invariably
breeds in its tenants.

The allotment was a different story. After the rain stopped
I once again made my shambling way up the hill to Omdurman Close, and so to the railway bridge. I was in fragile
condition, but I managed to get across without mishap. A
few minutes later I was standing at the gate of my father's
garden. A scarecrow stood among the potatoes (I must have
missed it before), five feet tall, made of sacking stuffed with
rags and tied off at the wrists and ankles with twine. Arms
outspread, it was nailed to a crude cross of two-by-fours, and
had clearly seen several seasons' service: its clothes were
weathered to a uniform gray-brown color, and the bowler
that was perched atop the lumpy, eyeless head, and nailed to
the backboard, was faded by rain and streaked with drop-
pings. For some minutes we stared at one another, this creature and I, until a gust of wind came up and ruffled the loose
sacking and gave me a start. It was hard not to notice that
the ragged edges of the sacking were stained a blackish color.
Overhead thick banks of gray cloud were moving in low
from the river, and the wind was freshening; it occurred to
me that we might have a storm. It also occurred to me to
make a gesture of remembrance, so I gathered a small bunch
of dandelions and a few sprigs of thistlegrass, and then (no
one was about) I opened the gate and slipped down the path
and scattered my simple bouquet on the potato patch. Then
I stretched out flat on the soil.

After a few moments I felt stronger, so instead of going
back the way I'd come I continued on down past the allotments to a steep path that gave onto a warren of streets and
alleys that for some reason had always been called the Slates.
Down the path I scrambled then stood a moment at the bottom getting my breath back. Off to the east I saw a long low
line of factory buildings with thin chimneys drifting smoke,
while to the south, two or three hundred yards away, there

was a corrugated-tin fence. But where *were* the Slates? All
around me the ground was scattered with bricks and rocks
and lumps of concrete with shorn-off iron cables sticking out
of them, and not far off the ground dipped to form a gully
in which water had collected, bleak tufty patches of grass
round the edges. Scraps of paper drifted across this wasteground as I turned in every direction looking for the Slates.
Had they gone? How could they have gone? Or was my
memory playing me false again? Arduously I made my way
back up the path to the allotments, then along to the railway
bridge again. Had I completely misplaced the Slates in my
mind? And if I had, was the rest of my "map" similarly faulty?
Oh, this was worrying, this troubled me sorely. It had been
a long day for the old Spider, and wearily he trudged home,
coming in very quietly so as to avoid Mrs. Wilkinson, who
would doubtless be wanting an explanation of his visit in the
night.

The next day I went down to the river, to a pebbly strand
where as a boy I used to watch the barges and steamers; in
those days they ran on coal, and constantly coughed cloudy
spumes of black smoke into the sky. You reached the strand
at low tide by a set of tarry wooden steps beside an old pub
called the Crispin. Down I'd go to sniff around the boats
moored there, old battered working boats with smelly tar-
paulins spread across their decks, all puddled with rainwater
and green with fungus. Often I'd climb onto the deck and
creep under a tarpaulin, in among the iron chains and the
damp timbers, and settle myself in a thick oily coil of rotting
rope—I loved to be alone in that damp gloom with the muted
screaming of the gulls outside as they wheeled and flapped
over the water. The Crispin was still there, and so were the
tarry steps, though they looked unsafe now and I didn't go
down. But I peered over the edge, and the beached boats
were there too, and across the water the cranes poked at the
sky just as I'd always remembered them. This was some
comfort, anyway; my geography wasn't totally skewed.

I CHANGED after my mother died. When she was alive I was a good boy, that is, I fell foul of my father's temper now and then and had to go down the cellar, but there was nothing abnormal in this, all boys make mistakes and are punished. But before my mother died I was a quiet boy, solitary and pensive, who read a good deal; I had no friends among the children of Kitchener Street, and I tended to drift off by myself whenever I could, down to the canal, or down to the river, especially in damp and foggy weather. I was tall for my age, tall and thin and brainy and shy, and boys like this are never popular, particularly with their fathers, who look for hardy, masculine traits. Mothers are different in this regard, this is my observation; my mother certainly was. She came from a better family than my father, she married down, you see, and she appreciated books and art and music; she encouraged me to read, and during those long evenings we'd spend in the kitchen while my father was out drinking she'd draw me out, encourage me to talk, to share with her my ideas and fantasies, and sometimes I would go to bed quietly amazed at all that I'd said, that so much was in my head, when so often I felt—or rather, was made to feel—that there was nothing in my head at all, that I was a gangling, tongue-tied numbskull with big knees and clumsy hands, unlikely ever to be of any use to anybody. Later I realized that my mother understood me because she too was alien to her environment—the women of Kitchener Street had no time for her taste, her delicacy, her culture, they were women like Hilda, primitives by comparison. So she understood what I suffered and she alone enabled me to be truly myself in those few fleeting hours we had together before my father stove in her skull with a spade. After that, you see, I was quite, quite alone, and without her love, her influence, without, simply, her *presence* I quickly went adrift. That's why I changed from a good boy to a bad boy.

Not that this happened without provocation. For Hilda I was, at first, a source of amusement. Later she came to fear me, but in those first weeks she used this big blushing lad, no longer a child and not yet a man, as a butt of her vulgar humor. She teased me, she laughed at me, she flaunted her body at me; and because she was so often in the kitchen, even when my father was out of the house, I could avoid her only by going to the canal (though this of course involved going out through the kitchen) or by hiding myself down in the coal cellar, or by staying in my room—though not even my room was a sanctuary anymore, for she felt no compunction about coming up and poking around to her heart's content. Did I receive any support from my father in this? Was he any sort of an ally? He was not. The very reverse, in fact; he shared her jokes, in that sly, quiet way of his, he exchanged winks and nods and secret smiles with Hilda when she set about "getting a rise" out of me. It quickly reached the point that whenever I was in the kitchen with Horace and Hilda I would see signals passing back and forth between them that suggested only one thing, ridicule, though if I said anything they denied it, and so I grew to mistrust my own perceptions, but that's what I *think* was going on. Why would they do this? Why would they so persistently taunt me in this manner? It was only years later, in Canada, that I realized I functioned for Horace and Hilda as an outlet for the guilt and anxiety that had settled on them in the weeks following my mother's death, settled on them not in any acute or panicky form but rather as a condition of existence, a way of being, in the wake of the murder. Much as Hilda could try to laugh it off, play the boisterous life-loving blonde as before—and extensive though my father's powers of repression were—at some level they were secreting the toxins that the act of murder will always and inevitably decoct in the human heart, and if they weren't to turn those toxins on each other then there must be an outlet, a conduit for it. I was that conduit, I was to channel and absorb the poison, and so I did; in the process I was contaminated by it, it shriveled me, it killed something inside me, made me a ghost, a dead thing, in short it turned me *bad*.

Perhaps the cruelest aspect of the situation was that my grief could be shared with no one. At first it wasn't grief, it was desperation. Where was she? Where was my mother? I could get no answer, and if I broached the subject with my father he would instantly grow tense and furious and remind me of the conversation we'd had on the Saturday morning I first saw Hilda with him in bed. But I always forgot that conversation, for the sense of loss I felt, the sheer panic of *not knowing*, would overwhelm whatever fragile inhibitions he'd instilled in me, and out it came, out it blurted; and again that terrible quiet anger, and all I took away with me was that I was *not yet to know*. And in time my feelings changed, desperation and urgency gave way to a chronic ache, a gnawing sense of absence, of emptiness, which left me curiously vulnerable to the sustained contempt that Horace and Hilda were directing at me. But it was not only that I was alone, for if I ever made reference to it in front of Hilda—and on two occasions, driven beyond endurance by her goads and gibes, I did this, I tearfully cried out: "You're not my mother!"—then she would pretend to be greatly surprised, she would turn to my father, who'd glance at her from hooded eyes, an almost imperceptible smile playing at the edges of his mouth—and she'd say: "Not your mother?" "No," I cried, "my mother's dead!" More silent mockery, another glance exchanged. "Dead?"—and so it would go until I fled the kitchen, unable any longer to hold back my tears, and clasping tight to myself a set of memories, and their associated emotions, that no one would confirm. So she lived only in me, now, this is what I came to realize, and the realization made me that much more tenacious, for I intuitively understood that if she died in me she died forever. You see, I'd heard my father tell the man next door that she'd gone to stay with her sister in Canada.

I developed in time my two-head system. The front of my head was what I used with other people in the house, the back of my head was for when I was alone. My mother lived in the back of my head, but not the front; I grew expert at moving from back to front and back again, and it seemed to make life easier. The back of my head was the real part of my life, but in order to keep everything there fresh and healthy then I had to have a front head to protect it, like tomatoes in a greenhouse. So when I was downstairs I would speak and eat and move and *to their eyes* be me, and only I knew that "I" wasn't there, this was only the greenhouse they were seeing; I was in the back, that was where Spider lived, up the front was Dennis.

Life became easier for me after that. I didn't mind being a bad boy, because I knew of course that it was *Dennis* who was a bad boy; and when my father took me down the coal cellar it was Dennis who went with him and leaned his head on the beam and curled his little finger round the rusty nail—while all the time Spider was upstairs in his bedroom!

I T followed that if my mother lived only in the back part of my head then so did her murder. Because if I couldn't refer to her by name downstairs, then how much greater by extension was my inability to allude to her death, and the way in which she'd been dumped in the earth like a sack of rubbish? During those first weeks I didn't realize what had happened to her, and I persuaded myself that indeed she had gone to Canada, as I'd heard my father say to more than one of the neighbors. But she didn't *have* a sister in Canada! Wouldn't I have known about a sister in Canada? Wouldn't she have mentioned her as we sat by the stove in the kitchen, those long winter evenings with the rain drumming on the windows and the ring of hobnailed boots on cobblestones as the men made their way down the alley behind the yard? She would have mentioned this sister, she'd have received letters postmarked *Winnipeg* or *Vancouver,* with stamps with the king's head on them, and she'd have showed them to me, read them to me, and together we'd have conjured scenes of Canadian winters, Canadian Christmases—her sister's family clustered about a dressed fir ("all your little cousins, Spider"), the smell of a fat duck roasting in the kitchen of a log house with a cedar-shingled roof and a stout brick chimney coughing woodsmoke into the damp Canadian sky. Together we would paint these pictures in the yellow gloom of number twenty-seven, and for an hour or so we would be far from that dreary slum, we too would be part of the family gathered at the open hearth, pine logs blazing and children—my little cousins—opening gifts with cries of pleasure. Why would she go to her sister's and leave me behind? This troubled me, up in my bedroom with my elbows on the windowsill, this provoked a sharp jab of bewildered pain until I remembered that there *was* no sister, no log house, no little cousins, there was only the absence of my mother, only, now, the memory of her, and downstairs a fat woman indifferent to me (when I wasn't the butt of her humor), and a cold, uncaring father. This, as I say, went on for several weeks, and it wasn't until we were close to our own Christmas that they began to take proper note of me, for by then, bad boy that I was (the Dennis part, I mean) I realized I no longer had to obey my father's order not to speak of her. And when I realized this, and they saw that I'd realized it, they couldn't ignore me anymore.

My father was still working at the time, so there was money coming into the house. This meant nights in the Rochester and people coming back to Kitchener Street afterwards. I'd see them spilling from the alley into the back yard, clutching bottles, their breath coming in a big cloud of mist so they looked like a single beast, a many-legged monster-horse stamping down the yard. They puffed steam, they roared in several voices at the same time, and I could never sleep when it was like this in the house, there was so much noise down there, loud voices and drunken singing, the clinking of bottles and stamping of boots on the floor. Often there were people in the house I'd never seen before, I'd watch them from my bedroom window as they reeled through the back door to the outhouse, or from my perch in the darkness at the top of the stairs I'd see them kissing and fondling each other in the passage below.

There was no Christmas tree in number twenty-seven, no decorations, no gifts, only a clump of mistletoe tied with string to the neck of the light bulb that dangled from the kitchen ceiling, and this permitted them to handle each other more licentiously than usual. Then bottles were opened as

Horace got down on his hands and knees to coax some heat from the stove. Hilda had had him bring in the armchairs from the parlor, and into one of these she'd settle herself with a large glass of ruby port as the singing and the hilarity started up. Despite the hubbub her laughter was always recognizable from upstairs even with the kitchen door closed. Once, I remember, I heard the kitchen door open—the noise swelled for a moment—and then came a furtive whispering in the passage. I was at the top of the stairs in my pajamas. I retreated into my room as I heard people coming along the passage. Through the crack in my door I saw a man and a woman come up the stairs: he was fat and wearing a dark suit, she, carrying her shoes, someone I'd seen in the house before, a friend of Hilda's, handsome in a way though as I think of her now I remember how life and drink had drained the color from her skin and the light from her eyes, she was a gray and sallow woman, and though she too laughed constantly her eyes were dead and so were her teeth, and her breath smelled foul. Her hair was dyed black and her name was Gladys. Along the upstairs landing they tiptoed and then into my parents' bedroom, pulling the door behind them though of course it didn't close properly, there was something wrong with it. Not very long after this I heard the bed creaking and Gladys quietly groaning; then there was silence. I crept down the landing, and getting onto my hands and knees as I had the day Hilda first came to the house I had a look at them. Gladys was lying on the bed smoking a cigarette. They hadn't turned the light on, so there was only the dim glow that seeped in from the streetlamp. The fat man was on the far side of the bed struggling into his trousers and at the same time counting out pound notes. I crept back to my own room, and five minutes later I heard the pair of them go back downstairs.

I stayed in my room, sitting by the window, and waited for them all to leave. It was after midnight when they went shambling off down the yard in twos and threes, no longer the horse-monster they had been earlier, too drunk for that now, and then I heard Horace and Hilda come upstairs. I waited another half hour before going down with a candle. The kitchen was disgusting: dirty glasses, empty bottles, overflowing ashtrays, Hilda's black shoes on the table, one upright, one on its side (why were they on the table?), and a foul stink of cigarette smoke and alcohol. Gladys was sprawled sleeping in one of the armchairs in her coat, and on the arm of the chair, close to where her sagging, snoring head lay pillowed on the shoulder of a dangling arm, stood a tumbler half-full of brown ale (black in the candlelight) with a cigarette butt floating in it, decomposing, shreds of tobacco drifting loose. I moved the tumbler to the kitchen table and took Hilda's shoes and set them on the floor. Then I stood gazing down at Gladys for a few minutes, holding the candle up under my chin so I could feel the warmth of the flame; the fire in the stove was dying and the chill of the night was creeping into the kitchen. And as I gazed at the woman sprawled there in the shadows I thought about the noises she'd made upstairs and the sight of her suspendered legs on the bed and her dress bunched up round her waist. There was someone sleeping in the other chair but it wasn't the fat man, it was Harold Smith. Then I went out through the back door into the cold and had a wank in the outhouse, and when I pulled the chain the water came right up to the rim before very slowly draining away: he still hadn't fixed it. When I came back in I found some old cheddar in the cupboard and a crust of a loaf in the bread box, so I sat at the table and, still by candlelight, among the snoring drunks, I ate my supper, washing it down with a glass of brown ale from an unfinished bottle by the sink.

The next day was Christmas Eve, and I didn't have to go to school. I wouldn't have gone anyway; since becoming a bad boy I'd missed a lot of school, for I didn't sleep at night anymore. I came downstairs at twelve o'clock. The kitchen had been cleaned up and Hilda was making mince pies. She smiled at me and I was immediately on my guard. Warmth in Hilda was a trap, for as soon as you relaxed she stuck a poisoned blade in you. I sat down at the table without a word. She was flattening out a lump of pastry dough with a rolling pin; her hands and arms were powdery with flour, though there was dirt under her fingernails and she smelled of jellied eels. She was wearing my mother's apron—it was tight on her, as you'd expect, particularly at the bosom. "What you looking at me like that for?" she murmured, her thick white arms bearing down on the rolling pin. "Here's your toast"— and she fished a plate out of the oven, on it a couple of stiff, charred slices of bread. "There's dripping if you want it," she said, "and the kettle's on. Your dad might be home early today."

What was her game? I examined the toast carefully and decided not to take the chance. I drank the tea, though, and detected nothing amiss. "Nora's down the butcher's," said Hilda. "It'll be a bloody wonder if everything gets done, you ask yourself if it's worth it." She glanced out the window over the sink. "I do wish she'd get a move on," she said, and I felt myself going rigid and shifting into the back of my head where Spider lived. As soon as I was there I knew that they must have worked out a new strategy—they hoped by "winning me over" to secure my silence and complicity. It was a trap, you see, it was as if Hilda was saying to me: "Yes it's true we murdered your mother but try and think of *me* as your mother now." This was why she was baking mince pies and talking about the butcher, she was acting *as if* she was my mother. It didn't come naturally to her, that was clear from the way she handled the rolling pin. My mother was far more deft with pastry, far superior to this ham-fisted prostitute putting on an act in a kitchen not her own; also, my mother never handled food until she'd thoroughly scrubbed her hands. Then this "Nora's down the butcher's"—what was Nora to me? Did she really think I would eat meat that had been touched by Nora? It was a subtle piece of theater but I was too clever for her. "What *are* you smiling at?" she said, pausing in her boisterous pastry-rolling and brushing at a strand of hair on her damp forehead. "You really have turned into a most peculiar boy just recently, I don't wonder your father's worried about you." Oh, she was good, in my head I was applauding her, she was just like a mother.

She carried on this way until Nora came in from the butcher's with the bird we were to eat for Christmas dinner. "Let's have a look at it then," said Hilda, wiping her hands on the apron once more. She snipped with the black kitchen scissors at the string tied around the newspaper the bird was wrapped up in. "Very nice, Nora," she said when it lay there on the kitchen table, its plump pink skin stippled with points where the feathers had been plucked. Me, I had no interest in this carcass until Hilda thrust her hand up its arse and cried: "Where's the giblets?"

"Not there?" said Nora.

"See for yourself!" And stepping aside, Hilda let Nora put her hand inside the bird. "He always leaves them in," said Nora, "I didn't think to look."

"Back you go and get our giblets, Nora. *And* the feet, *and* the head! What does he think, he can do us out of half our bird? And tell him, Nora"—Nora was halfway out the back door by this time—"if there's any more nonsense I'll be down to see him myself."

Shaking her head she turned the tap on and ran her hands under the cold water, then went back to filling her mince pies. I couldn't help myself, I had to peer into the bird's body: all I saw was a cavity in there, no organs at all, and it gave me a very queer feeling. I left the kitchen soon after and went down the cellar.

I was in my room when my father got home from work, and of course the first thing Hilda told him about was the bird coming back from the butcher's without any giblets, and how Nora had had to go back and get them. "What, no

giblets?" said my father—I was sitting at the top of the stairs
listening to this, barely able to suppress my laughter. Then
he too stuck his hand inside the bird, as I thought he might.
"What's this then?" I heard him say, and I knew exactly what
happened next: from out of the cavity he pulled a packet of
dead leaves, all tied up with string, and when he opened it
up little chips of coal fell out, a few birds' feathers, some
broken twigs, and right in the middle a dead rat!

I spent that night, Christmas Eve, in the shed down the allotments. My father had guessed immediately who was responsible. "Where is he?" I heard him say, and a moment
later he was stamping up the stairs. Then he was in the doorway of my bedroom, fairly trembling with fury, eyes blazing
and bottom teeth pushed out. "Down the cellar," he said,
"now!"

"Murderer," I said. I was kneeling on the floor with my
insects.

"Now!" And with that he crossed the room in a single
stride and, catching me by the collar, half dragged me across
the floor. Down the stairs we went then, me in front, choking,
him storming down behind me. When we reached the cellar
door he let go of my collar for a moment, and that's all I
needed. Out through the kitchen past a bewildered Hilda and
Nora, and into the yard, with him right behind me. "Get
back here!" he shouted. The gate in the yard had been left
open, fortunately for me, and I was through it in a flash and
off down the alley. It was just getting dark; close to the end
of the alley he caught up to me and crushed me against the
wall and held me there, pinned to the bricks, while he tried
to get his breath back. I went completely limp as he glared
at me furiously. "Murderer," I whispered, "murderer, murderer." His frown darkened, he screwed up his features with
perplexity—what was he to do about me, about *what I knew?*
His breath grew more even, and I remained limp; his grip on

me slackened slightly; I slipped out of his hands and again made a run for it. He chased me down to the end of the alley, but the spirit had left him, and as I darted off into the dusk, a fleeting, coatless, long-legged boy, he turned back, still in his shirtsleeves, and kicked in his anger at a dustbin standing against the wall. A black cat scrambled out from under the lid with a fishhead in its jaws and flickered away through the shadows. With his foot in some pain he hobbled back to the kitchen, where doubtless they talked about me for the rest of the night. I think, though, he must have taken off his boot and sock first, and found blood welling up under the nail of the big toe, turning it purple and black.

I F you've ever kept a journal you'll know how some nights it's almost impossible to squeeze out a single sentence, while at other times the words come flooding onto the paper hour after hour until you're empty, and then it feels not that you've been writing but that you've been *written?* I will never forget the night I spent in my father's shed. I had long since discovered how to break into it: you pried loose by a few inches the board to which the metal staple that took the neck of the padlock was screwed, and then you squeezed in through the crack and pulled the door tightly shut behind you, so the board slipped back into place. But before I went into the shed I spent some minutes kneeling in the potato patch. Nothing but black soil this late in the season, but it wasn't the potatoes I was there for. She felt my presence, I know she did, there was a *reaching up* to me, it was quite distinct, as I knew it would be, such was the bond between us: that was something my father couldn't destroy with his tarts and his violence, not a bond like that. As soon as I felt her I lay down flat on the soil and whispered to her, and I shall not write what I said. Darkness had fallen and it was rapidly growing colder; tonight it would freeze, and there had been some talk of snow. But no cold could touch me then, I whispered to her till I'd said all I needed to, then I squeezed myself into the shed.

I knew where to find the matches and the candles, and I lit them all and placed them on the shelves and the floor until the place glowed like a church. Then I curled up in the armchair as best I could, wrapped in sacks to keep out the cold, and watched the candlelight flickering in the cobwebs up in the gloom of the rafters. After a few minutes I had to climb out from under the sacks and cover the case with the ferret in it: the way the light caught its glass eye made me uneasy. So there I lay curled in the old horsehair armchair, watching the cobwebs, and it's strange to think of it now, for you'd expect me to have cried myself to sleep. But I didn't, instead I lay there wide awake and clear-eyed, and oddly enough it was the idea of the spiders in the rafters watching over me that kept this Spider secure.

I fell asleep. When I awoke, some hours later, a few candles still burned, and I had a moment of confusion and dislocation; then, faintly at first, but growing stronger every moment, a sense of peace and joy, for my mother was with me.

My mother was with me, dim and shadowy to begin with but becoming more distinct with each passing second. She was standing before me in the candlelit shed among the tools and flowerpots and seed packets. Her clothes were cloyed and damp with the soil of the garden and her head was covered with a dark scarf, but how white her face was! Spotlessly white, healed, whole, radiant, and glowing! Those moments are woven deeply into the fabric of my memory—the candlelight, the webs shining in the rafters in the cold, though I was not cold, how could I feel the cold, wrapped as I was in the warmth and peace of her presence and the low, soft murmur of her voice, and above all the sense of *plenitude* I knew then, a plenitude I have searched for since and never found, not here in the empty streets of the East End of London, nor in the plains and mountains and cities of Canada, where I wandered alone and despairing for twenty years?

Later I slept again, dreamless sleep, and I awoke early on Christmas morning still calm and joyful from her visit in the night. I squeezed out of the shed and along the path to where

I'd go down to the Slates, and so through the streets, deserted and silent so early in the morning, curtains still drawn closed and behind them sleeping men and women and children; and it made me feel queer to be out on the streets while behind the curtains of dark and silent houses families still slept. In some of those houses lived children who went to the same school as I did, and in my mind's eye I saw them curled up in bed with their brothers and sisters like little warm animals as the Spider loped by in the early morning.

Soon I began running, for the day was cold, there was frost on the windowpanes, and the puddles on the pavement were skinned with ice and crunched under my boots. It was a clear day, the slate-gray of the early sky turning slowly bluish as I ran on. I was filled with a sense of exhilaration now, the glorious feeling of no longer being alone, no longer the stranded object and victim of my father's house, for my mother was with me now, in a way she was flying with me through those cold streets down to the docks, and her presence inside me gave me courage and purpose and hope.

Later, bored and tired, I made my slow way back to Kitchener Street, where else was I to go? Through the streets I trudged and now there was light and life and movement in the houses I passed, smoke drifted from chimneys into the cold clear air and there was pain in my heart as I glimpsed through parlor windows the glow of coal fires with children gathered around them and the doors closed and the windows closed and me with nowhere to go but number twenty-seven and nothing to look forward to but a belting in the coal cellar and a night in my bedroom without supper.

Along the alley, down the yard, and in through the back door. My father wasn't home, it was just Hilda; grim silence as I came in. "Here he is then. Lucky your father's out, my lad, he's off looking for you. Here's your dinner." She took it out of the oven and set it before me and I was simply too hungry to care, I ate it all, and she watched me in silence as I did so. Nothing was said about the rat.

So I ate my Christmas dinner in the chilly silence of the kitchen, then went upstairs to my room and waited with no little dread for my father's return. It was around eight when I heard his boots in the alley, and then he was coming down the yard; he'd been at the Dog and Beggar, I could tell, and this was not good, a belting was always far worse when he'd been down the Dog for drinking seemed to loosen his anger. In through the back door, while upstairs I sat waiting for the summons, making a deliberate withdrawal as I did so into the deepest recesses of the back part of my head, where only Spider could go. Then—nothing happened! I was not summoned! I heard the scrape of chair legs as he sat down at the table, and then the murmur of voices—the door was shut, so I don't know what they were talking about, though I'm sure it was about me. My father never did come to the bottom of the stairs and call me down for my belting, and so that strange and in a way glorious Christmas passed.

I T was not hard, afterwards, to work out why I hadn't been belted for the dead rat: they had to keep me sweet. For what prevented me from turning them in? Simply, the prospect of becoming homeless, though they didn't know this. If I turned in Horace and Hilda I'd become a ward of the state, and be sent to an orphanage, and it was all too easy to imagine the sort of bullying that went on in such places, the loss of solitude, the regimentation. No, I was fond of my room in number twenty-seven, I took pleasure in my stark boy's life, my insects, the canal, the docks and the river and the fogs; and now, in a way, I had my mother too. So no, I had no desire to trade my lot for the satisfaction of seeing those two swing, not yet anyway. But they didn't know this, they couldn't be sure just what I would do next, so it was in their interest to keep me sweet. Hence no belting.

What I didn't realize until later was that Hilda to some extent enjoyed the same advantage as me. She too, you see, wanted that roof over her head—a man who owned his house was a rare creature in those days, and Hilda, being who she was, and *what* she was, would certainly have taken this very seriously. Consider, then, how she must have crowed when my mother was murdered—when she realized that *because* it was murder she could secure her own place under that safe roof! She wouldn't have taken the slightest interest in my father otherwise, of this I'm certain, she was a cynical, cold-hearted parasite, out to get what she could from a man over whom she now wielded the power, in effect, of life and death—for she, like me, could shop him whenever she chose, and if she was clever about it she'd avoid going to the gallows by his side.

At what point did my father realize what his position was? It seemed that the Canada story had been generally accepted, and as for Hilda's constant presence in number twenty-seven, this might have caused scandal in a street less inured to immorality and corruption, but on Kitchener Street such goings-on were commonplace. On Kitchener Street men routinely dispatched their wives to Canada and brought in prostitutes to share their beds; or themselves went to Canada while other men moved in to take their places. It barely aroused comment. So by Christmas, then, it looked as if they'd got away with it, as long, that is, as I kept my mouth shut.

I suppose my father finally understood the true state of affairs when Hilda came right out and told him. I didn't actually hear her say it, but I remember watching him in the yard one evening, and it was clear that something of the sort must have occurred. When my mother was alive, you see, my father had always had a tendency, if he thought she was nagging him, of just walking out the back door. The habit was deeply ingrained in him, and so when I saw him go storming out (there'd been voices raised in the kitchen), I knew she had angered him. He stamped furiously down to the end of the yard, pulling on his jacket, but he stopped at the gate and seemed to become immobilized by indecision, unable either to go forward or turn back. I felt a little panicky when I saw this, I'm not sure why—I think maybe the only thing worse than having Hilda and Nora in the house (and I hated Nora almost as vehemently as I did Hilda, she was a corrupt and cynical little drunkard) was having them there without my father. He did at least represent some sort of security for me, and I felt that if I was thrown on the mercy of those two monsters I would surely perish. So I did not want to see him driven out, not at this stage (though this would change). It was dark outside, and it had just started to rain; he seemed then to come to a decision, for he turned back into the yard and made for the house; but after a few steps he once again lost his nerve, and instead of coming to the back door he went into the outhouse. As I sat there at the window I saw the faint glow of the candle he had lit as it seeped through the crescent-shaped hole in the door. It was raining hard by this time, and I could see the rain falling across the crescent of light, and I imagined my father behind that door with his trousers at his ankles and his elbows on his knees, and it occurred to me that we were *both* at that moment estranged from the women in the kitchen; and I wondered if his feelings at all resembled mine? Then I heard the toilet flush, the candle was snuffed out, and he emerged. He came back into the house shortly afterwards, and once more I heard the murmur of voices in the kitchen.

I THINK what distressed me most after Hilda moved into number twenty-seven was seeing my mother's clothes being worn by a prostitute. It was not only the idea of trespass and violation, there was the daily spectacle of what happened to the clothes when Hilda put them on. My mother was a slender woman, she had a slim, delicate figure, boyish almost, whereas Hilda was all curves, she was *fleshy*. So my mother's clothes were tight on her, and became as a result provocative; what had been demure on my mother was tarty on Hilda, but then that was the nature of the woman, everything she touched in some way became tarty.

I began, I remember, to watch her, for she provoked in me a sort of appalled fascination. It's difficult to talk about this, but to see the dresses, the aprons, the cardigans that still, for me, carried the aura of my mother, to see them transfigured, charged with the sort of physical invitation that was stamped on all Hilda's gestures, all her speech, the way she walked, the way she swung her bottom—this affected me strongly. Often I followed her when she went shopping, or in the evening when she would slip on that mangy fur and go clicking down the alley in her heels, my mother's lipstick on her mouth, my mother's underwear next to her skin, my mother's *husband* on her arm—I'd slip down the alley behind them, move (like an African boy) from shadow to shadow, silent, invisible, a phantom, a ghost. When they drank in the Earl of Rochester I watched them through the windows, I

was outside in the cold and darkness, and I peeped in at them
as they basked and drank in the bright, sociable warmth of
the bar. I found a way into the yard at the back of the pub
and this gave me access to the windows of the lavatories;
standing on a barrel I would look down on Hilda when she
came out to the Ladies, I'd see her with her underpants at her
ankles and her dress hitched up, her bottom not touching the
toilet seat; then, having wiped herself, it was out with the
compact and a quick go with my mother's powder and lipstick. She never saw me, though once, I remember, as I craned
on tiptoe to see what she was doing, the barrel wobbled
beneath my feet and she looked up—but not before I'd ducked
my head and regained my balance. As I say, I experienced a
sort of appalled fascination at the sheer brazenness of the
creature, I watched her as you might some exotic wild animal,
with a mixture of awe and fear, and a sense of wonder that
such a form of life could exist. She was a force of nature, this
is how I thought of her at the time.

As for my father, for him my contempt knew no bounds.
He was no exotic, no force of nature; in a barbaric and cow-
ardly rage he had murdered my mother and now he was
enjoying the tainted rewards of that act. He would sit there
in the Rochester grinning and simpering as he sipped his mild,
a furtive, grinning man, a weasel with blood on his twitchy
paws, secretive, crafty, lascivious, cruel, and malignant. I had
reason to hate him, had I not? He murdered my mother and
turned me bad in the process; he infected me with his filth,
and the hatred I bore him was intense.

For a time I made a pretence of going off to school in the
morning, though after a week or two I didn't even bother
with this anymore. I no longer slept at night, and it was too
much effort to leave the house at half past eight and then
wander about down the canal all day, or go down the river
and mess about in the boats. No, I'd just stay in my room
and work on my insect collection and keep an eye on the
back yard, see who was coming and going.

Hilda often had her friends over during the day, tarts for the most part. Harold Smith and Gladys were the most frequent visitors. I would come down to the kitchen and sit in a chair with my knees pulled up to my chin and my arms wrapped around my shins, and say nothing, just listen, they didn't seem to mind, they chattered on, gossiped away about the various petty dramas that lent spice and tint to their seedy lives. Hilda was never slow to produce the sweet port. "Now not a word to your father," she'd say to me as she poured us all a tot in a teacup (I'd developed a taste for port myself, since Hilda moved in). Gladys always seemed to have a problem. "If it's not one thing it's another, eh Glad?" Hilda would murmur as she scrubbed the stove or peeled the potatoes and Glad sat at the table smoking Woodbines and patting at her black-dyed hair in a worried manner as she described some fresh calamity involving her landlord or her "gentleman" of the moment, while Harold Smith grinned his cynical dead grin and cleaned his fingernails and said nothing. But it was Hilda I was really watching, and as she went about her scrubbing and peeling I noted with secret fascination how her arms and thighs and breasts swelled and shifted beneath the skirts and aprons that had once graced the slender figure of my mother.

One incident stands out vividly from this period. In January it would be dark by five o'clock in the afternoon, so that by the time my father came home the streetlamps would be lit. I'd see him from my bedroom window as he wheeled his bicycle in from the alley and leaned it against the outhouse wall. His toolbag was slung over his shoulder, and he had a black scarf wrapped about his neck. He knelt down to undo the strings he'd tied round his ankles, and tucked them into his trouser pocket. Then, briskly rubbing his hands together, he stamped down the yard and in through the back door. Hilda was making dinner, I could hear the clatter of saucepans and the rumbling that came from the pipes when water was running in the sink. A murmur of voices, the scrape of chair legs—he'd have hung his jacket and scarf on the hook on the kitchen door and sat down at the table. Hilda would put a bottle of beer in front of him, then out with his papers and tobacco tin while she laid the table. How smoothly, you notice, Hilda had assumed my mother's role in the everyday domestic routines, she played the woman of the house to perfection; but notice also with what contemptible complacency my father accepted this!

I could tell something odd was going on as soon as I entered the kitchen. There was a way (I'd been aware of this before) that Hilda and my father would sometimes watch me from the corners of their eyes, and I could sense them doing it tonight. What used to drive me mad was that as soon as I became conscious of it they'd be looking elsewhere and behaving perfectly normally—*too* normally—and it was true of that night, there was a strange artificiality to everything they did. There was also a funny smell in the room, though I couldn't identify what it was. Not the food, I'm sure, for we were having kippers and I know what a kipper smells like. Without a word I took my place at the table; without a word I started on my kipper. I could still feel them glancing at me, and then at each other, though I was never able actually to see them doing it. Then I cut into my potato, and dead in the middle of the halved potato there was a dark stain.

I stared at it with some unease. Then a syrupy fluid began to ooze out of the potato, the thick, slow discharge of what after a moment or two I recognized as blood. I looked up, startled, to see my father and Hilda, their knives and forks poised aloft over their plates, openly grinning at me. The light bulb suddenly crackled overhead and for a moment I thought it was laughter. Again my eyes fell upon the oozing potato, and now the blood appeared to be congealing in a viscous puddle under my kipper.

What did they expect me to do? Something odd was happening to the light in the room; there was only the one bulb, unshaded, dangling from a braided brown cord, and the light it shed was harsh and yellowy. It seemed now to be fluctuating—for some moments to be growing steadily dimmer, until we were all engulfed in shadow, and all I could see of Hilda and my father were the whites of their teeth and eyes, and the *glitter* of their eyes—and then it slowly grew brighter again, and they appeared to be behaving perfectly normally. Then with sickening inexorability the light again thickened, and this time the crackling of the bulb grew suddenly very loud, it rose almost to a screech, and as I sat there barely daring to breathe it was impossible not to hear in its crackle voices of derision, and ridicule, and when I looked down at my plate—I was unable to watch Hilda and my father anymore, for they terrified me now, they were transformed, they were like animals of some kind, there was nothing in their faces that I could read as human, and this set the hair on my neck prickling—when I looked down at my plate the blood was faintly glowing, there was a pale incandescence to it, and I stared at it in a state now of frozen shock even as the light slowly came up again and returned the kitchen to that strangely unstable state of false normalcy in which knives and forks clattered on plates and Horace and Hilda ponderously chewed their food and drank their tea and the crackle of the light bulb was once more muted and intermittent, and the tap dripped steadily into the sink. On my plate the halved potato sat in a pool of congealed dripping stained brown by the juices of the kipper.

I would not get up from the table, I would not give them the satisfaction. "I thought you liked kippers," murmured Hilda, glancing up at me as she brought a freighted forkful to her own mouth, and I saw how my father's eyes slid toward her at this, and how his lips produced that fleeting twisty twitch of amused contempt, no sooner detected than it disappeared. I wouldn't give them the satisfaction; wordlessly I sliced into my kipper and began noisily to chew, my eyes now fixed on Hilda's face. "Whatever are you doing?" she said, picking up her teacup. "There—you've swallowed a bone!" I began coughing, for the kipper has a bony skeleton and I had been careless. I brought up onto my plate a damp gob of half-chewed fish with many tiny needle-thin bones embedded in it and sticking out; my father said, "Oh for God's sake, Dennis."

Oh for God's sake, Dennis—can you begin to imagine the fury this aroused in me? Was this not execrable treatment, this vile provocation? But *I would not give him the satisfaction*, and I held in my feelings, I bottled up my rage and my hatred, for my time would come, this I had known since Christmas, my time would come and then he'd be sorry.

Later they went out to the pub and I went back to my insects. When I heard them returning down the alley I turned off the light and watched them from my window as they came through the gate and into the yard. My father was unsteady, and Hilda was angry with him, this was clear from her unsmiling expression and the way she hurried across the yard and through the back door, while he clumsily closed the gate then made a visit to the outhouse. Footsteps on the stairs—Hilda on her way up to bed. But when, a few moments later, my father came into the house, I did not hear him come up after her, and as the minutes ticked by I realized he had settled himself in the kitchen, even though the light had not been switched on. After a while I tiptoed along the landing and watched Hilda as she slept; her clothes and underwear were draped over a chair, and one stocking had slipped off onto the floor. Then quickly downstairs, and as I'd suspected my father had stayed in the dark kitchen to drink more beer, then passed out. Silently I drew close to him. With his head back and his mouth open, and still in his cap and scarf, he was snoring gently in the chair by the stove, a quart bottle of beer and a half-empty glass on the floor beside him. By the pale gleam of moonlight that came sifting in through the window over the sink I examined him carefully; I still had all my rage bottled up inside me, and I realized I could do to him whatever I wanted; and with the thought came an enormously sweet sense of power, of control.

I opened the bread tin and took out the bread knife. I made

a few feints and thrusts with it, imagining how it would be to stick it in my father's neck. Soundlessly I waved it in front of his face, dancing around like an African boy; he didn't wake up. The moonlight flashed on the blade of the knife as round and round the kitchen I danced, lifting my knees high and wildly shaking my head, still without making a sound. Tiring of this I put the knife back in the bread tin and filled my palm with stale crumbs. These I then slowly dribbled onto my father's upturned face, and though he twitched and snorted, and brushed at the crumbs with a jerky hand, still he did not awaken, such was the depth of his stupor.

A F T E R the kipper and potato incident Hilda became far less sanguine about me. She decided, I think, that she could no longer tolerate the risk I posed to her new-found security—she had come too far to see it all snatched from her through the wild talk of a boy. For I'd seen the look in her eyes at the table that night, I'd seen the alarm when I'd coughed up a mouthful of bony fish; and with that alarm had come a new, worried watchfulness, I caught it often in the days that followed, she became alert to me in a way she'd never been before. And of course it wasn't simply the safe berth in number twenty-seven that she stood to lose; if they ever dug up my father's potato patch, and established that Hilda had been with him that night—then she'd lose a lot more than a safe berth. She'd swing.

And so the atmosphere of number twenty-seven became even more fraught with tension, there was a new edginess, a shortness of temper in both of them that I was quick to exploit. Hilda no longer dispensed teacups of port to Harold and Glad with the same air of merry complicity—no more "just a drop to warm you up, Glad, you've had a long night." No, Hilda was feeling the strain, she was snappy and preoc-cupied as she went about her tasks in the kitchen. I tried to make things worse. I stole her bucket and took it down the canal, where I filled it with stones and sank it. She was furious about losing her bucket, she searched high and low for it, for of course she couldn't scrub the floor or the yard or the front doorstep without a bucket. I can see her sitting at the kitchen table when my father came home from work that day (I was listening on the stairs); with a headscarf tied around her hair (all up in curlers) she sipped her tea and said: "I've searched high and low—buckets don't just *disappear*." Grunts from my father, and it was hard to interpret them. Was he indifferent to her lost bucket? Or was he knitting his brows, exposing his bottom teeth in that familiar grimace of angry perplexity, and perhaps, at the same time, casting his eyes at the ceiling, up at my room, laying responsibility for the lost bucket at my door? I suspect he was. When I came downstairs for supper Hilda came right out and asked me what I knew about her bucket. I sat in my chair, shrugged my shoulders, gazed at the ceiling and said nothing. "Dennis!" snapped my father. "Answer your mother when she asks you a question."

This was rich. "Mother?" I said, sitting forward in my chair, laying my hands flat on the table and staring straight at her through slitted eyes. "You're not my mother."

"Oh not this again!" said Hilda, turning toward my father. He frowned, took off his glasses, rubbed his eyes. "Let's have our supper," he said wearily. I exulted inwardly at the strained silence in which the meal was eaten.

Later that night I again heard them talking in the kitchen, so out I crept to the top of the stairs to listen. The door was only slightly ajar, and their voices were low, so I had to strain to catch what they said. But after a minute or two I made some sense of it. They were talking about me. They were talking about sending me to Canada.

I crept back into my room and closed the door. I turned off the light and settled by the window, my elbows on the sill, my chin in my palms. There was a moon that night, and beyond the alley it gleamed on row upon row of damp slate roofs. My father sent my mother to Canada, and she was down among the potatoes now. Then I thought of him passed out and slack-jawed in his chair in the kitchen below, and an idea started to take shape in my mind, and it had to do with gas.

*   *   *

In the days that followed I did nothing to make the situation worse than it already was. I couldn't get my mother's bucket back, it was gone for good, but at least I didn't steal anything else. I was quiet and normal at mealtimes, and there was no repetition of that distortion and crackling of the light. Nothing was said, but we were deeply suspicious of each other, and this increased the tension already stifling the house; none of us was eager to exacerbate it. A trying period, then, the only incident of any significance being my father's one clumsy attempt to throw dust in my eyes.

I was often down the allotments during this time—this would be late January, when there was little for gardeners to do. I liked it best at dusk, about half past four in the afternoon, particularly those ten or twenty minutes before darkness proper descended, when the sky was gray-blue but on the ground the shadows had thickened and objects were rapidly losing definition. Then that feeling I've always had for fogs and rainfall was aroused, and I happily roamed from garden to garden and felt only barely visible. But there was one afternoon—the allotments were deserted, except for me—when to my surprise I saw my father cycling down the path along the front fence, parallel to the railway embankment; I was in Jack Bagshaw's allotment, so I slipped behind his shed and, as I'd often done before, peered from round the side to see what he was up to.

He pushed open the gate to his allotment and wheeled his bicycle up the path, and leaned it against the shed. Then he came round to the compost heap and stared straight at me; I immediately pulled back. "Dennis," he called.

I said nothing; I barely moved, I barely breathed.

"Come on, son, I just want to talk to you."

I sank down on my hams and covered my ears. A few moments later I felt his hand on my elbow. "Come on, son, come over to the shed."

I allowed him to lead me back to his shed. He unlocked

the door, ushered me in, sat me down in the armchair while he lit a few candles. Then he settled himself on a wooden box, elbows on his knees, head bent forward, took off his spectacles and rubbed his eyes with the thumb and forefinger of his left hand. "What's the matter with you, son? What are you so angry with us for?" He glanced over at me, looking weary and perplexed. "Eh?"

I was curled up in the armchair and gazing at the cobwebs. My heart was beating very fast; with some relief I felt the Spider begin to withdraw, I felt him crawl quietly away, leaving only a dusty empty cell behind: that was Dennis.

"Why did you say what you said to your mother?"

"She's not my mother," I said, though I hadn't meant to say anything at all.

A snort of surprise. "Then who is she?"

But he would not trap me again.

"Who is she, son?" Anger stirring now.

I gazed at the cobwebs; Spider tried to creep into a hole.

"Who is she, Dennis?" The frown, the teeth.

"She's a tart."

"You cheeky monkey, I'll smack your bloody head!" He was on his feet now, looming over the armchair.

"She's a fat tart!"

He slapped me on the side of the head and I started to cry, I couldn't help it. "You killed my mum," I shouted through my tears. "Murderer! You murderer! You bloody murderer!"

"You what?" He sank back onto his box. "You having me on, Dennis? You know what you're saying?"

I relapsed into sullen and defiant silence; much as the Spider wanted to stay in his hole that slap on the head had smoked him out, and the hot, ringing sensation prevented him from sealing himself off again. My father frowned; he said he didn't know what I was talking about. Was I daft? he said. More scratching of his head as he sat there on his box. He kept glancing over at me as though he'd never seen me before, and then he'd look away. He started to tell me how daft I was acting, he said he didn't know where I got my ideas from, he said I spent too much time by myself, he said I should have some mates, he'd had mates at my age, every young lad should have mates, on and on he went and as the hot, ringing sensation faded I found I could pull away, pull back into the dark secret places once more, and as I did so a peculiar thing happened: my father seemed to shrink. It was suddenly as if he was very far away, though at the same time I knew he was just a few feet from me. But to my *eyes* he was distant and tiny, and his voice sounded as though it were crossing an immense expanse of space before it reached me, and when it did reach me there was a hollow, tinny resonance to it that obscured the sense and meaning of the words so they were just echoes, empty echoes in a gloomy shed in which up among the rafters spiders spun webs that winked and glistened and twinkled in the candlelight and made me feel soft, and time stood still until I clearly heard him saying: "Dennis? Dennis? You still think I done her in?"

I said nothing. He had swelled again to substance and reality, and the soft feeling went away.

"Answer me, son. You still think I done in your mum?"

What could I do? He frightened me. I shook my head.

"Well thank God for that," he said. "Let's go home."

We left the shed and made our way down the allotment path, him pushing his bicycle. As we passed my mother's grave it occurred to me that he hadn't offered to dig up the potato patch, but of course I didn't say this (though I doubt we'd have found anything, she'd risen by this time, but he didn't know that). Hilda was waiting for us in the kitchen. She looked anxiously at my father, who had a hand on my shoulder as we came in through the back door. Spider had by this point withdrawn to one of his most obscure holes. "All right then?" she said, and my father nodded, and with manifest relief she began to bustle. "Sit yourselves down," she said, "I popped out and got something nice for your supper." It was eels.

So I sat there quietly in the kitchen and ate my eels, but not for one minute did I forget that for all my father's talk they still planned to send me to Canada.

I T is very late at night as I write this, and I don't know if you can understand the anxiety I feel at committing these thoughts to paper. If she should find this book the consequences would be appalling, and I don't like to think about that, not in the light of what later transpired at Kitchener Street—when you learn the full story you will understand my trepidation. I am fairly satisfied with the fireplace as the site of concealment, although it does have the drawback of being very sooty in there—after only a few days the book became so filthy I had to put it in a brown paper bag before stuffing it away, using my mittens so as to keep my hands clean. This system worked well until yesterday morning, when I realized that if she found the sooty mittens her suspicions would be aroused and she'd go poking around in the fireplace to see what I was up to—which left me the problem (I'm being fastidious to the point of absurdity, you'll say, but believe me, I cannot afford to take the chance) the problem of finding a safe place of concealment for the mittens (under the linoleum perhaps?) or, alternatively, of getting rid of them. I chose the latter, I threw them into the canal yesterday afternoon, and watched them become waterlogged then finally sink. What this means is that (a) I have to wash my hands every time I extract and replace the book (which necessitates a trip down the corridor to the bathroom), and (b) at some point I shall have to explain to her that I have *lost* the mittens, and as you can imagine this is not an interview

I look forward to. But here is why it is so imperative that she not find the book: you see, *I think I know who she is.*

I was coming into the house one afternoon a few weeks ago after some hours spent walking the streets. I was crossing the hall, making for the stairs, when I happened to glance toward the kitchen, which is located at the end of a short passage at the back of the hall, off to the left of the staircase. The passage was dark, but the light was on in the kitchen, and she was standing in the middle of the room leaning over the table with her sleeves rolled up and a rolling pin in her hands. Nothing unusual in this, of course; she was helping the little woman, who was attempting a steak-and-kidney pudding, perhaps she was instructing her in the English method. But what riveted my attention to this brightly lit scene, framed as it was in the kitchen door at the end of that short dark passage, was the way she handled the roller, the way she rose up on her toes and *leaned* on the thing so that all the strength and weight of those beefy shoulders was transmitted down her powerful arms, through her wrists, and into the thick fingers of her hamlike hands, the nails of which, I saw with a very real thrill of recognition and horror, and despite the powdering of flour upon them, *were filthy*. For a moment past and present slid seamlessly together, assumed identity, and there was *one woman only* leaning on that rolling pin, and that woman was Hilda Wilkinson; at that moment the woman in the kitchen was transfigured, her hair was blonde with black roots, her bosom strained against the fabric of an apron not her own, and her sturdy legs were planted on the kitchen floor like a pair of tree trunks, lifting and sinking as she rose on her toes with every downard *thrust!* of the pin upon the pastry. I had drawn close by this time, I had entered the passage and was gaping at her as she turned, panting hoarsely, to the door, and brushed a strand of damp hair from her forehead. Her *chin!* How could I have missed it? She had Hilda's chin, big and puggy, *prognathous,* the very same! "Ah,

Mr. Cleg," she said—and I was back in 1957 with my land-lady once more.

A pause; I could think of nothing to say as she stood there at the table, turned toward me, a question in her face. "Did you want something, Mr. Cleg?"

"No," I said, but it came out in a sort of croaky whisper. "No," I said, more successfully, and it was only with the greatest of effort that I managed to get moving again, for I had become, for those few moments in the passage, uncou-pled.

"No?" she said, as I shuffled away, and the familiar spike of mockery was in her voice. "A nice cup of tea, Mr. Cleg?" But I had to get upstairs, so off I fled without another word. Once I'd gained the safety of my room I stood at the window and gazed down at the park and attempted to roll a cigarette; but my hands were trembling badly, and I spilled half the tobacco onto the floor, and it was some minutes before I was sufficiently recovered to get down on my hands and knees and retrieve it.

At first I didn't realize what I must do. I often find that it's not until everyone has gone to bed that I can think properly in this house, there's too much interference otherwise, too many *thought patterns* clogging the waves, if you know what I mean—this is not the least of the reasons I spend so much time down at the canal, because if I'm not careful these *thought patterns* of theirs crowd out my own, and I can't have that, I can't have other people's thoughts in my head, I had quite enough of that in Canada. It's the same when they're all awake in the house, even if I am in my room with the door closed, and let me tell you this: dead souls they may be, but the thoughts they think are grotesque, and this is connected to the creatures in the attic, but I'll get to them later. No, what I realized as soon as I could think clearly—that is, at the dead of night—was that I must confirm the very vivid impression I'd had in the hallway; there was no point in thinking about anything else until that was done.

It was about three in the morning when I realized that if I

knew who she was then she must know who *I* was—and the implications of that were very disquieting, though it was to take me some further days to think them through with any precision.

The following day was damp and cold. After breakfast I left the house as usual, but instead of going to the canal I went into the little park across the street. Now Mrs. Wilkinson's house stands on the north side of a square that must once have been impressive. Today though those grand houses with their stuccoed facades and Corinthian columns are shabby and decrepit, many have been torn down and those that remain are tenanted only by rats or ghosts or flotsam like me. So I sat on a bench in the park in the middle of this dilapidated square, beneath leafless trees and a slate-gray sky, amid empty bottles and cigarette packets, and tossed bread crumbs to the crows that live here; and with one eye I watched for her to come out.

It was after eleven when she finally emerged in her winter coat, a shopping bag on her arm, and without so much as a glance toward the park she marched off down the street. I gave her a clear five minutes; then back in, across the hall, and up the stairs to the top floor where she, like me, has her room, though she is on the other side of the house from me. I paused at the top of the stairs to listen; nothing but the radio going quietly in the dayroom, where the dead souls listlessly killed time. Then along the corridor to her door—another pause, another moment of listening intently to the house— then turn the doorknob, and—nothing! Locked! She'd locked her door!

A setback, this. I made my way back downstairs, out through the front door and across the street to the park once more, where I resumed my seat on the bench and tried to think the thing through. She locked her door. The only other door in the house that was locked was the one that opened onto the attic stairs (and of course the dispensary). Far from damping my curiosity, this development had quite the opposite effect, it inflamed my urge to know what the woman was hiding: I had to get hold of her keys.

Occupied with these thoughts, and making no progress at all, I absently pulled out of my pocket a slice of dried toast I'd saved from breakfast and began crumbling it in my fingers and scattering the crumbs on the ground around the bench. Soon the crows flapped down, and when the toast was all crumbled I took out my tobacco and rolled myself a thin one. And there I sat, deep in thought, my outstretched legs crossed at the ankles, smoking among the crows.

TH I S business of the thought patterns: it seems to have grown much worse over the last few days. Why should this be so? Full moon, perhaps? But no, the moon is just a clipping of fingernail, like the crescent of candlelight in the outhouse door. The dead souls, perhaps, have become animated, for some obscure reason, and are generating cerebral energy of an uncharacteristically heavy voltage? But I spent an hour in the dayroom after supper and there was no sign of any vitality at all, less than usual, if that's possible—they sat there in their accustomed chairs like a group of tailor's dummies, stupefied with medication, faces like suet, trembling hands, in ill-fitting clothes stained with food and drool (God how they do drool!), waiting for El Mustachio to appear with the cocoa. I should talk! I, too, drool, I tremble, I shamble, and as you know at times I become uncoupled; but God help me if I ever turn into one of them, pull the plug, please, if that happens, let me at least pursue the enigma of my childhood while I have the will for it, and if that dries up then string me from the nearest rafter and let me dangle like the Spider I am! Then in comes the little woman with her tray, and this is all the life we'll see in here tonight, the small dull ghost of a spark struggling to feeble life in the dead eyes of my companions at the prospect of a cup of weak cocoa made from milk powder and treacly with the sugar that produces these rolls of flab on their bellies and under their chins. They all have fat bodies here, you see—fat breasts, fat thighs,

fat fingers, fat faces, and dry hair that's always flaky with
particles of dead skin; and when they stir their cocoa, these
zombies, the dandruff comes drifting down into the cups like
clouds of light snow. I turn away, I turn toward the window
then and rub a hand across my own skull, which is shaved
to a stubble from ear to temple, and bristled on top with a
few thick tufts precisely the same shade of brown as my
mother's. I can scratch that nubbled skull of mine for minutes
on end without a *single flake* of dead skin coming away, for
my skin is like leather, stretched taut as it is over the sharp
bones of this long, lean, horse's head of mine: yes, stubbled
leather, this is my head; hooknailed spiderlegs, these are my
fingers; and my body just a shell with little in it now but the
fetid gassy compost of what was once a heart, a soul, a life—
so who am I to curl a lip at the zombies, I who have all the
brittle resilience of an eggshell, a light bulb, a Ping-Pong ball?
No, it isn't them crowding the air with thought patterns, it's
coming from somewhere else, it's coming from the attic.
Every night I hear them now, I haven't slept a wink, and all
that's held them off so far and given me relief is the writing
I've been doing in my journal.

My journal! Can it still be called that? Picture me at the
dead of night down on my hands and knees in front of an
obsolete gas fire, groping around for a brown paper bag
smudged all over with soot. Gingerly it's withdrawn, and I
clamber to my feet and tiptoe with it across the room to my
table. I wipe my hands on my trousers and take it out of the
bag. That poor exercise book, a few short weeks ago a pristine
thing with a shiny green cover—now it curls at the corners,
it's imprinted with the black smudges of my thumbs, it's
something you simply wouldn't handle unless you had to:
it's a dirty book. Having wiped my fingers and put the paper
bag to one side, I open this dirty book and turn the pages to
the most recent entry, adding, with every fingering, a little
more soot, a little more of the dirt of the house, transferring
it from the chimney to the fading whiteness of the pages

before me. I read over the last entry, then turn to a clean page, and pausing a moment, my eyes on the window, my pencil between my fingers, to frame the first words of the first sentence that will once more promote the flow of my memories and the construction, alongside, of a reasoned edifice of plausible conjecture, I begin to write.

I begin to write. And as I do a strange thing happens, the pencil starts to move along the faint blue lines of the page almost as though it had a will of its own, almost as though my memories of the events preceding the tragedy at Kitchener Street were contained not within the stubbled leather helmet of this head of mine but in *the pencil itself,* as though they were tiny particles all packed together in a long thin column of graphite, running across the page while my fingers, like a motor, provide merely the mechanical means of their discharge. When this happens I have the curious sensation not of writing but of *being written,* and it has come to arouse in me stirrings of terror, faint at first but growing stronger day by day.

Yes, terror. Oh, I am a feeble creature, yes I know it, I know it better than you do, I am so easily thrown into turmoil, so easily frightened and panicked, and it's getting worse, I haven't told you this for I'd been hoping that it might not be true, that I might be imagining it, that it might "just be me"—but it's not. The feeling of being like a light bulb: it is with me all the time now. I felt it during the interminable hour I forced myself to sit in the dayroom. It wasn't their thought patterns that so badly upset me, the thought patterns are coming from the top of the house; it was just their dead eyes, only their dead eyes, a single glance from a pair of those dead eyes has the potential to shatter me, to shiver my glassy identity into a thousand particles and leave the thin, barely glowing coil of filament within—the residue, the *ruin,* of what was once a heart, a soul, a life—leave it naked and vulnerable, smelling of gas, to the gale of the world that will surely snuff it to extinction in a second: and this is why, now, I must avoid their eyes, this is why I must skulk about by night, pursue my restless investigation of the opaque past like a creature of the shadows, like a halved thing, a body without a soul, or perhaps a soul without a body—ghoul or ghost it barely matters, what matters is that I nurse this glowing coil so that it can at least see me out, see me to the *end* of this thing, and this is why I am so prone to terror now, for I am conscious always of the danger of shattering, which in turns makes me crave *control,* which is why the sensation of being formed, framed, *written* makes me so desperately afraid. For that which can write me can surely also destroy me?

But I must go on, what real choice do I have? And perhaps, too (I have had a smoke and things never look quite so bleak after a smoke) I'm exaggerating my difficulties. I do, after all, have strategies, ways of coping, have had since I was a boy. For example there's the familiar withdrawal into the more inaccessible compartments in my head: it was not only Spider the boy who shifted into the back room after his mother died, and let Dennis face the world. No, over the years Spider has learned that it is often necessary to allow Dennis to face the world, or "Mr. Cleg" for that matter; not only this, but intermediate compartments have become necessary—with Dr. McNaughten, for instance, who knows my history. The front of my head does not satisfy the doctor so he is permitted contact with what *used to be* the back of my head but is now a sort of chamber occupied by a Dennis Cleg with "my history"—but Spider's never there! Spider's elsewhere, though the doctor suspects nothing. Similarly with the dead souls: all is well *provided Spider is elsewhere*—but let me for a single moment show myself on the outer wheel of the web in which my fragile and beleaguered being *lives*— and this is the moment I am destroyed. This is how it is with me.

But what is wrong with me, that in order to save my life

I must bury it within wheels, wheels strung on radials forming compartments—allotments!—containing only dead things, fetid, empty chambers where shadows and feathers, coal dust and dead flies, drift about, where the smell of gas is pervasive, and this is all there is—these *holes,* I mean, these smelly holes I've built around the Spider to save him from the gales and storms of the world? What sort of life is it, that can only take its existence dead at the hub of this ragged, wheel-like structure of empty cells?

WHEN I was taken away from Kitchener Street there was some delay before they made up their minds what to do with me. I remember very little of that period: a blur of men and rooms, and the air everywhere crowded with thought patterns, always a sense of terrible tension, like the tension my father could generate in the kitchen at mealtimes. Then I felt catastrophe was imminent, and I felt my own *wrongness* most intensely. The light was never clear, I seemed always to be in shadow and so did the others, the men who went with me from room to room, all in thick shadow, as though a permanent twilight had gathered in those rooms and rendered all forms and faces indistinct, and their voices too grew hollow, grew deep, they boomed and echoed from out of the shadows that clung to them and the air, the dusk, through which I moved was thick with thought patterns not my own. I lived and moved in terror then, constant terror, desperately reaching back into the back parts until at last I crawled, exhausted, into that hole where for some short period of time at least I could be safe.

Later the world came more sharply into focus again. Shadows receded and I no longer had this booming echo of voices in my ears, I came to distinguish one man from another and although I knew they meant to do me harm there was at the same time the feeling that it might not happen yet, or that when it did happen it would happen with such suddenness and from such an unexpected quarter that there was little point in maintaining more than a reasonable degree of vigilance as I went about my routines. Routines! These were the days of routine. From morning to night all was routine, each day like the one before it, and the one to come after, and there was in this some comfort for me, at least during the quiet periods when I felt that I could cope with the thought patterns, when they didn't mount up and mount up against me, filling the air with their staticky buzz and hum and click and clack like a blizzard of germs in constant excitation around my ears and the back of my head until there was no escaping them, not even back there in the quiet flaps and recesses where only the Spider could crawl—when that was happening then no routine on earth could dull the harrowing of the terror of the disaster that was imminently to befall me. Later though they always seemed to know when it was about to happen and they took me to a safe room, kept me out of harm's way until I was quiet again. But what makes it all so disturbing to remember now—and I didn't tell you this earlier, for I have only just remembered it—was that at those times there was always, always, *always* the pervasive and overwhelming and filthy smell of gas.

Time passed. Twenty years, this was my Canada. Oh enough. My Canada—my *Ganderhill!* With your walls of faded red brick, your barred gates and locked doors, your courtyards and corridors, your flower gardens where men in ill-fitting flannels and squeaky shoes sat twitching and writhing on wooden benches, while their restless mad eyes gazed out over the terraces to a cricket field far below, and beyond that the perimeter wall, and beyond that rolling farmland and the wooded hills of Sussex in the distance . . . During the later years in Ganderhill I worked in the vegetable gardens; I wore stout black boots and baggy yellow corduroy trousers. I remember in the summer the smell of fresh-mown grass, a smell that comes back to me so strongly now that I stop writing, almost convinced that it is in the room—the smell of fresh-mown grass, here in this chilly midnight garret! Here, in this bleak season of fogs and rain, at the top of this morgue of a house—fresh-mown grass! Outside in the dark wet streets dead leaves clog gutters and drains and drift in heaps between high black metal railings with spiked, spearlike tips; and the Spider smells fresh-mown grass! Oh, see me seated at this rickety table in all my shirts and jerseys, pencil poised over the smudged page of the journal and the long horse-head lifted, heavy with shadow in the hollows of the cheeks and the eye sockets, a knobbled stubbled bulb of a head as it lifts, sniffing, a dead thin one hanging from its lip, into the gloom as the memories of asylum cricket come drifting back and bring in their train the smell of fresh-mown grass! Fool, Spider! But better you smell grass than gas.

What to tell you of those years? Mr. Thomas was the first of them to grow distinct when the world began to come back into focus; he never threatened to shatter me with his eyes, the way other men did. Those mild brown eyes of his: the skin around them was crosshatched with tiny crinkled lines, and they reassured me, I don't know why. There was the pipe, too, the constant pipe, and I don't know why that reassured me either but it did, the steady sucking, punctuated, every few minutes, when he took it from between his lips, by the exhalation of smoke; perhaps the smell of the tobacco, the fragrance. After supper I'd stay on the ward, I'd read, I'd play cards, do a jigsaw. It was a quiet life.

The first ward I was on in Ganderhill was what they called a hard-bench ward. Not difficult to find the reason for that: there wasn't a soft chair in the place (apart of course from in the attendants' room by the stairwell). Men did a great deal of sleeping in those wards and I was no exception. After breakfast I stretched myself out on a bench, the woodwork all cankered with cigarette burns, and using my shoe for a pillow I'd doze off and try and stay comatose for as much of the day as I could. Who cared? Nobody cared. On the hard-bench wards men were mute, incontinent, hallucinated. If I couldn't get a bench I simply curled up on the floor under a blanket. Nobody cared. We were all immobile and with-drawn up there, and in this there was a certain comfort. What I didn't like were the doorless lavatories, I could never get used to them, it was an agony of humiliation to me to sit on the toilet in a doorless lavatory, exposed to the stray glance of any passing eye: it occurs to me now that much of the later trouble I had with my intestines (they were pulled to the back of my body and twisted about my spine from arse to skull like a snake) may have originated in the disturbance of the excretory function that I suffered on the hard-bench wards.

I learned to roll fat ones and thin ones on a hard-bench ward, we took our tobacco seriously there. It's an odd thing, no matter how deep a man may be sunk in his own melan-choly, his own madness—adrift, you'd think, all lines to the social body cut—yet he'd never fail to give you his butt to light your own with, there is no madness so deep that it excludes you from the community of tobacco. Here's another odd thing: a man gets a proper cigarette from an attendant, a Woodbine, a Senior Service. He sits on a bench and smokes. A second man stands nearby, arms hanging limp at his sides, face blank, dumbly waiting. In due time he is given the butt. This he smokes until it burns his fingers, and then he drops it on the floor. A third man immediately picks it up, and careless of burning his fingers he smokes the rest of it.

On a hard-bench ward nothing was expected of you except that you fail. You were there because you *had* failed, failing was what you did, you would fail again. In this there was comfort for the Spider, a certain vigilance could be relaxed. What was comforting was the indifference: nobody cared about anything but his own damage. Routine was basic and solid, a few rude struts to give the day shape: lining up for meals at the front of the ward, shuffling there for twenty minutes, then down the narrow stairs, gates clanging, keys on bars, the shouts of distant attendants, a file of gray patients in ill-fitting shirts and trousers, flapping shoes—no belts or shoelaces on a hard-bench ward—to line up in the vast clattering barn of a dining hall, and pass along trestle tables behind which kitchen workers in greasy white aprons dolloped onto your plate soggy servings of mashed vegetables and horsemeat, or dogmeat, or stale cod. For pudding, spotted dick and custard with lumps. In the late afternoon the day shift went off, and for the hours before supper we were locked up or else herded together in the dayroom under the supervision of a single attendant. This I hated, to be crowded in with the others like that, and vainly I begged to be allowed to join the two or three privileged men who wandered the ward by themselves.

From time to time someone became upset—I remember John Giles, a big man, furious about the withdrawal of his privileges, storming up and down his room; as I passed on my way down to the dayroom I remember thinking: John's about to blow. I may have mentioned it to someone, I don't remember—then suddenly the sound of a window smashing, and it was John Giles of course. Out of the dayroom we poured, but not before the attendants were running down the ward from either end—what a racket their boots made on the tiles!—to where John, spitting and cursing, stood trembling in his doorway and clutching a great ugly jagged piece of glass. They didn't rush him, not with that piece of glass in his hand. "Put it down, John," one of them said, "come on, John, do us all a favor"—but John was way over the top, he spat and snarled and told them what he'd do to them if they got any closer. Two of them then went into a room. A moment later out they came, at a run, with a mattress held up before them like a shield. Then they were on top of poor John and all I could see were his arms and legs flailing from the sides of the mattress as he struggled there, pinned against the door, his shouts muffled by the mattress. In due course he let go of the glass and shortly after that they trussed him up in buckles and stout canvas webbing and marched him off to a safe room at the end of the ward, where he shouted himself hoarse and then fell asleep. But I tell you the story only for the sequel. Down in the yard a week later, poking around in a flower bed, I found a shard of glass shaped like a dagger, and looking up, realized it came from the window John Giles had smashed. I took it back up to the ward and showed it to Mr. Thomas. He led me into a side room, where on the table he had reconstructed the entire window, every fragment in place as though it were a jigsaw puzzle—every fragment, that is, but one. He took my glass dagger and slipped it into the last thin gap, it completed the shattered window, and with a grunt of satisfaction he turned to me and said, "I was worried about that one, Dennis, I lost sleep over that one, I could see someone losing their eye." And then he put a hand on my shoulder, and I walked back out onto the ward—odd thing, this—almost choking for the sheer joy of that hand on my shoulder.

A quiet life, then, for I did settle down. And it was only after I had settled down that I could bring myself to think about Kitchener Street again. Often, as I sat on a bench on the terrace and watched the men working in the vegetable gardens, hoeing, or seeding, I would think of my father in his allotment on a Sunday, perhaps doing the same work as them, for one potato patch is very much like another. But having thought this I would immediately remember that my father's potato patch was in fact very different from any other, for the simple reason that my mother had been buried in it. And with that thought, unless I was careful, such a *flood* would be set roiling and seething within me that at times it was your old Spider who got trussed up in canvas webbing and marched off down to a safe room (his head twisting to escape the smell of the gas)! But in time I learned that there were ways of thinking about Kitchener Street and the tragedy without losing control (it all has to do with compartments) and in time I was able to think such thoughts even when, in later years, I had a job in the vegetable gardens myself. A particularly rich seam of memories was uncovered, I recall, when I was

forking the institution's compost one very blustery day in the
autumn.

I pause; it is very late now. I take a moment to relight the
dead one. The house is utterly silent around me; outside, the
rain has stopped, and the streets too are silent. An odd thing,
to sit here with the book before me, the pencil in my fingers,
remembering a time of remembering. Is it always thus, I
wonder? Smoke is drifting in lazy coils toward the faintly
crackling light bulb overhead; I lean back, fingers linked behind my head, my outstretched legs crossed at the ankles,
and watch it diffuse in the gloom. Is a memory always and
only the echo of its last occasion? Which in turn is just an
echo of the one before? A flicker of unease in my belly at
this, a small spurt of alarm: like the cross-strutting of the
gasworks uprights, the horror of multiplicity is there, the
horror of reproduction; and yet what I remembered that blustery day in the vegetable gardens (I was leaning on the handle
of a garden fork, the smell of the compost strong in my
nostrils) what I remembered seems now so fresh, so crisp, so
sharp and clear to me that I cannot doubt, I cannot doubt,
for the simple reason that I saw it, I was there, hanging around
the allotments in the days after Christmas in case my mother
came back again. And my father, you see, was working his
compost.

A well-made compost heap (this is the gardener speaking)
is a layered structure that heats up and decomposes quickly.
Kitchen rubbish, dead leaves, plant residue—all this makes
for good compost, all this contributes to the good dark crumbly matter that enriches even the thinnest soil. Add a layer
of manure, or even blood meal, then some soil, and dust it
with wood ash. This is how my father built up his compost
heap over the autumn, layer by layer to a height of five feet,
the whole contained in an enclosure of wooden posts and
wire-mesh fencing. He'd moistened each layer as he'd built
it, and with his hands he'd scooped out a shallow depression
in the top to make a puddle where rainwater could collect.

The day I remembered he was turning the heap, letting it air so as to ensure uniform decomposition and prevent overheating; but barely had he lifted the first forkful than to his astonishment he saw that the heap was moving, that the exposed interior was *alive*. He took out his spectacles (I was watching him from behind the shed in the next allotment, Jack Bagshaw's; it was a gloomy damp day, and cold) and he found that his compost was infested with black maggots.

He had never seen maggots like these before. They were swarming all over the compost, all over the decaying horse manure, the potato peelings, the grass clippings and ground bone, swarming and seething, these plump little black things, and what insect, my father must have wondered as he stood there scratching his head (I am still peering round the side of Jack Bagshaw's shed), what insect laid eggs that hatched so late in the year—though he would then have realized that the heat generated by the decomposing compost would be enough to incubate the creatures, and *beetles,* he would have thought, *beetles*. But what English beetle produced a grub like this? I saw him pick one up and examine it on the tip of his finger: a sleek, fat, soft-bodied, humpbacked grub, and as it squirmed there he must have felt the slime of it moisten the soil that grimed his finger so he wiped it off on the seat of his trousers and then with his fork uncovered a deeper layer of the heap. Again the swarming of innumerable black grubs, and he knew that the whole heap was infested. I watched him lean on his pitchfork and gaze, frowning, at his ruined compost, but even as he began to turn over in his mind how he would rid his garden of its parasites the chill of the winter air began to be felt by the maggots, and as they lost their heat so their activity slowed, and they began to die. And it was at that moment that I saw my father suddenly stiffen, and shrink back, and clutch the fork to his chest as though to defend himself—and his eyes darted about him in what looked like terror, intense terror, and I knew, I knew, that he'd felt something brush by him.

I didn't move, I didn't breathe. I saw him shiver, then throw down the pitchfork and turn toward the shed—but then the shed began to shudder (it was growing dark), to shudder as it must have shuddered the night he'd copulated with Hilda in the armchair, the night my mother discovered them there. Then it started to rain, and I watched my father backing away from the shed, his face alive with horror, backing down the path as the shed heaved and shook on its foundations with ten times the violence it had the night Hilda sprawled in the armchair with her skirt up round her waist, and him on his knees on the edge of the chair with his trousers open and his pencil of a penis sticking out between the buttons. It was a mockery, this, a dark travesty of the spectacle my mother must have observed the night she was murdered, and before he'd even reached the gate he could hear the awful gasps and groans of Hilda at pleasure, and by this time the air was dense with that terrible black energy, and he fled, I watched him go, I watched him push his bicycle up the path and scramble onto it as if the very devils of hell were after him, and only then did I climb over into the allotment and begin shouting and jumping up and down, making mud of the soil, as the dusk rapidly descended.

I was there the following Sunday when my father destroyed the compost heap. I came up through the Slates, up the slope at the back of the allotments, and along behind the sheds to Jack Bagshaw's. My father had not been idle; during the week he'd been coming after work to spread mulch on the soil to prevent beetles from reaching his potatoes in the spring, and he'd cleaned up the cuttings and dead weeds likely to harbor larvae clusters. But Sunday was for burning the compost and destroying the maggots inside it, and so I watched him dig a shallow pit (needless to say on the far side of the allotment from my mother's grave) and in the pit he laid the foundations of a bonfire, clumps of newspaper, kindling wood, and a few old planks that he'd stored under a tarpaulin behind his shed all winter. He soon had a good blaze going, I could feel it from where I was hiding, then he began to fork on the garden debris, much of which was damp, and the bonfire smoked profusely. But when he added the first mounds of compost the smoke grew so dense that all I could see of him was a shadow moving back and forth and forking up compost and flinging it onto the fire, and I remembered a picture I'd once seen of hell, a sort of cavern with dripping black walls and thick black smoke from somewhere down below, and in the smoke the devil was clutching a pitchfork not unlike my father's, his long barbed tail flicking up behind him in the gloom. Damp though it was the compost somehow burned, or smoldered at least, and the smell of it, the manure and the rotting vegetables, was so bad I had to creep away, back behind the sheds and down to the Slates, and from there I made my way to the river. Even from down by the Crispin I could see the smoke as it climbed into the gray wintry sky, a long thin column that leaned to the west the higher it rose and eventually drifted away into nothingness off toward the setting sun.

When it was almost dark I made my way back up to the allotments. I saw no sign of my father, so I climbed the fence and approached what was left of the bonfire. The pit was still heaped with compost, and in the middle of it a round core glowed and smoldered in the gloom and crackled suddenly as the heat caught a stray twig or stick of straw and consumed it. Over by the shed all that was left was a patch of pale damp ground inside a wire-mesh fence. I unbuttoned my trousers and pissed into the smoldering compost, and as the piss hissed in the pit a column of steam rose into the darkness, stinking of charred manure.

All this I remembered as I leaned on a garden fork in flapping yellow corduroys and gazed out over the Ganderhill wall, over farmland and wooded uplands, at fat white clouds kicking across a blustery blue sky one fresh autumn afternoon in the early 1950s.

W H A T else to tell you? Almost all I know about what happened at Kitchener Street I worked out during that period. For when I settled down and was able once more to think about that time—the terrible autumn and winter, I mean, of my thirteenth year, when my father first met Hilda Wilkinson—what I found was a jumble of partial impressions: scenes viewed from my bedroom window, scraps of talk overheard from the top of the stairs, mealtimes in that poky kitchen, and glimpses of my father at work in his allotment. But as regards the order and meaning of those scraps: that was what I pieced together, like a shattered window, in the quiet years that followed, fragment by fragment until the picture was whole. And oddly, as my childhood took shape, so did I, Spider, become more coherent, firmer, stronger—I began to have substance. Hard to believe, no? Hard to believe, given the sorry creature I am today, tonight, as I sit here scribbling (out of terror) in the crow's nest of this shabby ship of a house and swamped, almost, by the surge and flood of sheer *life* that crashes round me—a fragile vessel I am today, but back then, it seems, building on the bedrock of routine, and bit by bit reconstructing the events of that time (the appearance of Hilda and the subsequent murder of my mother, the destruction of my home, and the tragedy that followed), back then I looked, for a while, before my discharge, like a man.

Picture me then, a young man: Spider at twenty-five, tall and lean as I am today but there's something about me—can you see it?—a vitality, a flame, even if it is a mad one, still it's there, in the sheen of my skin, in my restless energy as I work in the vegetable gardens from morning to night, it's there in my eyes—not like the dull filmed glaze that clouds the hollowed eyes of the Spider these days. A handsome man, even! See me in the gardens in shirtsleeves and yellow corduroys, a wiry, muscular figure turning the soil on that Sussex hillside, in that brisk air, framed against the sky—can you see me?—leaves swirl about me, red leaves, golden leaves, swirling down from the elm tree by the wall, and I pause in my work, I thrust my spade in the soil and turn, again, to the landscape I grew so to love, the sweep of the terraces, the cricket field, the perimeter wall with its old bricks glowing a soft rufous-red in the fresh clear air, and beyond the wall the farm and the hills, the trees a vivid slash of color this autumn afternoon. Oh, out with the Rizla, and the paper flutters wildly between my fingers as the tin of Old Holborn appears, and the wind molds the rough fabric of the gray asylum shirt to the bones of my lean trunk, and the thick yellow corduroy flaps about my shanks! Tonight you see me in decay, a brittle bulb housing a flickering, faltering coil, but in those days I had a body, and a vigorous spirit burned inside it!

But enough, enough of this pathetic nostalgia, this romantic drivel. What am I saying, that I was a hero? Standing on my windy hillside, clutching a spade? A hero? This lunatic? I lived among the criminally insane, and I knew routine, community, and order. Whatever strength or structure I had, it came from without, not within, and if you need proof of that then look at what's happened since my discharge—look at me *now,* scribbling *out of terror* in this lonely room, engaged in some pitiful attempt to drown out the voices from the attic. And not even institutional structure was enough at times! At times the Spider collapsed, the whole flimsy scaffolding came to bits and he fell, poor fool, he tumbled to earth with a crash, and awoke in a safe room with his shell all in pieces around him.

But the important thing is that slowly I pieced together an account of what happened, and as the story grew firmer then I grew firmer with it. Conversely, when the story collapsed then so did I, but I rebuilt, I rebuilt, and each time the edifice grew stronger, better buttressed, the struts and braces pulling it together till it was tight, till it was whole. And so was I. And then they discharged me.

There's irony here, as you will learn. Much was changing; there were pills now, for people like me, and there were also changes afoot in Ganderhill—most notably, the departure of the medical superintendent, Dr. Austin Marshall.

Dr. Austin Marshall was a gentleman, a tall, kindly gentleman in well-tailored tweeds who walked with a limp as a result of a motorcycle accident in medical school that had left him with a steel pin in his hip. A gentleman: it was a rare day I didn't see Dr. Austin Marshall limping across the terrace, and he had a kind word for each man he encountered; he remembered one's name, too. "Ah, Dennis," he would say, pausing to lean on his stick. "How are we today?" He would turn his head to the south and gaze out over that magnificent view, a squire, so he seemed, surveying his demesne. "Good day to be out on a horse," he'd say. "What about that, Dennis? Fancy a canter, do you? Of course you do!" He'd pat me on the arm and then chuckling gently off he'd limp, and on encountering another inmate he'd again stop, again turn his head to the south and, addressing the man by name, again make his friendly remarks about horseback riding. His conversational gambits were few, but the warmth behind them was genuine; he was a fine medical superintendent, and we all loved him, with the exception of John Giles, who tried to murder him whenever he could.

I rise to my feet and stare out of the window. The first pale suggestion of dawn is apparent, a faint gray smudging out there over the North Sea somewhere. All is quiet in the attic now and my terror has abated, to some extent. My relationship to this book is changing: when I began to write I intended to record the conclusions I'd arrived at about the events of the autumn and winter of my thirteenth year; and in the process I thought I'd buttress and support myself, shore up my shaky identity, for since being discharged I have not been strong. But all this has changed; I write now to control the terror that comes when the voices start up in the attic each night. They have grown worse, you see, much worse, and it is only with the flow of my own words that I am able to block out the clamor of theirs. I dare not think of the consequences were I to stop writing and listen to them.

AN D so began another day. I no longer knew which was worse, day or night. The silence and solitude of the night had once been my haven, my safe place away from the eyes and the voices and the thought processes, which seemed to be most active when others were awake in the house. Now I dread nightfall, for those damn creatures in the attic give me no rest. I was out there on the landing a few minutes ago, shaking the handle of the door that gives onto the attic stairs—no good, of course, it's always locked. They're her creatures, I must not forget this, this is why the door is always locked; but surely I can think of some way of getting at her keys?

I smoke until breakfast time, watching the sky. Banks of billowing blue-gray cloud—this will be a damp day, today the rain will be spitting. I am wearing all my shirts and on top of them a black polo-neck jersey, and on top of that the jacket of my shabby gray suit. Suit trousers, thick gray socks (two pairs), and a large pair of thick-soled black leather shoes with ten close-set lace holes (eyelets) and a sort of flame-shaped strip of leather stitched around the toecap and pricked with decorative perforations. Asylum shoes, these, made by the Ganderhill cobbler. I also have strips of brown wrapping paper and thin cardboard taped to my legs and torso, which crackle when I move.

Breakfast was uneventful—dead, fishlike eyes over porridge bowls, the usual squeaky farts. Then straight out into the spitting rain, and off toward the canal, and the streets, thankfully, were empty save for the odd hurrying figure with an umbrella and a blind girl tapping along with her cane. I was noticing details of the world that were new to me, how the corrugated tin that fenced off a patch of wasteground was sharpened at the tips, like a line of spears; the way a brick wall had had bits of broken bottles set in a bed of concrete on top, and painted beneath it in large black letters the words NO RUBBISH. There were weeds sprouting from the concrete, stiff, thistlelike growths, hardy, bristling things. Then under the viaduct, its arches stained black by the rain, and I was damp now, I could smell the dampness on me. A wind was blowing, there was dog shit on the pavement. From a wall dangled a piece of striped cloth and as the wind caught it it flapped at me, a message of some sort. I paused at the main road and waved the traffic on, waved it past me until I could cross over. I seemed to be making for the river; I'd thought I was going to the canal.

The wind was stronger by the river, I had to button my jacket and turn up the collar. I found a bench: two concrete uprights each with a protruding arm to which the three gray-scarred greenish planks were bolted, three more bolted to the uprights for your back. It was damp, I didn't care, I was damp. In front of me a rusty black railing then the river, gray-green and running strong and choppy in the wind. A structure of wooden pilings a few yards out. On the far side a terrace of houses beneath a forest of cranes leaning drunkenly in all directions as if about to collapse. Gray sky, the great bellying rolls of clouds ponderously pushing east before the wind. The drizzle is a haze that mists me, makes me damp, makes the black wool jersey smell strange. Out with the tobacco, and with the first good lungful comes the thought: today I shall try her room again.

I C A M E in from the river very damp, late in the afternoon, and went straight upstairs. I had had an idea that I might cross the canal, that I might go to Kitchener Street, finally see what it looked like, twenty years later; but once again something inside me—some deep-seated anxiety, some reluctance, or fear—would not allow me to set foot on the bridge, and I'd followed my usual route along the canal and so back to the house. Now I stood at my window and smoked a fat one as the light thickened and the crows flapped their wings in the bare branches of the trees in the park, and as I did so I heard the front door slam and a moment later I saw her going off down the street with a shopping bag on her arm. I stubbed out the roll-up in the tin I use for an ashtray and made my way quickly to her bedroom. This was something I'd done a few times now, whenever I knew for certain that she was out of the house. This time her door was unlocked; so without any hesitation I went in.

Nothing unusual at first glance. You know what a messy woman she is, how she leaves her underwear all over the room, how she clutters her dressing table with cosmetics and so on, how she never makes her bed: clearly the years have gone some way to repairing these sluttish habits, for this room was neat and tidy, the bed made and not a scrap of underwear in sight. I quickly went through the chest of drawers and found nothing of interest, nor was there anything on or in the bedside table. There were, I noticed, three framed pictures on the walls, two scenic views of the Lake District and over the bed a Madonna and Child. At that point I came back out onto the landing to make sure she hadn't returned: no sound, only the muted tones of dance music from the wireless in the dayroom. Then back in again, and over to the large dark wardrobe that stood against the wall facing the door. As I stealthily approached I found myself reflected in its long mirror, still in my damp black polo-neck jersey and shabby gray suit; and what a queer furtive creature I looked, tiptoeing long-legged across this gloomy bedroom, what a *spider!*

I paused at the wardrobe, a hand on the door, and turned my head, once more to listen to the house, for five, ten, fifteen seconds: nothing but the faint, far-off wireless music. I opened the wardrobe—and there it was, the first thing I saw, though it was pushed way down to the end of the rack and almost concealed: that ratty old fur of hers.

Then I heard the front door slam (fortunately it's a door that's hard to close quietly) and I rapidly crept away, leaving the room just as I'd found it, crept back to my own room, and, by this time literally trembling with emotion, stood at my window and tried to stay calm.

There I stood for many minutes, my left arm pressed across my chest and the fingers clutching a bony shoulder, and between the still-trembling fingers of the other hand a fat one, I needed it. Slowly the trembling grew less violent, and as that happened the damp smell of the wool jersey rose once more to my nostrils, and finally I shook my head, shook off the last of the emotion, and took off my jacket. I hung it on the back of the door, then off with the ill-smelling jersey. But the odor persisted, and it was only then that I recognized it as gas.

It was a long night. I still don't know how I got through it, for it was probably the worst one yet. Despite further layers

of brown paper taped to my torso, despite the layers of vests
and shirts and jerseys on top, the smell of gas was with me
until dawn. Of course I had the journal, and this alone, I
believe, saved me from doing harm to myself or anybody
else. A new strategy from the creatures in the attic: I kept
my light on all night of course, and the bulb crackled at me
as it usually did, and I paid it no attention—until, that is, the
crackling grew suddenly loud, as it had in Kitchener Street
the night I've described, but this time it was the *voices* that
had taken over, and were producing a sort of chant that came
out of the bulb, and the chant went: KILL her kill her kill
her kill her KILL her kill her kill her kill her. At this I sat up
rigid from my writing and focused my attention on the bulb,
but when I did that the noise immediately decayed to a staticky buzz and I lost it. Back to work then, though as soon
as I was absorbed in the writing the crackle again resolved to
that terrible chant, and again I stopped, up came the head,
and the chant turned to laughter that slowly faded away and
all there was then was a faulty light bulb in an ill-wired house,
and a desperate man tormented by messages that issued from
he knew not where, the attic above him, the light bulb over
his head, or some deep hole in the back reaches of his own
sick mind. Oh it was a bad night, may I never, ever see the
like of it again.

Toward dawn it grew less intense and I paused, rolled a
cigarette, looked over the pages of my book. They were
scribbled and smudged, covered with words I had no real
interest in reading, not now that the night was almost over.
Something was happening to my handwriting, there was a
definite slant and flow to it now, it was now a *hand* and not
merely the cramped markings of a man who had read much
but written little. It was a fluent hand, the hand of a writer,
and in other circumstances, I reflected, I might have regarded
these writings with satisfaction, with pride, even. But the
circumstances of composition permitted me no such complacency; I took heart only from the faint gray hint of dawn

tentatively fingering the eastern sky, and the promise it brought of some respite from these torments, at least for the few brief fleeting hours of daylight. Somewhere in the house a toilet flushed, the pipes rumbled, and in my mind's eye I saw a dead soul in threadbare, grubby pajamas emerging from a lavatory with bleary eyes crusted with yellowy sleep-matter, foul of breath and yawning stupidly, and shuffling back to his narrow bed to slip again into the sweet oblivion of sleep; and at that moment I would have traded a hand, or an arm— or an arm and a leg!—to be a dead soul with an empty mind and the sweet possibility of sleep before me. To be awake is to be available to torment, and this is the full complete meaning of life.

And would I today return to Kitchener Street, I asked myself, once more picking up my pencil? What would I find there? Would it bring me peace, or relief, to stand outside number twenty-seven, to see some stranger's lace curtains drawn across the parlor window? Perhaps a new coat of paint on the front door, and the fanlight over it, the setting sun, scrubbed clean of the dust and grease that congealed there after Hilda moved in? Would I make my spidery way down the alley at the back, pause by the dustbins, perhaps dare to push open the gate into our yard, and see someone else's washing flapping on the clothesline, someone else's bicycle leaned against the outhouse, in which, perhaps, the water still came up to the rim of the toilet when you pulled the chain, and sometimes slopped over? What would this do for me? Perhaps I'd turn away, shuffle down to the end of Kitchener Street, slip into the Dog and Beggar and nurse a half of mild by the fire. Cast surreptitious glances at Ernie Ratcliff, in his fifties now but weaselly as ever with his quick thin hands and his oiled hair and his damnable subtlety—though he wouldn't recognize me, no, he wouldn't see in this shabby ruin the shy lad who used to come looking for his dad when dinner was ready, he wouldn't see that at all, he'd see a slow sad man, broken by mental illness and with barely the coppers in his pocket to buy the smallest glass of the cheapest beer in the meanest pub in London!

No, I won't go back to Kitchener Street, not today, I'm not strong enough. When I'm feeling better—when I get through this bad patch—then I'll go home again, then I'll go back to number twenty-seven, and maybe it'll do me good.

I lay down my pencil, cross the room and turn off the light, I don't need it anymore. I stretch out on my bed and gaze at the ceiling: silence. Soon the pipes will be rumbling, the wireless will be turned on, I will hear people in the lower parts of the house. But for now, silence, blessed golden silence.

Down to the river again today. For some reason that I haven't bothered to work out I no longer want to sit by the canal, though it may, it now occurs to me, have to do with the prospect of the gasworks over by Spleen Street. Misty today, not as damp as yesterday, and the smell of gas has almost disappeared. I find some comfort in this rickety structure of wooden pilings in the river, greenish where the water washes round it, dark brown for the rest, stained with creosote, and I can smell the creosote from here if I try hard enough. Otherwise there's wood smoke in the air, I see it rising from the tin chimney of a battered Dutch barge a hundred yards downstream, and about halfway across the river begins the mist, a soft curtain that contains the eye, that permits me to review, without distraction, the brief glimpse I had in her shadowy bedroom of the ratty fur. That she *still has it*—what am I to make of this? I am calm now, I can turn these things over quietly in my mind. A sea gull alights with a scream on the pilings and from somewhere off behind me a hooter sounds, some factory. A schoolboy stops by my bench and tries to make me give him a cigarette. "Go on, mister," he says, "just one." But I shake my head, I don't even shift my gaze from the pilings heaving up from the gray-green Thames and the misty curtain beyond. You'd think my resolve would be strengthened by what I saw at the back of Mrs. Wilkinson's wardrobe. Why wasn't it then? Something was confusing the logic of it all. What was it? That the creatures in the attic should be urging me to kill her, was this it? Were they not her creatures? Perhaps not. Perhaps they were anybody's creatures; or nobody's. Or perhaps they issued, as at times I was convinced they did, from some deep hole in the back reaches of my own sick mind—what then?

EARTH; water; gas; and hemp: these are Spider's elements. When I returned from the river I went straight up to my room and got out my rope. I have had it in the grate behind the gas fire for the last ten days. I found it by the canal one afternoon and knew immediately that I'd need it. It's not the sort of thick rope in whose oily coils I used to curl up as a boy, down on the boats, it's much thinner rope than that, cord, you'd call it, three wiry braided strands of dark green hemp. It's not clean; the oil and grime of long service have stained it black in places, and also, now, there's the soot of the fireplace on it. It's about twelve feet long, fraying at one end and woven into a loop at the other, the loop reinforced by a steel ring. I take it up between my fingers; I like its rough grimy texture. I grip it in my fists and snap it taut: it is good strong cord, still serviceable. I loop it over my arm and lay it on my bed. I sit at my table, chair turned toward the bed, I smoke a thin one and look at my rope. A knock at the door: suddenly she is in the room with me.

"*Mister* Cleg," she says, in that way of hers—she has a bundle in her arms—and then she sees the rope. I am still on my chair. "Not on your bed, Mr. Cleg," she cries, "that filthy thing!" Clutching her bundle in one arm she picks up my rope and tosses it onto the floor, where it sprawlingly uncoils with a sort of dull muted ropy clatter. She brushes at the blanket with the side of a fat hand and then sets down her bundle. At the top of the heap is an umbrella, tightly

furled. "Mr. Cleg, if I can't stop you walking in the rain I
can at least give you an umbrella. One umbrella. Now this"—
she lifted up a rubbery thing, pale orange, shaped like a flat-
fish, and dangled it at me—"is your hot-water bottle. You
can fill it in the kitchen before you go to bed. This"—she
picked up an overcoat that looked third-hand at least, probably the offcast of some tramp she'd met—"is your winter
coat." It was pale gray with a fine herringbone pattern that
immediately gave my eyes trouble, all those thin slanting
parallel lines in zigzag rows. "And this"—she brandished a
threadbare blue blanket with a number of cigarette burns—
"is your extra blanket."

I stared at this bizarre collection in silent perplexity. What
did these objects have in common? She had turned her back
and bottom to me, she was fussing with my bed now, putting·
on the extra blanket. She glanced over her shoulder. "Nothing
to say, Mr. Cleg? Cat got your tongue?" (What a revolting
idea.) Did she realize, I suddenly thought, what I wanted the
rope for? Sudden intense anxiety in the Spider. "There," she
said, finishing with the bed; then, glancing at the floor: "Can
I take this away? It's really too dirty to be in a bedroom."

Immediately I reached for it, pulled it to me and clasped
its tangled coils in my lap. "Just please don't put it on your
bed then," she said. "I think that's oil and I'll never get it
out." She was standing at the end of the bed now. She seemed
very huge today, terrifyingly huge. "Nothing to say, Mr.
Cleg?" She set her head on one side and folded her arms
under her breast. "I'm worried about you."

I shrank back, tightly clutching my rope. How desperately
I wanted to withdraw from the gaze of those eyes, they bored
into me, they splintered me, I was about to shatter and I could
not get away, I was hypnotized like a rat before a snake.
Overhead the bulb leapt to sputtering crackling life though
the light was not switched on. The room grew darker, her eyes
glittered at me. "You do remember," she said—and her voice
came as though from the depths of a deep stone well, hollow

and booming and ominous—"you do remember that you're
seeing the doctor again tomorrow." BOOM boom boom
boom—the words kept booming in the room even after she'd
left. I went to the window and stared at the streetlamp, which
had just been lit. I was trembling uncontrollably; the rope
slipped from my fingers and tumbled to the floor with that
same ropy clatter, and slowly the echoes faded away. But oh,
I thought, this will be a bad night, this will be a nasty one,
how will I get myself through this one?

What a Spider was seen in the first pale light of dawn! What
a broken haggard shadow of an echo of a *joke* of a man! What
a husk, what a wreck, what a wretch! But he lived, he lived.
I stood at my table leaning on my hands and gazing at the
sky: the night was over, I had come through. There was
silence; the shrieking had ceased, the furor was ended, I was
the fragile vessel caught on the open sea in a storm by night
that limps at dawn into some small cove or harbor with his
mainmast splintered and his helmsman roped to the wheel,
bleary with fatigue and spent terror. Small comfort, the haven
of daylight, but comfort nonetheless. Cardboard crackled as
I shifted my limbs, moved to the bed, lay on my back and
gazed at a damp-stained ceiling that an hour before had been
a demon's dark canvas of hellish forms in coils and knots that
squirmed, spat, *oozed* with filth and violence. But for now
the ebb of night, the heave and swell of silent dawn: my
Pacific.

The beached Spider lay on his bed with his legs crossed at
the ankles and watched the smoke of a thin one rise in a
slender column that broke into whorls and faded away. He
thought of his rope in the fireplace, and he knew it was almost
finished, this sorry jig of his, this jig in hell; enough, he
murmured to the silence, enough enough enough.

D R. McNaughten was in Mrs. Wilkinson's office when I left the kitchen after breakfast. "Good God, man, what's happened to you!" he cried as I shuffled in. "Sit down!" I sat. He peered at me, frowning, then went to the door and shouted for Mrs. Wilkinson. "Has this man been taken off his medication?" he said, not troubling to lower his voice.

"Of course not, doctor," said Mrs. Wilkinson in hushed tones, drawing him away from the door so that I could hear no more of their conversation. A few minutes later he was back with me. "Dennis," he said, "I believe you've been hoarding your medication. Tell me frankly: have you?"

What did it matter now? A shrug, a sigh from the weary Spider. The doctor frowned at me, then went to the window, where he stood with his back to me; one hand was in his trouser pocket, the other was drumming on the sill. Silence; after some minutes the door opens. It is Mrs. Wilkinson. She goes to the desk and spills onto it a dozen or so soot-stained tablets; she is also carrying my rope, and this too she puts on the desk. I sit up with an involuntary start of alarm: where is my book? Dr. McNaughten looks at me, shaking his head. "Thank you Mrs. Wilkinson," he says. He returns to the window, and again stands with his back to me, gazing out. Eventually, and without turning, he speaks. "I'm almost convinced that I should commit you," he says, "but I want to give you one last chance."

* * *

When I got back up to my room I found to my great relief
that the book was safe. I was not to be sent back to Ganderhill;
Dr. McNaughten had a number of reasons for this decision,
one of which was that before I stopped taking my medicine
I was apparently making "progress." Toward what, he didn't
say.

E V E N when a man has nothing to call his own he finds ways of acquiring possessions; he then finds ways of concealing his possessions from the attendants. What you did on a hard-bench ward was tie one end of a piece of string to a belt loop, and the other end to the top of a sock, then have the sock dangle down the inside of your trousers. In it you kept tobacco, sewing materials, pencil and paper, other bits of string—whatever you had that was of use or value. Men grew attached to their socks: life was cut to the bone on a hard-bench ward, and this was a way to flesh it, make you feel more than a mere creature of the institution. Men fought bitterly to retain their socks, when the attendants decided to confiscate them. When that happened you'd lose your clothes as well as your sock and be thrown into a safe room in an untearable canvas gown, or you'd be straitjacketed, buckled and trussed like a game bird lest you break your knuckles hammering on the wall.

During the later years in Ganderhill I had a room on a good downstairs ward in Block F and enjoyed all the privileges the institution could give me. But in the early years I was usually up among the sad men, and often in a safe room in a strait-jacket. I remember the first time it happened, how a couple of attendants had begun talking about me while I sat smoking on the other side of the dayroom. Glancing over at me, the one attendant then told the other that I was here because I'd murdered my mother. Naturally I disputed this; I told them

it was not me but my father who had killed her. They laughed
and then for a while they talked of other things. But after a
few minutes they were again discussing me, and again it was
said that I'd killed my mother. Again I contradicted them;
they told me not to get upset, not to get myself into a "state."

This was rich. I remember that I began to rock backwards
and forwards on the bench (a thing I couldn't control) and
my fingers were trembling violently. The Spider was making
desperate scurrying movements, back and forth, backwards
and forwards, so it felt, seeking with growing desperation
some niche or cranny to crawl into. Rapidly the dayroom
grew dark, and the two attendants sat watching me with
animal intensity as my rocking grew violent. There was noise,
screaming, then they had me pinned to the floor as the light
ebbed and swelled. Then came the weirdly familiar clank of
buckles, and the frenzied Spider, with the sensation of sudden
constriction as they tightened the straps, at last saw his hole
and slipped into it, and nothing more until he found himself
in a safe room, trussed like a Christmas chicken and the single
thought going round and round and round in his head that
it was his *father*, his *father*, his father his father his father . . .

Not easy to think of those times now (perhaps it's a mark
of my so-called progress that I can dwell upon them at all)
but it was to a great extent the work of those first years in
Ganderhill to learn to endure such goading—which eventually I did: there came a time when I could hear them attempting to awaken the violence in me, when they'd murmur,
one to another, about my mother, and instead of growing
agitated—starting to rock and tremble, to scuttle about like
a crab in search of a stone—instead of all that the Spider
developed structures that could withstand provocation, he
tirelessly rebuilt, he rehearsed with constant industry, and so
became able to withstand the goads, and as this began to
happen then so did the goading subside, and he was left alone.
Life in Ganderhill began at that moment to improve.

I am sitting by the river, my furled umbrella leaning against the bench beside me. An overcast day, and very windy. I am drowsy from my medicine, perhaps this too helps me think of the early Ganderhill years without agitation. Other patients—John Giles, Derek Shadwell—would never do to me what the attendants did: with each other we had no reason to doubt, or lie. It occurs to me though that a function of the goading, deliberate or otherwise, was to force me to face and understand what had happened in Kitchener Street: this was why, you see, when I *did,* it eventually stopped, though this was not effected speedily, no, it took years, there were frequent collapses that would see the Spider once more curled like an infant under a blanket, or asleep on a bench with his head on a shoe. But what was happening during this period was the further development of the two-head system: back there where the Spider lived, that's where we find the sad, true tale of Kitchener Street (the one I'm telling you now). And on the ward, in the dayroom, Ganderhill inmate Dennis Cleg moved unperturbed, a mask, a ghost, a puppet, among false rumors, scandalous imputations and provocative goads—for the Spider was elsewhere! (Until, that is, Dr. Austin Marshall retired and a new medical superintendent took over, and this man managed, in the space of two afternoons, to undermine all my work; but of him more in due course.)

Bad years, then, the early years, years of persecution. The first months were the hardest in this regard, before I adapted to their ways. (It is much more difficult to speak of those days: see how upright I sit on my bench now, staring at the pilings in the river as a screaming sea gull sweeps by in the gusting wind, and how white-knuckled my bony hands are, clasped on the handle of the umbrella.) For they would have made me their creature had I not found the means to resist. See me, then, in a cold tiled room at the front of the admissions ward, bathed and disinfected, stark naked and shivering: a long, ribbed, skinny boy, his pimpled skin white as milk, with terror in his eyes. They have taken my clothes away and are about to issue me the standard grays of the institution. So the old me, the lad from Kitchener Street, the Spider of London, has been stripped away; and before I assume the uniform of a lunatic there are these few minutes that I am naked in that bleak tiled room, that I am truly nothing, neither the one thing nor the other, and here's an odd thing: I am seized, in those minutes of bare shivering nothingness, with a feeling so intense as to make me laugh out loud; and the attendant turns from the table, where he is busy with my few pitiful possessions, and frowns at me as I hop from foot to foot and try to stifle waves of an inexplicable joy—soon extinguished as I struggle into a shirt too small and trousers too wide, and a pair of thick-soled asylum shoes from which the laces have been removed. He has taken my pencil, and the few coppers I possessed, and sealed them up in a brown envelope with my name and the date scrawled on the front, and told me they'll be returned to me when I leave. So while I entered that room as Spider of London, I stepped out of it a lunatic, unrecognizable to myself; and the terror, momentarily extinguished by that brief odd gush of hilarity, returned then, and all I was aware of was the touch of alien material on my skin, and the alien smells in my nostrils. Now I was afraid, desperately afraid, more frightened than ever I remembered being in my life before, and all I wanted was to be back in my room above the kitchen in number twenty-seven. But that odd laughter: I believe, now, that what I was feeling was relief.

John Giles was the first patient I encountered on the admissions ward, John with his great shoulders and shaggy eyebrows. He was admitted to Ganderhill the same day as me: when I first saw him he was facing a wall near the front of the ward and chattering to himself with great rapidity and animation. Beyond him, further down the ward, a little bald man sat on the floor moaning gently as he plucked repeatedly at the collar of his shirt, and beyond him, frozen to his spot like a statue, a man stood gazing at his own open palm and splayed fingers. I must have paused, there on the threshold, for I remember the attendant murmuring, "Come on, son, down we go."

Down we went. A few men wandered the ward, most were locked in cells with barred gates for doors and bunks of solid concrete. These men wore canvas gowns and lay sleeping on the concrete with their knees drawn up to their chins. One man, his eyes wild and his hair standing up off his head in damp spikes, rushed to the gate as I passed and gripping the bars cackled at me till the attendant moved to- ward him with an uplifted hand and he shrank back with a whimper of distress. Halfway down the ward the gate of an empty cell was unlocked and rolled back on rattling metal casters. "Here we are, son," said the attendant. "I won't lock you up for the time being." I stood there staring in: a small barred window high in the wall, a lidless, seatless concrete toilet, and a concrete bunk. "Just stay out of trouble, son," he said, "and we'll soon have you downstairs." He was as tall as me, this man, whose name I later learned was Mr. Thomas. He turned and made his way back down the ward, glancing from side to side as with one hand he gently slapped a large key into the palm of the other. See me then: sitting on the edge of the concrete bunk with my elbows on my knees, my hands dangling limp between my legs, and my head hung low. There was a hot choking feeling in my throat; I stared, blinking, at the floor and watched two or three tears fall between my feet. A shadow fell across the cell; I looked up, startled: it was John Giles, the giant. "Got any snout?" he said. I shook my head; he shuffled off.

I ate my supper in my cell, from a paper plate with a wooden spoon, and shortly afterwards I was issued a pair of blankets and three sheets of toilet paper. Then my gate was slammed closed with a great clattering *bang!* and the lights were turned off, all but one or two that spread a dim glow down the middle of the corridor, enough for me to see the man in the opposite cell. I lay down on my bunk, and for the first time learned to use a shoe for a pillow. The sounds of the ward changed; the men I'd seen curled on their bunks with their knees pulled up to their chins seemed to awaken with the darkness, and now there arose such a piteous clamor of groans, and cries, and whimpers that I clapped my hands to my ears and lay there, on the concrete, rigid, my eyes wide and staring at the ceiling, where the glow from the corridor cast a weirdly elongated grid of bars across the plaster. Even so I couldn't escape the voices, and after some minutes I was pacing back and forth across the cell, still clutching my head and muttering feverishly to try and drown out with my own voice the unbearable anguish of theirs. Then there was an attendant at my gate. "Settle down, son," he murmured, "don't get upset." I said nothing; I stood in my cell and gazed at the man. After some moments he said, "Lie down, son," and I did. He went away, and I heard him silence the moaning and whimpering, until the ward was almost quiet. I lay there for what seemed an eternity, watching the skewed grid of shadows on the ceiling, and then I began to see the cobwebs in the roof of my father's shed; from this I derived comfort of some kind, for I managed to sleep then.

The next days passed in alternating cycles of monotony and hell. I easily became distraught and agitated—hardly surprising—and soon I'd lost my shirt and trousers and was locked up in an untearable canvas gown. Oh, this was the low point; I shudder, now, to think of what I must have been going through to do the things I did. Such was my despair, my pain, the sheer bloody wretchedness and misery of my isolation that I flung off my gown and used my own feces to write my name on the wall—my real name, that is, *Spider,* I mean, daubed and smeared in damp brown clots across the plaster—and *now* see me, hunkered naked on my hams and grinning at the wall where my own name drips in shit in letters two feet high, and for a few brief minutes I am my own creature, not theirs, not theirs. But then see how I'm marched ungently down to the bathroom while my cell is scrubbed down with hot water and coarse bleach, confirmed, *in their eyes,* as a lunatic, by this dirty deed, though *in my own eyes* the reverse!

Bad days, then, though in time I learned, as I say, to build up the old two-head system and give them a lunatic while the Spider stood aloof. This was partly due to tobacco: in Ganderhill tobacco was one of those rude struts men used to give their days shape. There was an issue after breakfast and an issue after supper, from the tin at the front of the ward. I soon learned to join the others when they lined up for it, though it wasn't so much the tobacco that yielded the plea-sure, it was, oddly, the scarcity of the stuff, the paltriness of the morning issue that made you impatient for the evening (having smoked it all by noon) and then in turn it was fin-ishing the evening issue that made you look forward so avidly in the long sleepless hours of the night to the morning. The pleasure was all in the delay, the anticipation; and this is how they made you their creature, for if you got into trouble you lost your tobacco, and the whole sweet rhythm of anticipation and satisfaction disappeared from the day; and what a bleak and dreary day that made it! So this too prompted me to build up the old two-head system, for if I gave them a good lunatic they gave me tobacco, twice a day, for me to hoard or smoke as I chose. Not that tobacco could do everything: men still banged their heads against the wall till they bled, they tore out their stitches, they burned holes in their flesh with cig-arettes, they stuffed their gowns down the toilet then flushed till the water flooded the cell and went streaming down the corridor. For this was a hard-bench ward, and we were there because we failed; but I did learn to give them a good lunatic, and it was at that point they decided I was ready to see Dr. Austin Marshall.

The interview was not a long one. It took place in his office; he sat, I stood, with Mr. Thomas behind me at the door.

There was a file open on the desk; I realized that this was my file; somehow it hadn't occurred to me that I had a file. He poked at his pipe with a matchstick. "You're very young to be so sick," he murmured, gazing up at me with the pipe clasped between his fingers. "How are you getting along on the ward?"

"Fine," I said. (I'd been told to say this.)

"Sir," said Mr. Thomas quietly.

"Sir," I said.

"Like to try and make a go of it downstairs, Dennis?"

"Yes sir," I said.

"Yes," he murmured as his eyes returned to my file. Then: "Why did you do it, son? Any idea?"

"I didn't mean to, sir. It was a mistake."

"Sorry you did it, then?"

"Yes sir."

"Well that's a start. Eh, Mr. Thomas? That's a start, eh?"

"Yes sir," said Mr. Thomas from the door.

"Don't suppose you'll ever do it again," said Dr. Austin Marshall. "Only got one mother after all." He looked up with raised eyebrows; I had been told on no account to mention what my father had done. Mr. Thomas cleared his voice, a reminder. I stayed silent. The superintendent scribbled in my file for some moments, then said briskly: "Let's try him out on a downstairs ward, see how he gets along. Block B, Mr. Thomas—can I leave the details to you?"

"Yes sir."

"Jolly good. Don't know any naval history, I suppose, Dennis?" he said, rising to his feet and waving vaguely with his pipe stem at a painting in oils of a sea battle. I couldn't look at the thing, all that smoke and blood, screaming men in a burning sea as mainmasts were shattered and cannons belched flame, I could hear it, I could smell it, I wanted no part of it. "No, of course you don't," he said. "Still, you should, East End boy like yourself. It's the Royal Navy made this country great, am I right, Mr. Thomas?"

"Quite right sir."

"Jolly good then. Well off you go."

Off we went, and so began my first stint on a downstairs ward. In later years I found it to be generally true that you only got to see Dr. Austin Marshall when you least needed him. Odd, eh?

The sea gull has settled on the pilings in the river and I seem unable to tear my eyes away from it. Ugly fat thing, with its beady eyes and webbed feet, now it lifts its hooked beak and lets out a screechy croak, you can imagine that beak coming at your face, pluck out an eye like a cockle, leave an empty socket and a bloody cheek—bloody cheek! Bloody nerve! Bloody nerve, nerve, nervous disease—I hate birds. The water's boiling and frothing round my pilings now, whitecaps further out, strong current running, wash you out to sea like a scrap of flotsam, death by water, death by gas, death by hemp hemp hemp: they should have strung Horace up by the neck and let him swing. Horace—Horrors! Horrors Cleg! Horrors and his bird Hilda, they should've strung'em both up! Tower Bridge a dim gray structure of pencils and string against the failing light of this blustery afternoon, long strips of dark gray cloud sweeping out across the western sky, a few ragged, jagged tears between with the light shafting through, me on my bench leaning on the umbrella as the wind spits bits of river in my face and the gull lifts off the piling with more screechy croaks and an untidy flap of dirty wings before wheeling off on the wind and letting me rise at last to my feet and shuffle off home.

Upstairs without being seen and out with the book. Like a fox, the Spider, for when she found my rope and tablets in the fireplace she didn't find the book: I was *just too clever* for her. For inside the flue, directly behind the mantelpiece that sticks out over the gas fire, there's a narrow shelf, a ledge, and I stand the book on this ledge and wedge it firm with an upright brick. Only one way to retrieve it when it's wedged on its ledge: flat on my back with my head up against the gas fire, my arm through the gap, into the fireplace, up the chimney—I grope, I stretch—and my fingers are just able to reach the brick and lift it down, and the book comes tumbling after; and despite the brown bag it is dirtier than ever now. Pencils: these I've been stealing from around the house, no sense letting her know what I'm up to, and I'm using the old Ganderhill system for these, the sock down the trousers. So out with my pencil, open the book, and gaze out the window at the sky, now dark, and return in my mind to the old days.

L I F E was certainly better on a downstairs ward. Tobacco and books; a room with a door; fresh air out on the terraces. This last was my great joy. There were benches on the terraces (my life has been a journey from bench to bench, and will end on a bench with a lid!) from which I had a clear view over the vegetable gardens and the cricket field, the wall down at the bottom, and beyond it farmland that gradually yielded to wooded hills in the distance. When the wind blew from the south it carried up from the farm a rich smell of manure, and this too gave me pleasure. For a lad who'd grown up on Kitchener Street, for whom the allotments and the working Thames were all he knew of nature, this sweep of countryside was true glory. And the skies it gave me! My skies were London skies, but these were blue, with high white clouds moving across in stately caravan, and my spirit exulted, something was awoken in your old Spider when first he met those skies, and it's still there, faint now, and burning low, but it's there. And I remember how, one day, sitting on a bench at the back of Block B, I watched the men at work in the vegetable gardens, in their flapping yellow corduroys and their green jerseys, and when I went back in (they gave us only half an hour on the terrace) the men in the vegetable gardens were still there, and I thought: this is the work for me.

It took years. At times I'd become agitated, I'd do something stupid, and back upstairs I'd go. Always John Giles was there to meet me, though his grin was a goonish one now, for after he bit off an attendant's ear they'd pulled all his teeth out. John only got downstairs once in twenty years, even after they began giving him electric shocks; he's up in hard bench today. But I was different, I was learning to give them a good lunatic, and as time passed, and Spider made his life more secure in the back parts, it became less and less vital to maintain my claims on the ward. The goading diminished, the agitation subsided, and I spent longer periods downstairs. I sat on the terrace and watched the men in the vegetable gardens, thinking: this is the work for me.

Yes, this was the work for me. Ah dear God, are they starting again? Is this them with their voices crackling at me from the light bulb again? And me thinking I wouldn't go through another night of it. I look at my fingers—they seem so far away from me, at first I think I see a crab of some type lying there on the open page, a yellow crab with horny pincers, a creature unrelated to me. I follow it up my arm to my shoulder, I need to do this to confirm that the thing is a part of me, or at any rate connected to this composite, this loosely assembled and unraveling weave of gristle, husk and bone. For I am almost empty now, the foul taste in my mouth attests to this, and of course the smell of gas, and I wonder (such are my thoughts at night) what they will find when they cut me open after death (if I'm not dead already)? An anatomical monstrosity, surely: my small intestine is wrapped tightly around the lower part of my spine and ascends in a taut snug spiral, thickening grossly into the colon about halfway up, which twists around my upper spine like a boa constrictor, the rectum passing through my skull and the anus issuing from the top of my head where an opening has been created between the bones joining the top of my skull, which I constantly finger in wondering horror, a sort of mature excretory fontanelle (my hair would be matted and stinking but for the blessed rain that daily cleanses me). Since this occurred (late one night earlier in the week) I have tried not to eat, for the movement of matter through the intestines has become painfully vivid to me, a series of jerky spasms as though a worm of some kind were crawling round my back-bone. Other organs have been compressed against my skel-eton so as to create a void or emptiness in the trunk of my body, and I haven't yet learned why this is occurring. One of my lungs has disappeared; there is a worm in the other but fortunately smoking remains possible. A single thin pipe takes water from my stomach (squashed flat and ridged against my rib cage) and this pipe alone drops through the void and connects to the thing between my legs that hardly resembles a formed male organ at all anymore. There is ma-terial rotting slowly inside me, the composting remains of organs I no longer need, and it is because the odors given off by this process have begun to seep through the pores of my skin (my skin! my husk, my shell, my *rind!*) that I have now wrapped my torso and all my limbs in newspaper and cor-rugated cardboard held in place with string, sticky tape, rub-ber bands, whatever I have been able to steal around the house. All this, all this I can live with; what preys upon my mind now is the thought that my body is being *prepared* for something, that I am being evacuated internally so as to *make room for something else:* and even as I write these words, even as I draw a wavering line beneath them, a loud cackle suddenly comes from the light bulb, and from the attic a volley of stamping that shakes the walls and sets the light bulb swinging on its cord, and I sit here terrified, clutching the table with both hands as the swinging bulb throws the room into wildly shifting blocks of light and shadow.

It subsides to a flicker and a crackle and I stand up from the table, I must leave the room if only for five minutes. I shuffle to the door and there's an ominous howl from above as I lay hands on the knob and turn it, but their wrath I can endure for a short time at least. Down the darkened landing to the lavatory, where I stand over the toilet and with trem-bling fingers unbutton my trousers. A small pipelike apparatus, something from a plumber's toolbox, protrudes and begins urinating tiny black spiders into the bowl, where they curl up into points and float on the water. I appear to be infested; I appear to be playing host to a colony of spiders; I appear to be an *egg-bag*.

Back in my room I stand at the table leaning on my hands and gaze out at the leafless trees in the park below. Illuminated dimly by the glow of the streetlamp, their fingery boughs form a pale tracery against the darkness. The night sky is cloudy, there is no moon. Nothing is moving out there. I sink with a rustle of newsprint and cardboard into my chair and pick up my pencil. I'd thought I wouldn't go through another night of it; in this as in all else I am wrong, I delude myself with the idea that I am *free,* have *control,* can *act.* It is not so. I am their creature.

This is the work for me, I'd thought as I watched the men in the vegetable gardens. After numerous requests I was given my chance, and I did not disappoint them. By this time I had spent almost ten years in Ganderhill and was a well-known figure. I had a room on Block F and a few legitimate possessions (a few illicit possessions too, squirreled away in one hole or another). I was comfortable, I had my niche; I was known as something of a solitary, though I did maintain a sort of friendship with Derek Shadwell, a man from Nigeria who, like me, had been wrongly accused of murdering his mother; Derek and I played billiards together in the dayroom every evening. I was on good terms with the attendants, and was regularly greeted on the terraces by Dr. Austin Marshall. It was in a way the apex of my career in Ganderhill, to claim a place on the working party in the vegetable gardens; and I was confident that by application of what my father had taught me as a boy I'd be able to do all that was asked of me there.

At the eastern end of one of the terraces a set of stone steps descended to a patch of lonely ground about the size of a football field, enclosed on one side by a section of the periphery wall, in the shadow of which stood an old elm tree. Perpendicular to the wall on the southern side another set of steps descended a slope that gave onto the cricket field, while to the north there was a steep climb through an uncultivated patch of bushes and trees to the higher terraces. It had a derelict, forsaken look to it, this lonely field, and had once been a tea garden, for a few pieces of old-fashioned garden furniture—a pair of wicker chairs, a wrought-iron table—stood rotting and rusting under the elm. Elsewhere flourished clumps of weeds and patches of wild grass, and this being October dead leaves lay heaped against the wall in damply moldering drifts in which colonies of spotted toadstools had sprung up. Close to the wall at the foot of the wooded slope there was an unsightly heap of waste lumber and dead branches. My first morning in the vegetable gardens I was put to work clearing this ground for planting in the spring. I had a wheelbarrow and a garden fork; there were spades and mattocks in the shed, when I needed them.

I went to work. I was younger then, I was strong, I could lift heavy boulders into the barrow, wheel them to the steps and carry them up to the pile behind the shed. It was a windy spot, and though the work warmed me I kept my donkey jacket on, with the collar turned up. I'd also been issued yellow corduroy trousers, black boots, and a green jersey. It took me a day to clear the boulders and make a start on the dead leaves; the work tired me, but it exhilarated me too, and when I stopped briefly to smoke a roll-up I leaned on the fork and gazed out over the landscape, and felt at peace. Previously I'd had a job in the Ganderhill workshop, standing beside Derek Shadwell hammering pallets all day, with nothing but a small barred window with a view of a wall, and no light but what came from a dusty, crackling fluorescent tube.

I made progress with the leaves, wheeling my barrowloads up the slope and along the terrace to the compost heap, this one much bigger than my father's, for it claimed the organic refuse of the entire institution. In the course of these journeys with my wheelbarrow I passed the other men in the working party, who would say, "All right, Dennis?" or, "Take it easy, Dennis," and I would say, "All right, Jimmy," or whatever. With the leaves and the boulders cleared I set to work cutting the weeds down, and when this was done I grubbed out the roots with a mattock. It was on the third or fourth afternoon, having dumped a load of weeds and roots on the compost, and while wheeling my empty barrow back along the path toward the shed, that I saw a small figure in a black coat and headscarf at the top of the steps, her back toward me; no sooner had I seen her than she slipped down the steps.

I stopped dead in my tracks and dropped the handles of the wheelbarrow. I had not been expecting to see her, not after so long, not after being disappointed so often. I ran past the shed to the top of the steps and gazed down at the tea garden. It was deep in shadow, for it was after five by this time and the sun was low in the sky. I stood at the top of the steps—to either side of me a squat brick post with a stone ball on top—and raked the area with my eyes. There!—by the tangled pile of branches and lumber in the far corner— surely I saw for an instant a figure slipping through the gloom! I came quickly down the steps, and then I was running across the field; reaching the wall I peered up the wooded slope that climbed to the higher terraces. Did I see her? I clambered up the slope, twigs and dead branches snapping beneath my boots. Halfway up I stopped and gazed wildly about me: a profound silence hung there in the trees, and it was too dark now to distinguish anything clearly. For several minutes I stood there, making no sound or movement; then I crunched back down to the field, which looked more desolate than ever as darkness rapidly came on. My immediate excitement sub- sided somewhat, and was replaced by a vague thrilling of anticipation, a sense that something momentous had just been set in motion. I went back across the field and back up the steps, gathering my tools on the way, and put them back in the shed before returning to Block F with the rest of the men.

Ah, she tormented me, like they torment me. Listen to them now! Surely I must be damned and twisting in hell to endure this, surely I must be dead already, dead and gone, and this wrapped corpse of mine animated merely by some odd freak gust of ghoul's breath, to endure this! And yes, she tormented me: in the months and years that followed, on countless occasions I caught glimpses as fleeting, as tantalizing, as the one I've described—that small slim figure in coat and headscarf, clutching her handbag and standing, say, in the dappled shade of the elm tree by the wall, on a summer afternoon, her head turned away, and me on my knees in a bed of cabbages or lettuce or spring onions, and I would drop my trowel, rise to my feet, and a moment later be leaping the rows of vegetables (thinking always, in my madness, *this* time, *this* time)—and finding only a mocking play of light and shadow as sunshine sifted through the canopy of leaves overhead. There was one summer, I remember, when her presence was especially vivid, when I would see her almost daily, and I even heard her say my name as I worked alone in the gardens, heard her whisper: "Spider! Spider!"—and I whirled around to nothing, nobody, silence. But late that summer—it must have been September, we'd had one of the best summers in living memory, and Ganderhill was so rich in fresh vegetables we were selling them to neighboring villages—late that summer there was a string of afternoons when I'd gaze south from the terrace and the sky was transformed: a bluish golden light of extraordinary intensity, a great broad strip of radiance centered on a point due south of my own precise position, was spread across the sky, filling somewhere between a sixth and a quarter of it from the horizon up as high as the eye could see—and I understood something, then, in my wonder at the sheer splendor and magnificence of the spectacle, of the nature of my mother's presence in Ganderhill. Sad thing, though, that later in the year, in the late autumn and winter, when she stayed among the shadows and only came at dusk, I lost the insight, and felt again frustration and at times angry impatience that she could go on teasing and tormenting me like this. Yet I would rather have had her phantom presence than nothing.

These then I call the good years, Spider at peace. In the evenings I played billiards with Derek Shadwell, and later (Derek died in Ganderhill) with Frank Tremble. I read the paperbacks that passed from hand to hand in Block F, very occasionally a newspaper, almost never did I listen to the wireless (large events were unfolding, apparently, during the early years, but I wanted no part of them). I held my mother's presence close, in the back parts where I'd always held her, and mentioned her to no one, not even Derek when he was alive. I became a good gardener, and fresh vegetables being generally a scarce and valued commodity in Ganderhill my access to these goods contributed much to my status in the institution. Dr. Austin Marshall maintained an affable warmth toward me and almost always remembered my name when he came limping across the terraces with his cane. Often he had his dogs with him, a pair of large glossy-coated Irish setters toward which I displayed an affection I did not feel; I used to think with some pleasure of what John Giles would do to those dogs after he'd finished with the superintendent.

(See me out on the landing now, both hands gripping the handle of the door to the attic stairs, shaking it and weeping brokenly as their laughter shrieks and howls about my ears, useless of course, it's locked of course, so see me shuffle back to my table where I sink, stiffly crackling, onto my chair and reach for the tobacco to roll myself a fat one, I need it. It ebbs now as with trembling fingers I light my cigarette and get a good harsh mouthful down, feel it sucking down the pipe, pushing down the terror, emerging in thick cloudy coils and whorls into my one remaining lung where a worm lies dozing in the lower part, the segments of its plump white body heaped atop each other in a circular formation. Smoke rapidly fills the sac, is absorbed by grayish spongy tissue, enters the system of lacelike filaments that trace their forking circuits (still!) across the pulpy inside surface of my rind, and so to skull and brain. Nothing looks so bleak after a smoke.)

Every afternoon at about four o'clock we would gather in the shed for a cup of tea, the half-dozen of us who worked in the vegetable gardens, with Fred Sims, our attendant. Sims was a quiet fellow who could be relied on to give us news. I remember the day he told us that the superintendent was retiring. Rain was pattering on the roof of the shed, we were inside on wooden boxes, us in our yellow corduroys, him in his black uniform and peaked cap, and the door was open. There was an uneasy shuffling at this piece of information; men in our position did not welcome change. "Retiring?" said Frank Tremble. "What, Dr. Austin Marshall?"

Sims nodded, his eyes on the floor as he removed a shred of tobacco from the tip of his tongue. More shuffling. "Why's that then, Fred?"

He lifted his eyebrows and shrugged. "Too old, they want a younger man."

"Younger man, eh."

He took off his cap and scratched his head. He was very thin on top. "Seems they've picked him already," he said.

"Who is he, Fred?"

"It's a Dr. Jebb, from London."

"Jebb," said Frank.

"Never heard of him," said Jimmy. "What's he like then?"

"He's got new ideas," said Sims.

A very uneasy silence at this point, a good bit more shuffling of boots on floorboards. Around us in the gloom tools hung from nails in the walls, spades, rakes, forks, mattocks, hoes, trowels, shears. On the floor, battered watering cans, piles of flowerpots, stacks of wooden boxes. Shelves with bundles of markers held together by rubber bands, flats for seedlings, coiled hoses, balls of twine, knives, pencils, spoons, scissors, bales of netting, old newspapers. Strong smell of earth and dampness. Outside, a steady downpour of rain. "New ideas," said Jimmy. "Looks like you're out of a job then, Fred." We had a good laugh about that, but even so there was planted in all of us, that afternoon, the seeds of anxiety, for none of us wanted change, not Frank, not Jimmy, not Sims, not me.

(Derek, of course, didn't live to see the changes that came with Dr. Jebb, and he was fortunate not to. I remember him once telling me that every time he smoked a cigarette his mother had to sleep with a sailor. Poor old Derek, his mother was dead, though of course I didn't say this to him. We were playing billiards at the time, and the worst of it was, he said, shooting a cannon and sinking the red ball, he was smoking more than ever! I think it might have been this that finally drove him to it.)

AFTER the summer of splendid light, as I came to think of it, my mother's phantom presence in Ganderhill became increasingly rare. That summer was the peak, the acme, in this regard, and there was even a period—a few days, no more—when the weather came under the control of my own thoughts and actions. Those were exhilarating days, but the effort involved in maintaining splendid light proved in the end too much for me, so I slowly allowed it to slip away. After that, as I say, her appearances became more fleeting and irregular, and in the last years I barely glimpsed her more than three or four times, and always at dusk, in the vicinity of the old tea garden, now planted with beds of cabbages, spring onions and potatoes, with a line of cucumber frames along the south side.

One day Sims told us that Dr. Austin Marshall had cleared out his office and left. There was a farewell banquet in the staff social club, where he was presented with a handsome wheelchair specially constructed in the Ganderhill workshop, for apparently his bad leg was now making it impossible for him to get around. There were speeches, and everyone was very moved. There was talk of a knighthood in the New Year's Honors List.

After this, a breathless pause, so it seemed, in Ganderhill, as we awaited developments. The news Sims told us was alternately alarming and reassuring. Jebb reportedly intended to hire more psychiatrists. On the other hand, he generously increased the tobacco allowance. Sims' attitude toward the new superintendent was cagey and watchful, and so was mine.

I was called to his office one morning at the end of June. I'd seen the man on the terraces, though only from a distance; not for him the tweeds, the dogs, the genial affability of his predecessor. No, Jebb stormed along in a turbulent cloud of purpose and vigor, which only served to deepen my foreboding; he wore a dark suit. I sat outside his office on a hard chair in the corridor, soil under my fingernails and clad in my yellow corduroys: I'd come straight from the vegetable gardens. I sat there for thirty minutes, not smoking, and finally the door opened and a group of senior attendants came shuffling out, looking grim. Dr. Jebb then peered at me from the doorway. "I won't keep you a minute," he said, and went back in, closing the door. Fifteen minutes later he called me in.

The first shock: he told me to sit down, frowned at my file, lifted his head, took off his spectacles—and I was staring straight into eyes the same cold shade of blue as my father's! I shrank back in my chair (a hard wooden one). He had the same hair as my father, black, lank, and oily, combed straight back off a narrow forehead and flopping about his temples: he frequently pushed a hand through it when he frowned. The same narrow nose, the same pencil-thin mustache neatly hedging the top lip, the same wiry build and tone of pent explosive energy: what jest was this? "You've been in Ganderhill," he said, without preamble, and I was relieved to discover that his voice, at least, was his own, "how long?"

I shuffled on my chair and cleared my throat. All I could seem to manage was a sort of helpless croaking sound. He frowned at me. "Almost twenty years, Mr. Cleg. You were very disturbed on admittance"—here he replaced his spectacles and read from the file—" 'negativistic . . . withdrawn . . . uncooperative . . . aggressive.' You settled down fairly quickly, however, you formed friendships, became a steady worker, and for the last ten years you've held a position of trust in the vegetable gardens, a trust you haven't abused." He took off his spectacles again and glared at me with those familiar glacial eyes. "How would you like to try life on the outside?"

This was what I'd dreaded. Even so, I had no response prepared. I stirred uneasily, I looked out of the windows, I looked at the walls: happily the naval battles were gone. "Well?" said Dr. Jebb, tapping on his desk with the point of a pencil: tap tap tap tap tap.

Still I said nothing, still I squirmed there in perplexity and dismay. "Mr. Cleg," he said, rubbing his eyes with the thumb and forefinger of his left hand, "let me see if I can guess what you're thinking. On the one hand"—he stopped rubbing, lifted his eyes to the ceiling, formed a steeple with his fingers and rested his chin on the peak—"on the one hand you're anxious about leaving Ganderhill. You have friends here, a routine, work"—he began counting my blessings on his fingers—"a certain"—here he lifted his eyebrows, communicated irony—"seniority in the patient community, and a deep familiarity with the workings of the hospital." (Hospital now, was it?) "To leave all this—to enter an unknown world— this is threatening, you sense the difficulties, the dangers that lie ahead—and you're right, of course, there will be difficulties, your trepidation is perfectly understandable." He laid his hands flat on his desk and glared at me with understanding. My own hands were behaving very strangely by this point, they appeared to be twisting round, rotating on their wrists, turning back to front: I pressed them between my thighs and clutched my sock for comfort. "On the other hand," said Dr. Jebb, "you imagine what life must be like outside Ganderhill—without locked doors and high walls. You imagine how it must be to drink a glass of beer in the evening, meet women. The prospect goes some way to overcoming your apprehensions." (Drink beer? Meet *women?*) "It is, I agree, a dilemma, please don't think I'm unaware of this."

Some response, clearly, was expected of me, but I could not speak without smoking, and I could not smoke without speaking. After an uncomfortable few moments he resumed. "Mr. Cleg, let me see if I can sum up your career here. When you first came to Ganderhill you were a very sick boy; in fact you were displaying most of the classic symptoms of schizophrenia. You were hallucinating floridly in the visual, auditory and olfactory spheres; your affective reactions were bizarrely inappropriate; you suffered marked body delusions, you were regressed, you had ideas of persecution and thought injection." He glanced at the file. "You were aggressive on the ward and frequently had to be isolated in a safe room, in restraints. You showed no awareness of your environment, nor any awareness of why you'd been brought to Ganderhill in the first place. My point is," he said, closing the file, "that all that has changed."

"Changed," I murmured.

"Changed," he said. "You have for the past ten years assumed a steadily increasing measure of responsibility for your own life. The hospital milieu has imposed demands on you, Mr. Cleg, demands relating to grooming, punctuality, competence, sociability, and cooperation; these demands you have met. Your therapy has been implicit in your daily round of tasks and contacts: there's no more we can do for you."

"No more," I said faintly.

"I need your bed, Mr. Cleg."

My *bed!*

"Ganderhill is overcrowded, and I find you are well enough to leave us. Is there any reason why I shouldn't discharge you to community care?"

"Yes!" I suddenly cried, without at all meaning to; shocked at my own temerity I fell silent.

"And that is?"

Silence.

"That is, Mr. Cleg?"

Nothing.

"Mr. Cleg, I wonder if you trust your own ability to function adequately in society. Is this the problem?"

Still nothing.

"I think perhaps it's time we talked about your mother."

"She's none of your business!" I shouted.

"Ah. So that's it. None of my business." He took off his spectacles; a small smile played about his thin bloodless lips, a smile I knew well from my boyhood, a smile that augured no good for me. "Mr. Cleg," he said, suddenly serious and stern, "I am your responsible medical officer. *None of your business is none of my business.*"

By the time I got back to the vegetable gardens the men were coming in for lunch, so I came back in with them. I was silent and morose in the dining hall, and they left me to myself. At about half past two in the afternoon I abandoned what I was doing (tending a bonfire of garden rubbish) and made my way up to the shed. I closed the door behind me, sat on a box, and with the knife we used for cutting the eyes out of potatoes for seeding I opened my wrists. Twenty minutes later Fred Sims found me there with my blood dripping into a flowerpot full of earth. They stitched me up in the infirmary, and by suppertime I was in a safe room on a hard-bench ward, wearing an untearable canvas gown and being very closely watched.

I SCRIBBLED on through the long slow hours of the night. I smoked thin ones almost continuously, lighting each from the butt of the one before. The worm in my lung did not waken, I believe as a result of the smoking. Sporadic outbursts from the attic, nothing I hadn't endured before. I was very attentive to sensations from the empty space in my torso, for I now had reason to think it infested with spiders. I pictured webby constructions glistening in the darkness, damp silk traplines flung from breastbone to backbone, pelvis to rib. Scuttling creatures, weaving and spinning inside me— to what end? For six days I was on hard-bench, and after my ten years in Block F the shock was a rude one.

It all came back to me. Doorless lavatories, the humiliation of being always visible, always accessible to hostile eyes. And the smells! Coarse bleach, most vividly, those chipped tile floors were mopped two, three, four times a day with boiling water and coarse bleach: there always seemed to be someone working his way up the corridor, or back and forth across the dayroom, with an old institution mop, its head a floppy tangle of gray hemp, and a tin bucket with a metal attachment on the inside lip and a handle that you depressed to make the teeth of the thing come together on your mophead and squeeze out the filthy water. I had forgotten too the daily humiliation of having to ask for the smallest quantities of the most basic suplies: a few sheets of toilet paper, a pinch of tobacco, a drop of hot water. Perhaps the request would be granted; but more usually you stood there shifting your weight from foot to foot as the attendant frowned with annoyance and told you to come back later—that, or he subjected you to a glance of cold appraisal, permitted a dead pause to occur, then ignored you—all for three hard sheets of toilet paper, for a few coarse strands of pale tobacco from the tin! Oh, civility is wasted on a lunatic, this was the message chiseled into the cold brick heart of Ganderhill, wasted on a lunatic on a hard-bench ward.

Six days I was on hard bench, and then one morning they brought me down to the end of the ward to see Dr. Jebb. He showed me into the side room and we sat down. Green walls, a barred window, a light bulb, a table, two wooden chairs—nothing else. A tin ashtray in the middle of the table. I was in gray shirt and trousers, and laceless shoes. He was in his black suit, and wearing a tie that immediately riveted my attention, for this tie, dark green, had no design but a single crest, in which the dominant figure, a shield flanked by a pair of dragons and surmounted by a sort of winged helmet, displayed a snake coiled around a staff. At the time I had no way of grasping the full meaning of Jebb's crest; only later was I able to interpret it in terms of the changes occurring inside my body, and my death. Nonetheless it provoked a sensation of unease in me. "Please smoke," he said. Silence, then, for some minutes as with trembling fingers I rolled myself a thin one, and he removed his spectacles and produced that familiar rubbing of the eyes with thumb and forefinger—how often had I seen that same gesture, that same weary impatience, in the kitchen of number twenty-seven! Then, with a small dismissive wave of the fingers at my bandaged wrists: "Quite unnecessary, Mr. Cleg, and very melodramatic. I'm disappointed in you."

I was not strong. I had been on hard bench for a week, I had been thoroughly humiliated, I had nothing I could call my own, no shoelaces, no belt, not even a sock down my trousers. I was in no condition to hold off this cold-eyed creature, this copy of my father—this Cleg-Jebb!—or whatever he was. Silence was my only weapon, the retreat of the Spider into the back parts, down some hole, and this I attempted as the voice rose and fell, boomed and hissed, and "Jebb" shrank away, became tiny, and vast distances opened up in that green-walled bleach-stinking room. But after a moment or two—panic. Long years in Block F, long years being my own man in the vegetable gardens—something had atrophied, and struggle as I might I could not escape the tiny booming figure on the far side of the vast table. It grew dark in the room, the familiar nightmare was upon me, and I was stiff and heavy and pinned, squirming, in the front of my brain, unable to escape the boom and hiss, the eyes, the hands, of this Cleg-Jebb creature across the table. "A cry for help," he boomed, "sheer panic," he boomed, "the necessity of facing up," he hissed, as I squirmed, not the Spider anymore, *he* was the Spider and I the fly! "Escape responsibility for the accident," he hissed, "you killed your mother," he boomed, and I rose wildly to my feet and pointed a trembling finger at him. "You did!" I shouted. "Not me, *you!*"

The door opening—attendants—smartly down to a safe room and only then, only then did the Spider at last regain the old nimbleness, and down a hole he scuttled and left me rocking back and forth in the corner.

Three more months I spent in Ganderhill, one on hard bench, two back in Block F. There were more interviews with the superintendent, in the course of which he reconstructed my "history." Then, one cool and misty morning at the beginning of October, he discharged me. See me standing in front of the main gates, under the clock, in a shabby gray suit, and clutching a cardboard suitcase with very little in it; see me turn my head from side to side, imagine my dismay. In my pocket three pound notes, some coppers, and a scrap of paper with Mrs. Wilkinson's address written on it.

CLEG-JEBB had reconstructed my history, but he had reconstructed it wrong wrong wrong, it was bad history. If he knew anything of my father's plan to send me to Canada he did not indicate it; if he understood my terror at the prospect, if in other words he'd learned the truth about what really happened to my mother—he didn't indicate this either. It was not hard to imagine what would come next: I'd be lured down the allotments some foggy night, and there, fortified by drink and Hilda, my father would batter me senseless with a gardening tool. He would dig another hole (again displaying that weirdly incongruous solicitude for his potato plants) and then, still under the approving gaze of Hilda, he'd dump me in and cover me up, and without the benefit of even a winding sheet I would soon become a meal for the maggots, the beetles, the flesh-worms, leaving nothing behind me but a heap of long bones, detached and uncoupled and growing more so with every shift of the earth until my brittle frame lost what little coherence and integrity it may once tenuously have possessed in life and was scattered widely in London soil! Then, down at the Dog and Beggar, when the men said, "Where's that boy of yours, Horace?" or, "Where's young Dennis?" my father would say, with his twitchy little smile, perhaps wiping the beer froth off his lip: "He's joined his mother in Canada"—and Hilda would be unable to suppress a hoarse belch of unlovely laughter, and that would be my epitaph.

I sat in my bedroom and heard them murmuring in the kitchen below. Then the scrape of chair legs, Hilda came upstairs briefly, and a few minutes later they left by the back door. I came downstairs and went out after them. I saw them go down the alley, arm in arm, and turn right at the end, off to the Rochester. Back upstairs then, where I took out from under my bed a stolen ball of brown string. I cut a length and tied one end to the leg of my bed. The other end I let out through the window, and it landed in a tangled coil in the yard outside the back door. Then downstairs again, and I brought the string in through the kitchen window (opened half an inch) and tied it to one of the knobs on the gas stove. Back upstairs, and sitting by my open window I reeled in the string till it was taut between my fingers. At this point I began gently to tug it; you can guess my purpose.

I was upstairs and downstairs for the next half hour, adjusting the string, trying to make it work. The string would tighten but the knob on the gas stove wouldn't turn, and if I pulled harder it frayed where it rubbed against the bottom of the window. I began to think of some sort of mechanism that would make it run smoothly, some sort of spool mounted on a spindle or bobbin, but how to attach such a thing inconspicuously to the kitchen window? Then I heard the ring of hobnails in the alley, and raised voices, so I untied the string from the knob, ran upstairs and hauled in my line. Into the yard they came, Horace and Hilda and Harold and Glad, arm in arm and much the worse for drink—Hilda roaring with laughter at her own unsteadiness as she broke free of my father (who was the soberer of the two) and went crashing into the outhouse, where I heard her shouting and banging against the door, trying to light the candle. The others came in and the kitchen light was turned on, then Hilda emerged, still pulling her skirt down, and even before she reached the back door she was loudly expressing her astonishment that she should live with a plumber unable to fix his own toilet. It was a proper disgrace (she didn't mind telling us) and by this time Gladys was shrieking in the kitchen, and then I heard Hilda say: "Come on, Glad, 'ave something, it'll do you good." I closed my door and returned to the window, and tried to block out their noise. When at last Harold and Glad went off I listened carefully by my door: Hilda came up first, my father close behind her; he would not pass out in his chair by the stove tonight.

The days that followed were filled with strangeness and terror. I couldn't stay in the house, and when I got outside my steps would seem always to lead me, and against my conscious will, down to the allotments, down to my father's vegetable garden—despite the fact that I knew he intended to kill me there. On very cold days I broke into the shed, where I lit candles and wrapped myself in potato sacks for warmth. Once, at dusk, I caught a glimpse of my mother by the remains of the compost heap; but when I ran over she disappeared. Another time I saw from the railway bridge that the shed was on fire, a furious, glorious blaze against the stillness and gloom of the afternoon; but the closer I approached the dimmer it became, and by the time I reached the gate the shed was as it always was. Frequently I lay on the frosty soil in order to feel my mother reaching up to me; often I was disappointed, but several times she called me to join her: this tore me sorely, the love and terror rising in my heart in equal measure, with equal passion, so it felt.

At other times I went down the cellar and sat in the corner smelling the coal and watching the black germs dance in the few shafts of daylight that penetrated the hatches in the pavement above. It was cold down there, down in the hold, so I'd cloak my head and shoulders in a piece of dirty sacking like a monk's cowl and pull my knees up to my chest and wrap my arms around them; I'd shiver and blow cold breath at the shafts of light and see the little germs, the imps, go spinning and swirling wildly round and round, and this made me laugh. One afternoon I sat very still and very quiet and a rat came creeping out and scurried along the wall in short runs, pausing every few feet to twitch its snout. After that I took the cheese out of the traps and scattered it in little pieces across the floor; then I could watch several of them at once. I loved their tails, how long and plump and *pale* they were, and furred with a down of light bristle as they twitched about behind them like wormy ropes on the deck of a ship. Hilda heard me laughing down there once and the door opened, light spilled in from above. "What you doing down there?" she cried. Sitting in my corner, in my cowl, in the shadows, I said nothing; she came down a little way in that queer sideways manner she had of descending stairs and then she saw the rats. A cry of horror, back up she went, and the door slammed shut behind her! More laughter from the shadows. When my father came home from work she had him go down and set the traps. The next day there were two dead rats, I put them in my pocket, I reset the traps myself, I liked them just as well dead as alive. Once when I was down there in the corner I heard a voice say: "Spider!" It wasn't my mother's voice, it was a cracked and growly voice, like an old woman's voice, and I realized it was the night-hag who lived in my wall. I didn't go down the cellar after that.

I took to hanging about under the bridge by the canal, where it was dark. There was much in the visual world by this point that caused me terrible anxiety—I constantly had the sensation that some awful catastrophe was about to occur, and this feeling became at times so overpowering that I sank to the ground against the wall beneath the bridge and covered my eyes and ears with my arms. It was the fear I had of my father sending me to join my mother in Canada, it was the fear of being attacked with a gardening tool at the moment I least expected it. I attempted not to let them know what I knew but I could not sleep in number twenty-seven anymore, and I barely ate a thing, why would I? Why would I touch meat or vegetables prepared by Hilda? Their faces were changing now: I could see them eating, their jaws moving, their eyes shining in the kitchen's gloom, their teeth closing on pieces of food, but each feature was fixed in space separate and distinct from the rest, and it was only by combining fragments of their broken-up faces and hands that I could keep them in focus and remain alert to their activity. They soon lost whatever veneer or crust of humanity they may once have had, and in their broken-up aspect they showed their true nature, their deadness and animality, and when I saw this the sensation of impending disaster almost over-whelmed me and I fled the kitchen in terror, heedless of their cries and squeals of frustrated hunger, for they planned to eat me, I'd realized, they planned to eat me up.

At night I grew calmer, partly as a function of darkness and partly because they were so often out of the house. Some-times I followed them when they went to the Rochester, I watched them through the windows while they were at their drink, and when Hilda went to the Ladies I climbed on a barrel to see her pee. Other nights I stayed in the house and experimented with lengths of string dangled from my win-dow down to the knob on the gas stove. Once when I was twitching the string and trying to get the knob to turn I felt my mouth fill up with small birds, which I crunched between my teeth, and then their feathers and blood and broken bones started to choke me, and I retched and retched but nothing came up. Another time I found a bottle of milk by the canal and in it was the putrefying corpse of a man my father had murdered the night before, and I opened the bottle and drank the milk. Another time I found a baby with a hole in the top of its head, and through the hole I sucked up and swallowed everything in the baby's head until its face collapsed like an empty rubber mask. Later I remembered that this was how spiders devoured insects. That night I accidentally fell asleep and my father came in and compressed my skull with a plumber's wrench, and when I woke up my head was pear-shaped; this was so that it would fit the sack they'd prepared for me to be murdered in.

They grew hungrier and hungrier as the days passed, and I knew it would soon be time. When Hilda looked at me saliva dribbled from her mouth and ran down her primitive chin. My father was more furtive in his display of appetite, he watched me always from the corners of his eyes. His hands I noticed looked like paws now. Deadness and animality: I had no name for creatures like this, I still don't despite the fact that one of them at this moment lies sleeping on the other side of the house, secure in the knowledge that her creatures in the attic (despite their occasional treachery) will preserve her from harm. Listen to them!

Listen to them. There is a rhythm to their activity, three distinct waves, each one rising and falling, each one separated from the last by a lull or hiatus during which I experience both relief and the torment of anticipating the next (the anticipation as intense as the wave itself). Each begins at the level of highest vehemence of the one preceding, so there is a massive increment of scale in volume and frenzy from the early part of the night to the later. And what is it that they do? Impossible to be precise: there is chanting and stamping, also hissing, screaming, cries and shouts that are only partially intelligible, gales of laughter, voices of people I have known saying wildly uncharacteristic things: Dr. Austin Marshall reciting filthy verses for example. They use my name freely, they play on it, they invert it: gelc, they call me, gelc, and recently they invented the chant: gelc SINNED gelc sinned gelc sinned gelc sinned gelc SINNED gelc sinned gelc sinned gelc sinned . . . They repeat it over and over, louder and louder, stamping all the while so the light bulb swings back and forth on its cord and I am plunged into shadow, then brought to lurid life, plunged into shadow, then back to lurid light—and I huddle on my chair with my legs drawn up to my chest and my head between my knees and my hands over my ears weeping weeping weeping as they push me to the very limits of what I can endure—then it breaks apart in screechy laughter—this gradually subsides, is followed by mumbling—and slowly I lift my head and catch trembling hold of the side of the table, perhaps pick up my pencil or roll a quick one while they gather themselves for the next— which *begins,* as I say, at the pitch of fiercest frenzy of the last!

Three waves, followed by exhaustion. Finally I rise from my chair and stand gazing out the window, gazing east to catch the first faint hint of dawn, and again I tell myself: no more. I wander through the sleeping house, past doors behind which dead souls dream, I patter down the stairs and into the kitchen, out into the hallway again, glance in Mrs. Wilkinson's office—and it is then that I see them: on top of her desk, splayed there in the gloom, her house keys. *Her house keys.* A quiet cry of joy inside your old Spider as he silently crosses the room and in one smooth swooping movement pockets the bunch. Then off, in long spidery strides, back up the stairs, back to his room, unseen, unheard, unbound.

WITH my cardboard suitcase in my hand, and my three pound notes in my pocket, I turned for a last look at the gates of Ganderhill. Flanked by a pair of square towers, they were fifteen feet high and came to a sharp arch above which hung a huge clock that read one minute past ten. It was a fine clear morning, and the autumn sun was mellow on the bricks. A small door was set into the left-hand gate, and it was through this door that I had emerged. Mr. Thomas stood in the doorway; he was a senior attendant now, and had seen to the details of my discharge; he had also slipped me a couple of packets of Capstan Full Strength. He lifted his hand, I lifted mine; he stepped back in, and the door closed.

Somehow I found my way into the village and boarded the correct bus. I sat by a window and smoked; I gazed at the countryside as we rumbled toward London, attempting to control strong surges of bewilderment and loss that at times almost overwhelmed me. I felt, in a way, as I had after my mother's death—the same sense of friendless isolation in a strange and threatening world. Twenty years in Ganderhill, how well I knew the place! Its courtyards and passageways, its gardens and outhouses—imbued, all of it, with the fleeting whisper of her presence, as she showed herself shyly to me, now and then, in the dappled shade of an elm tree, on a lonely terrace at dusk. And oh, the rhythms and rituals that governed the life there—in all of this I had a place, and was seen to have a place. As I sat there on that slow bus to London, among the housewives with their shopping bags, I knew with utter certainty that I could hope for no better than that, not me, not the old Spider; and now it was gone for good, for Jebb would never have me back, he'd made that clear enough. There was an ominous cast to my thoughts now, for I felt the first dim stirrings of approaching disaster—out there on the far horizon something large and black and dreadful was moving toward me. For what had I to give this world into which I'd been so abruptly thrust, and what had it for me?

Then we were on the main road and going at some speed. I tried to see what lay ahead, but could not, I could not imagine the way of life I was now to pursue. How would I live? Who would I be? Dennis Cleg, from Ganderhill? The lunatic? Oh surely not that—I could imagine, at least, the effect of that, the cold eyes, the sneers, the whispering contempt—the *thought patterns,* in short. Suddenly I saw myself hurtling into a void, and for a few minutes I became uncoupled with terror and froze rigid in my seat with my cigarette halfway to my lips. Immediately I felt the eyes of the women on me, their heads inclining toward one another, the murmuring, the stifled laughter, the muffled snorts of scorn. It passed off soon enough thank God, and with an effort I stayed calm. Later I began to see streets and buildings and I knew we were on the outskirts of the city, and this gave me some small comfort; I *am* the Spider of London, after all! Over the river by Westminster Bridge, the Thames alive with light, sparkling green in the autumn sunshine, and the sight of it did me good. A little familiarity, that's all, a little of what you know, this buttresses a soul, gives strength. I pulled out the slip of paper with Mrs. Wilkinson's address on it: I knew the place, I'd often been over that way as a boy. It was in the East End, you see.

A bit of trouble with the crowds at first—the eyes! the thought patterns! The air was thick with them, and again I became uncoupled, I stood in the middle of Victoria Coach Station gripping my suitcase and frozen like a statue. But this

was London, after all, and I knew London, and soon I was
shuffling off to look for a number twenty-seven bus, or was
it a thirty-seven, or a hundred and thirty-seven?

In the late afternoon I fetched up at Mrs. Wilkinson's door
I'd got lost several times, for the city had changed in ways I
couldn't understand. I knocked; she opened the door. "Mr.
Cleg?" she said. "We've been expecting you." I shuffled in,
exhausted and confused and very close to tears, and not for
one moment did I realize who she was. It's only now that I
can appreciate the implications of those first words of hers.
"We've been expecting you," she might have said, "so we
can finish the job we started in Kitchener Street, twenty years
ago."

I WRAPPED my limbs with fresh newspaper, I found clean socks in the chest of drawers and threw the old ones into the hole behind the gas fire. Then flat on my back on my bed, hands behind my head, legs crossed at the ankles, to watch cigarette smoke curling and coiling beneath the ceiling. Down my trousers, between my thighs, in my sock, the thick solid pressure of her house keys. They are bound together with a stout rubber band to keep them from clanking against each other and so betraying their presence.

The bell at last, and I am up off my bed and smartly down the stairs even as the first of the dead souls emerge blinking from their holes. All as usual in the kitchen—the mustached one dripping ash into her saucepans, the tarpaulin on the table freshly wiped and smelling of bleach, the hissy bubble of porridge as steam rises from the pot and mingles with cigarette smoke in the glare of wintry sunshine at the window over the sink. Dead souls shuffle in, I drink tea, no milk, much sugar. I do not eat now, my intestines coiled about my backbone as they are, but I do drink tea, it flushes out the spiders.

Then Hilda is filling the doorway, glowering from a great height and asking have we seen her house keys? A spasm of guilty excitement down there where the weighted sock sprawls between my wrapped thighs. Oh she is frowning, oh magnificent terror, oh the fury, oh to imagine surrendering and with delicious shame extracting my sock and handing it over with trembling fingers and averted eyes, cheeks burning, and *craving* punishment, begging for humiliation, abasement, pain! But I hold my peace, I gaze (foxlike!) with blank eyes and open mouth, shake my slow head as her gimlet eyes wheel round to me, burn into my soul, but the truth of it is there *is* no soul, only spiders now, only spiders! Then frowning like thunder she is gone, and I drink more tea, touch my sock, roll a fat one, conceal my glee.

Then out, out into the sharp clear air, but not without a final encounter by the front door, not without her asking me was I *sure* I knew nothing of her house keys? Blank mute useless shrugging from the wily Spider, whose whole secret presence is down in his sock while the face above registers only dumb bewildered ignorance.

I walk quickly at first, quickly for me, past the park, where the crows flap in the bare branches, past the padlocked church-yard, then sharp left and down along the railway viaduct (glimpses of the gasworks through the arches), and then, with steadily slackening pace, to the canal. Greeny-black in the morning light, sudden bursts of sparkling diamonds on the water, wintry sunshine—and there's my mother on the hump-backed bridge with her back to me, and I stop dead, become uncoupled, stare with astonishment, with giddy elation, at the clarity of her form against the light. With her face still obscured by the headscarf she crosses over and is lost behind a wall on the other side, on the Kitchener Street side.

And now at last I move down the path to the bridge, and for the first time in twenty years I clasp the iron railing, feel how cold it is, and shuffle forward. Oh, terror now! Oh with that first shuffling footstep a chaos of turbulence and a roiling of fluids inside me, and voices start up, cackles of incredulous laughter, groans of dread, but in spite of it all I cross the bridge; groping blindly forward with both hands on the rail-ing, I do cross the bridge.

And now I am shuffling along streets both familiar and strange, oddly empty, oddly desolate somehow. I come upon a man with a horse. They are standing down the end of a dead-end street under a high brick wall. The man is wearing a white shirt with the sleeves rolled up; the horse wears only a bridle. I stand at the other end and watch as the man takes the hanging reins and, half-turned toward the horse, leads it slowly down the middle of the street. He begins to run, shouting at the horse now, which lifts high its hooves, the iron shoes ringing on the cold cobblestones, and pulls back its lips from its teeth as the long head comes up and utters a loud whinny. They come toward me up the empty street, the half-turned running man in white shirtsleeves, and the high-stepping horse, tossing its head; clouds billow as their breath turns to mist in the cold air. The man slows the horse as they approach my end of the street, slows it to a walk, then turns the beast—I gaze at its heaving flanks!—and trots it back to the wall at the other end.

I drift away, looking for my mother. On the corner I see a pub burned out by fire, its white brickwork seared and blackened with smoke and its windows merely black holes, empty of glass, sightless eyes. Over the door, which is boarded up, hangs the sign, but the metal has been warped by heat and the paintwork so badly singed that the name is unreadable. I turn another corner—*and find myself in the shadow of the Spleen Street gasworks.*

Oh Christ the knob on the gas stove the knob the knob the knob on the kitchen stove oh Christ spare me this: a fluted nubbin of some hard material fixed by a recessed screw to a pipe attached to the gas ring. In one of the knobs a screw with its face to the window: a couple of turns with a screw-driver and it protruded enough to let me tie a piece of string to it, and the string I then led not out the window but down to a staple nailed to the floor then across the floor and under the door to a nail I'd hammered into the side of the staircase, just off the floor, then straight up vertically to the top of the stairs. When I pulled it it grew taut from knob to staple, from staple to nail, and from nail up to me; and when I gently

tugged it the knob turned a fraction and gas began seeping
into the kitchen—

Oh I tear my eyes away, I turn my back on the massive
domes, their flaking rust-red paintwork horribly vivid in the
morning sunshine and their crisscross struts and uprights mul-
tiplying endlessly over my head; horror is here, the horror
of reproduction, so with eyes averted I shuffle off. I must go
home, I tell myself, I must go home, I must go home to
Kitchener Street, where my mother is waiting for me by the
back door.

Now the streets are achingly familiar and memories rise in
clusters from the deep forgotten recesses of my mind and I
become uncoupled for minutes on end and have to lean against
a wall and with fumbling fingers try and roll one, and the
worm in my lung seems to be stirring. A woman with a
string bag bulging with parcels wrapped in brown paper and
tied with string stands in front of me and asks me am I feeling
poorly? I push myself off the wall and lurch away. I must go
home to my mother! Then I am coming down Victory Street
and not this corner, not the next, but the one after is Kitchener
Street. Listen to them now! What a filthy racket! But on he
comes, the game old Spider, flannels flapping on newspaper
limbs, thirty yards, fifteen—oh a great pounding in my chest
now, the worm awakens, and then I am at the corner, and
turning the corner, and gazing at—

Nothing. A fence of corrugated tin. What is happening to
me? Through a gap in the fence I see a cratered wasteground.
It is strewn with heaps of brick and rubble, and weeds with
purple flowers, and here and there lengths of black rubber
piping, rusty tin cans, old shoes, car tires. What is happening
to me? Gales of laughter, a barking dog. Is this my doing?

B A C K at my table now. Badly shaken by what I saw this morning, very fragile, very brittle. I had plunged down the street in wild panic, reeling from lamppost to lamppost like a drunkard until I reached where number twenty-seven ought to be. A hole in the fence: I'd pressed my eye to it and found another hole, a shallow pit littered with chunks of brick, slate, lumber, rubbish, the same purple-flowered weeds bristling in the breeze; and a voice had said: this is your doing.

And then, as I leaned against the fence, helpless and weeping, a smell had come, and then a memory, dislodged from the underside of some deep flap of my mind: I saw myself sitting at the window of my room above the kitchen, watching Horace and Hilda leave for the pub. Then I saw myself walking slowly down the stairs, along the passage, and into the kitchen. I saw myself attach my trapline: I tied one end of the string to the screw on the knob of the gas stove, then led it carefully through the staple and under the door and out into the passage to the nail in the side of the staircase. From halfway up the stairs I gently pulled it round the nail and then, climbing to the top of the stairs, I tied it to a banister. Then I went back into my room and waited for their return.

I saw myself again sitting at the window with the light off. I remember there was a sort of buzzing in my ears that drowned all other sounds, so that when Horace and Hilda returned they seemed to be weaving down the yard in utter silence, and in slow motion; their movements were clumsy and uncoordinated, and I had to stuff a blanket in my mouth to stifle the wave of laughter the spectacle provoked in me. Finally they reached the back door and came in; I heard loud voices for some minutes, and then Hilda's slow heavy tread on the stairs, Hilda's *alone*. This produced a silent cry of exultation in the tense young Spider, how hard it was to stifle my laughter then! I waited, for five minutes, ten minutes, twenty-five minutes—twenty-five minutes that felt like twenty-five years! Then I crept silently out of my room: the house was dark and silent, the kitchen door was closed. Barely daring to breathe I sat at the top of the stairs and untied my string from the banister. Gently, oh gently I reeled it in; in my mind's eye I saw it grow taut from knob to staple, from staple to nail, and from nail to me; I held it a long moment, thinking: my string in my fingers, his life in my hands. Then I tugged—it moved—enough. I tied the string to the banister and slipped back into my room.

Sleepless with triumph I sat cross-legged on my bed in the darkness. I rocked with silent laughter. Then slowly, slowly from below, at last there rose to my eager, waiting nostrils the faint but unmistakable smell of gas—

Yes, this was my doing all right. I'd pushed myself off the fence; the panic had subsided and I felt strangely calm (though in all the excitement the worm in my lung had awoken). I noticed then that the even-numbered houses on the other side were intact, though their windows were boarded up; and that there were buildings still standing on this side down the end. I moved on, steadier now, I set my course for the end of the street. There I found three houses: number fifty-three, boarded up; number fifty-five, also boarded up; and the Dog and Beggar. The Dog and Beggar! I leaned against the wall and I laughed, yes, imagine that, imagine your old Spider at this point leaning against a wall with his big chin lifted high and giving out a brief hoarse wheeze of silent laughter. But after a moment or two he pushed himself off the wall, shuffled up to the door of the public bar, and went in.

The door swung shut behind him. Nothing had changed. It was eleven o'clock in the morning and cold sunshine washed in from the window by the door. A small coal fire was burning in the grate, and at the table close by sat an old man with a glass of beer, otherwise the room was empty. The wooden floor, the mirror over the mantelpiece, the brass rail at ankle height under the chipped old bar—nothing had changed here. The smells of the old man's pipe, last night's beer, the crackle of burning coal; on the bar a newspaper folded to the sports page . . . In shuffled the Spider and sank onto a chair near the door. All was still and silent; dust danced in the streaming wintry sunlight and a clock ticked somewhere off behind the bar.

Spider sat as though entranced and listened to the ticking clock, watching the motes of dust. A man appeared behind the bar, polishing a glass on his apron. It was him! It was Ernie Ratcliff! The same thin hands, the same narrow eyes, the same air of weasel cunning, though the hair was sparser now, the bitterness was etched deeper in the lines of the face. He glanced at Spider: "What'll it be?" he said. Spider gazed at the man. Ernie Ratcliff—one of the last people to see his mother alive! "Looking for your old man, Mrs. Cleg? He was here but I believe he's gone." Almost the last friendly words she'd heard, and not so friendly at that, Ratcliff was never what you'd call a friendly man. "What'll it be then?" he repeated, setting down the polished glass and wiping his hands on his apron. Spider shuffled to his feet and dug through his many pockets, unearthing a few coppers, a threepenny bit, some halfpennies. He came to the bar and spilled the coins onto the counter. Ratcliff glanced at them and word-lessly reached for a glass.

Spider sits by the door with a half of mild. Nothing happens. A second old man joins the first, they murmur to one another and then fall silent. Spider examines the pattern on the frosted glass partition; it suggests to him a leafy plant of some kind, the flowering sprout of a root vegetable, a turnip perhaps. Yes, this was his doing, gelc sinned all right. He tries the beer—an immediate hiss of distaste from the lung-worm, a flurry of activity among the spiders. He remembers his mother's story about the spiders in the elm trees, and thinks of his own insides, and the creatures that have hatched there. I am an egg-bag, he thinks, and I should be dangling by a thread from a branch. He sits there in the warmth until half past three, when Ernie Ratcliff kicks him out.

I N the days that followed Spider was often in the Dog
and Beggar. He would wander up and down Kitchener
Street for an hour or so, hoping for a glimpse of his mother,
though at some level he knew from the moment he laid eyes
on that pitful of rubbish where number twenty-seven used
to be that he'd never see her again. So what drew him back?
God knows, perhaps merely to regard the desolation and say
to himself, this is your doing, you did this. After the third
or fourth time he was able to brave it without becoming
hopelessly distressed; a curious calm then, a sense of slowing
down, of a coming to resolution, not unconnected to the
constant reassuring presence of the loaded sock hanging down
his trousers. It was a sad, vague, sleepy calm, more a melancholy, and it was only disturbed by the nightly shrieking
from the attic and the writhing of the lung-worm trapped
inside his body. He moved slowly but with purpose now
within his given compass, and whiled away some hours each
day in the public bar of the Dog. It remained to him only to
settle accounts with Hilda.

Then one afternoon he left the Dog and followed the old
familiar route down to the canal, over the bridge and up the
hill to Omdurman Close, and so to the allotments. By this
time of the afternoon the sun was sinking toward the river
and there was a perceptible thickening of the light. Down the
path he shuffled to his father's gate; the place was deserted.
He entered the allotment and got to his knees in the potato

patch, then stretched out flat on the wintry soil. He lay there motionless for several minutes. There was an odd silence on the allotments, its depth and stillness intensified somehow by the faint and distant barking of a dog. There was silence, too, in the earth, so he scrambled slowly to his feet and made his way round to the back of the shed, where he had a clear view over the wasteground that had once been the Slates, beyond it a sprawl of warehouses and docks, and beyond that the river. The sun by this time had chalked the sky a sort of powdery reddish color that grew deeper and richer even as he watched. Already the river was shimmering with the lights of the city, and now a flotilla of little flecky-edged clouds formed a long streaming sinking line above the sun, their undersides burnished by the last rays as they followed it down. Tower Bridge was etched black against the red, and directly above it he saw what looked like a few broken lines of illegible molten script. Then he turned and shambled off through the gloom of the garden, in the fading, the dying, of the day . . .

Oh I throw down my pencil with disgust. I am not mellow or melancholy or maudlin, I am in foul humor, these last days have been utter hell. I cannot sleep, I cannot eat, and I cannot escape the constant, pervasive, almost paralyzing sense that everything around me is turning silent and empty and *dead*. The very air seems filled with death! It's occurred to me more than once that *I* am dead—the presence in my body of the worm and the spiders would seem to suggest this, the withering of my vital organs, the smell of rot and decay that seeps continuously from my rind now—aren't these signs of death? When did it happen? Was there a moment of death, a moment at which you could say *then* he lived, *then* he was dead? I don't think so. I think it's been gradual, a slow death that began the day I stood beneath the Ganderhill clock with my cardboard suitcase and my three pound notes—though it occurs to me even as I write this that perhaps it began even earlier, that it began the night my mother died, and that since then I've just been burning down, smoldering to ash and dust inside myself while preserving merely the outward motions, the jerky gestures and postures of life. So perhaps it's not been a life at all, but a crumbling, held together by sticks and bits of string, a child's construction; and now all that's left is ash and dust, and the spiders that feed on such compost. There's the bell for supper but I shall not go down. Hilda is down there somewhere, probably still hunting for her house keys. I know she thinks I have them, for she's been in here looking for them, her smell is in the room and won't go away. They're still in my sock but the irony is I can't seem to pluck up the courage to use them—I have the idea that were I to unlock the door to the attic stairs and go up I'd be torn to pieces and eaten; so I suffer their outrages rather than confront them. And as always it's the journal and the tobacco alone that provide what little scaffolding I have.

Later I hear the wireless playing dance music in the day-room, and later still the plumbing groans and thumps and clanks to life as dead souls shuffle into bathroom and lavatory to scrub their crumbling teeth and empty their shriveled bladders. Dead souls! I am the deadest of dead souls now, see me lying on the bed smoking a thin one to keep the lung-worm down, regard the weary zombie!

Later still the house grows quiet, and in the early part of the night, before they start the chanting, I often prowl from floor to floor, for I like the shadows. I specially like the way the light from the streetlamp sifts in through the frosted glass panels of the front door and spreads a dim glow across the hallway, I often sit in the darkness at the top of the first flight of stairs and watch the glow, for I find it makes me tranquil. What makes me even more tranquil is being in the kitchen late at night, when everything is quiet. One night I discovered the cupboard under the sink, and by means of my lighter was able to examine its contents carefully: there was a U-shaped pipe descending from the sink above; there was a toolbox; there were bottles of bleach and ammonia; rags; detergents;

a stack of yellowing newspaper; a tin bucket with a scrubbing brush and a bar of carbolic soap in it; I even found my rope in there. I spent half an hour sitting cross-legged gazing into the cupboard, the lighter burning fitfully on the floor in front of me. Then I took everything out, set it all neatly on the kitchen floor, and climbed in myself—not an easy task, I am not small! But with my head on my chest, and the U-shaped pipe in my lap, and my arms round my knees, I was able to squeeze in and pull the door shut. For ten minutes I sat there squashed up in the darkness, and felt great peace. Then I climbed out and turned the taps on; with the sound of running water in the pipe the little cupboard was heavenly, and now I am spending thirty or forty minutes in there every night.

But if I stay too long they make me suffer for it, so you'll see me suddenly emerge from under the sink and go scuttling back up to my room in a fine state of guilty panic! Ah, the creatures. Often now they work on the ceiling, they use the ceiling as a screen, and upon it they project images and even entire scenes that are distortions, or elaborate parodies, of pieces of my past. They have learned, too, the insidious technique of taking the content of my day's thoughts and rendering it filthy or absurd or grotesque, and sometimes even as I'm writing, and can't stop myself looking up, I see a skewed imitation of the very matter on the page in front of me—see now! See them do it now! See how huge my hands are, disproportionately huge, and my face long and yellow with the skin flaking off in a shower like the scales of a cod under the fishmonger's knife! Oh see him fumbling there, the poor monster, fumbling with his pencil with those great misshapen paws—the pencil so tiny and delicate now as he tries to grasp and manipulate it—and I tear my eyes away, *force* myself back to the book and as I do so up comes a shriek of laughter, and it's impossible not to hear Hilda's voice in it, the touch of hoarseness and the fierce hiss of *threat* in the tone.

Breakfast is a trial, for their eyes possess the means to destroy me; more hazardous still is crossing the hallway to

the front door, and my nightmare is to become uncoupled
halfway over. Fearing it makes it occur, so I find myself at
the end of breakfast attempting not to think about becoming
uncoupled; I rarely succeed. Then she comes out of her office
and I am gripped with terror. "*Mi*ster Cleg!" she'll cry.
"Where is your overcoat?" Or, "Where is your cap?" One
day she said: "We really must get those fingernails clipped."
Her face has started to break up the way it did in Kitchener
Street, eyes and chin and hair and nose separated one from
another and all afloat so I must bring them together *with my
mind* in order to make a face. She doesn't try to conceal her
deadness and animality now, it's evident in her fingers, which
clench and unclench with barely suppressed rage and hunger.
She wears the same cardigan she did the night she took my
father down the gasworks canal, and I sometimes think she
will open it and push her breasts at me, as she did that other
night, and there's movement in my lung at this thought. She
is biding her time though; every encounter breaks off abruptly
and uncertainly, leaving me bewildered. Once she said to me:
"Mr. Cleg, what do you know about the bread knife?" That
day she was up in my room again, I could smell her when I
got back. It was as though a pack of wild animals had been
living up there, not even tobacco and an open window could
rid the room of the odor.

The streets give me no comfort: everything is losing color,
becoming bleached and dry. The weather is part of it: a string
of these cold, clear days when the light is so strong and bright
that my eye has no warm pockets of color or shadow or
dampness into which it can slip for safety. There is always
this glare now, the streets and walls and windows all look
hard, like metal, the way they push white light back at me
and make my poor eyes dart this way and that to escape it,
and I can no longer sit by the canal or the river so I go down
Kitchener Street and while away the hours in the Dog and
Beggar. One visit I remember vividly: I was crossing the
bridge over the canal when I became aware of a thought

pattern not my own: Everything I touch dies. If you love me you die. If I touch you you die. Everything I love dies.

This stopped me. Whose thought pattern was this? My father's. It was my father for the first time *coming out in me*. More strangeness followed. When I reached the Dog I didn't shuffle over to my usual table at the back. Instead I leaned on the counter with my foot on the rail, just as he had always done. Again it was him coming out in me, and I had no power to control it. Ernie Ratcliff was hostile, his face too breaks apart when he gets close to me, and it occurs to me that he is dead and either a ghost or a zombie like me. I bought my half of mild and stood there for more than an hour. Out with the tobacco and papers, and again it was *him,* it was Horace at the bar rolling a thin one, and I the helpless victim or vessel of his imposture. I had been appropriated, I felt, dragooned, impressed, and I watched in futile rage as he behaved in his old ways, leaned on his elbows, let the cigarette dangle from between his lips, turned whenever the door opened, kept himself to himself. What he didn't do was drink his mild—the lung-worm has forbidden this, so he stood in the Dog without drinking, stood there in a world of wet, dying of thirst, so it seemed! As in a way was I.

My father began taking over my thoughts and movements more and more frequently after that, and the Spider was helpless to prevent it. It was my father who began slipping into Hilda's room at night, and during the day, whenever he was in the house, he watched her hungrily from shifty, furtive eyes that always slid away when she became aware of him. He began to take note of when she went to the bathroom and the lavatory, and he tried to catch glimpses of her through the keyhole, but I don't believe he succeeded more than twice. Then, to my horror, in the Dog one afternoon, he attempted a conversation with Ernie Ratcliff.

Oh dear God the humiliation! He had no aptitude for it, no ease, it had been years since he'd practised casual conversation with a stranger. He stood at the bar in the way I've described and just blurted it out. Ernie Ratcliff was down the end of the counter murmuring in low tones to an old man with no teeth and a white stubble on his chin. "Remember Horace?" my father said, and it came out in a load croak that immediately silenced Ratcliff and the old man. "What's that, mate?" one of them said. Their eyes bored into him; he tried again.

"Remember Horace?"

"Now which Horace would that be?" said Ratcliff.

"Cleg," said my father. "Horace Cleg."

Ernie Ratcliff exchanged a glance with the old man, and then began polishing a beer glass with his dishcloth. "Friend of yours, was he?" he murmured.

My father tried to laugh but it didn't work; he was close to panic. "Died in the war, did Horace Cleg," said the old man. "Died in the Blitz."

Ernie Ratcliff produced a bitter snort. "Took out the whole bloody street, that one did. Still, he was beyond caring by that point."

The old man shook his head. "Beyond caring," he said. "I never seen a man lose his interest in life like Horace Cleg did. Destroyed him, what happened."

"Destroy anyone," remarked Ernie Ratcliff, "lose your missus like that."

"Gassed, she was," said the old man, turning toward my father. "Gassed in her own kitchen. Nice woman, too. Hilda, her name was, Hilda Cleg, her boy turned the gas on." The old man paused, lifted his glass with a trembling hand. He fixed my father with a watery eye and whispered: "She were dead by the time Horace got to her!"

There was a silence then, and the clock could be heard ticking somewhere off behind the bar. "Whatever happened to that boy?" said Ernie Ratcliff after a while, but my father didn't hear the answer, for he'd already fled the pub, never to return.

*   *   *

The days that followed grew increasingly strange for the Spider. The oppressive sense that everyone and everything
around him was dead rarely left him now, and for this he
knew himself to be responsible. He became aware too that a
terrible catastrophe was about to occur, but he had no clear
idea what it was or from which direction it would come. It
was at around this time that he decided to be buried at sea.

Then one night as he sat in the cupboard under the kitchen
sink a fresh memory erupted into consciousness. He was in
his room in Kitchener Street, and he was dreaming. He was
standing on a dusty road that stretched in a straight line to
the distant flat horizon, and there was nothing in the landscape
at all except for a low wicket fence of white posts that ran
beside the road at ankle height. He was walking toward the
horizon when he fell into the carcass of a chicken and was
trapped in its bones. Then the night-hag came out of the wall
and stuck her fingers through the bones, trying to get at him,
hissing, "Spider! Spider!" Then he noticed that he was naked
and covered with a soft black fungus. He stroked himself,
which made him piss, and when this happened it immediately
started to rain, and the rain hammered so hard at his window
that he woke up to the smell of gas in the room. All perspective was distorted, none of the lines of the floor or the
ceiling seemed to join up, and the door was a vast distance
from the bed, though the walls on either side of him were
so close together it was like being in an alley. On the floor
were the fly boxes he had been working on before he fell
asleep, so he climbed off the bed and sat on the floor, picking
the flies off the ends of the pins and putting them in his mouth.
All the time the smell of the gas was growing stronger and
making him laugh, though the odd thing was that while he
laughed he felt nothing. Then after some minutes he felt sick,
and with that came a sudden overwhelming sensation of guilt
and desolation. He went to the window and opened it and

hung over the sill in the driving rain, limp as a rag doll until it passed, and then he began laughing once more, though again there was only a dead feeling inside. He had earlier stuffed a blanket under the door; he heard the door being pushed open and then, still limp, he was half dragged, half carried down the stairs and out the front door into the rain. He noticed then that he'd wet his pants. He stared at the open door of number twenty-seven and saw his father lurching out backwards dragging Hilda behind him, and this made him laugh more, though it puzzled him in a vague sort of way. Later he noticed the neighbors standing on the pavement in small groups in the rain and he could see at once that none of them was alive, that they were ghosts. After that he remembered a black car with its headlights on, and he remembered the way the rain was caught slanting across its beams, and there was also an ambulance with a red cross on the side. He remembered Hilda being loaded onto a stretcher and covered with a sheet, and this started him laughing all over again, but even so he was puzzled, and dimly sensed that some sort of mistake had occurred.

Late one night before the chanting started Spider lay on his back by the fireplace and groped for his book. Out it came, the filthy thing, and he took it to his table and opened it to the last entry. He picked up his pencil and began to write.

The presence in my body of the worm and the spiders (he wrote) has borne home to me that I am a dead man. This is what I shall do. When this entry is complete I shall put on my overcoat and leave the house. It is a clear night and the moon is close to the full. I shall quietly leave the house and make my way down to the river, down between the warehouses to the slimy steps. On my way I shall pause frequently to pick up stones, the heavier the better, and with these I shall fill the many pockets of the various garments I am wearing. Doubtless my progress will grow slower as my clothing grows heavier, but on I shall go, on through the empty moon-lit streets, and by the time I reach the slimy steps I shall be very heavy indeed. A curious figure I shall cut then, your old Spider—empty within but for the worm and the spiders, wrapped without in cardboard and newspaper and layers of garments all weighted down with stones—and dead! Strange zombie, no? I will stand at the top of the slimy steps and watch the moonlight on the river, and I will think of the North Sea. I will think of that empty sea heaving beneath the moon, as I begin gingerly to descend, and I will picture in my mind's eye the pale light gleaming on its swells, and even as the river churns about these large flat asylum shoes of mine, even as it catches and tugs at the turn-ups of my flapping flannels, even as my leg wrappings turn soggy and my sock gets wet—I will think of the silence of the moonlit sea. And when I'm up to my chest in it I'll still be thinking of the North Sea, and I'll be exulting inwardly, oh yes I will, I'll be exulting at the prospect of silence and darkness and damp-ness and sleep. But by that time the river will have its arms around me and down I'll go, and there'll be nothing left of your old Spider then but a dirty book stuffed up a chimney.

That's a pretty picture, eh? That's a pretty death. But it's not for me. I shan't do it that way, attractive as it all sounds, the silence, the dampness, the moonlit swells. No, there's only one way out for me, and it's not the river. I've been thinking about it for weeks now, ever since I came across that nice bit of rope—which Hilda thought she could take away from me! Well I found it. I found it in the cupboard under the kitchen sink, and now I'm going to use it. Where? Up in the attic of course, where those bloody creatures of hers can see what they've brought me to! They can cackle, they can drone, they can chant and stamp their filthy feet, they can get the dust dancing in the moonlight and paint pictures in the roof, but will it stop your old Spider climbing onto a broken chair, with the loose end slipped through the ring end to form a noose? Will it stop him lashing the rope to a rafter? And putting his head in the noose? Will it stop him kicking the chair away? It will not, no it will not!

Oh enough. Listen, the house is so quiet you can hear the dead souls coughing and mumbling in their sleep. But here's a question: why do I keep thinking about John Giles' teeth? His false teeth, I mean, the ones he got after they pulled out the originals? They lived in a glass of water on a shelf in the attendants' room, and before every meal he'd go up and get them, and return them after he'd eaten. Well, there was one summer when John had been very quiet for some months, and it was decided for the first (and only) time to try him on a downstairs ward; and it was also decided that if he was well enough to go downstairs then he was well enough to wear his teeth. I was working in the vegetable gardens at the time, and one of the great joys of summer for me was the cricket, for from the old tea garden I had a clear view of the field below. So one afternoon Ganderhill was hosting a team from a nearby village, and the men from the downstairs wards went down to watch, John included. Perhaps it was the sun, but right in the middle of the game he became agitated. I'd been aware from where I was working of the crack of leather on willow, the ripples of applause, the sudden cries to the umpire, all these sounds carried clear up the hill—when suddenly I heard a voice roaring: "Austin Marshall, where are my brains? Where are my brains, you bastard!" I looked down, and in among the cricketers was John. He was staring up at the buildings at the top and waving his fist. "You *bastard!*" he yelled. "Where are my brains?" (John believed that while he was asleep the superintendent had stolen his brains.) Three or four attendants were cautiously moving toward him across the grass when Dr. Austin Marshall himself appeared on the top terrace and called down: "What's the matter, John?" I turned toward him, shielding my eyes from the sun. But the sight of the superintendent only enraged poor John the more, and he made a run for the steps. The attendants soon overpowered him, and struggling wildly, and still shouting, he was manhandled up the steps to the top terrace, then straight up to hard bench. It was discovered only when they got him there that somehow in the fracas he had lost his teeth.

Well, for a day or two this gave us something to talk about, and then we forgot about it. But two weeks later I was picking lettuce from the beds close by the path. They were lovely lettuce, the ones I grew that summer, Augustas, a crisp, green, loose-headed variety. It was a cool summer, and this is good for lettuce, for hot weather turns the leaves bitter and triggers bolting. I've grown all types, but it's the Augustas I like best, they're the sweetest and most buttery. I was picking my Augustas then, when close to the path I came upon a particularly glorious specimen. I pushed back the thick green outer leaves, and there, dead in the heart of the thing, were John's teeth! Grinning at me! And *then* I thought I heard the lettuce say: "Where are my brains, you bastard!"

Odd thing, no? Quiet wheeze of laughter from your old Spider as he gropes for his tobacco. One last thin one, one for the road, then it's out with the sock, out with the keys, and off up the attic for me!

FOR THE BEST IN PAPERBACKS, LOOK FOR THE

In every corner of the world, on every subject under the sun, Penguin represents quality and variety – the very best in publishing today.

For complete information about books available from Penguin – including Puffins, Penguin Classics and Arkana – and how to order them, write to us at the appropriate address below. Please note that for copyright reasons the selection of books varies from country to country.

In the United Kingdom: Please write to *Dept JC, Penguin Books Ltd, FREEPOST, West Drayton, Middlesex, UB7 0BR.*

If you have any difficulty in obtaining a title, please send your order with the correct money, plus ten per cent for postage and packaging, to *PO Box No 11, West Drayton, Middlesex*

In the United States: Please write to *Dept BA, Penguin, 299 Murray Hill Parkway, East Rutherford, New Jersey 07073*

In Canada: Please write to *Penguin Books Canada Ltd, 2801 John Street, Markham, Ontario L3R 1B4*

In Australia: Please write to the *Marketing Department, Penguin Books Australia Ltd, P.O. Box 257, Ringwood, Victoria 3134*

In New Zealand: Please write to the *Marketing Department, Penguin Books (NZ) Ltd, Private Bag, Takapuna, Auckland 9*

In India: Please write to *Penguin Overseas Ltd, 706 Eros Apartments, 56 Nehru Place, New Delhi, 110019*

In the Netherlands: Please write to *Penguin Books Netherlands B.V., Postbus 3507, NL–1001 AH, Amsterdam*

In West Germany: Please write to *Penguin Books Ltd, Friedrichstrasse 10–12, D–6000 Frankfurt/Main 1*

In Spain: Please write to *Alhambra Longman S.A., Fernandez de la Hoz 9, E–28010 Madrid*

In Italy: Please write to *Penguin Italia s.r.l., Via Como 4, 1-20096 Pioltello (Milano)*

In France: Please write to *Penguin France S.A., 17 rue Lejeune, F-31000 Toulouse*

In Japan: Please write to *Longman Penguin Japan Co Ltd, Yamaguchi Building, 2–12–9 Kanda Jimbocho, Chiyoda-Ku, Tokyo 101*

Blood and Water
and Other Tales

'Bewitching . . . a unique vision . . . written with high style and unapologetic perversity' – Clive Barker

'The gothic is strongly characterized by decay, by a movement towards death . . . seeing a culture that is fading out gives a lovely feeling of decadence' – Patrick McGrath

'Severed hands, dead monkeys, swarming insects, pickled body parts and menacing pigmies proliferate in *Blood and Water* . . . ancient Southern plantations, isolated manor houses, places where ghosts like to lurk, and everywhere spiritual and physical decay presides . . . Combined with his gothic imagination and dark splendid humour, the result is fiction that can be as powerful as it is strange' – *The New York Times*

'Stylish, original stories . . . McGrath takes pleasure in the play of words on the page, and the conscious manipulation of fictional form. Of course, it's impossible to resist a book in which a character demands, and not rehetorically, "But how can you love a man with a hand growing out of his head?"' – *Washington Post*